John Hill Aughey

The fighting preacher

John Hill Aughey

The fighting preacher

ISBN/EAN: 9783337135638

Printed in Europe, USA, Canada, Australia, Japan

Cover: Foto ©Andreas Hilbeck / pixelio.de

More available books at **www.hansebooks.com**

THE
FIGHTING
PREACHER.

BY
REV. JOHN H. AUGHEY, A. M.,
CHAPLAIN UNITED STATES ARMY.

An Unvarnished and Truthful Story, full of Pathos,
Humor and Adventure, and a Vivid Record
of Personal Experiences.

Copiously Illustrated by H. S. DeLay.

COPYRIGHT 1899.
CHICAGO:
RHODES & McCLURE PUBLISHING CO.
1899.

PREFACE.

A celebrated author thus writes: "Posterity is under no obligations to a man who is not a parent, who has never planted a tree, built a house, nor written a book." Having fulfilled all these requisites to insure the remembrance of posterity, it remains to be seen whether the author's name shall escape oblivion.

It may be that a few years will obliterate the name affixed to this Preface from the memory of man. This thought is the cause of no concern. I shall have accomplished my purpose if I can in some degree be humbly instrumental in serving my country and my generation, by promoting the well-being of my fellowmen, and advancing the declarative glory of Almighty God.

JOHN HILL AUGHEY.

March 1, 1899.

CONTENTS.

SECESSION SPEECH BY COL. DRANE.......... 22
   SECESSIONISTS' REJOICING AT THE ELEC-
   TION OF LINCOLN....................... 25
CAPT. LOVE OPPOSSING SECESSION.......... 26
A SECESSIONIST SPEAKS.................... 30
SERMON AGAINST SECESSION.............. 34
VIGILANCE COMMITTEE AND COURT MARTIAL 46
   The Unique Summons.................... 48
   Skull and Crossboness.................. 48
   Coffin, Graves, Gallows and Victim........ 48
   The Trial and its Results............... 50
   The Midnight Attack by the Vigilantes..... 60
   Their Incontinent Flight 60
ATTEMPT AT ASSASSINATION................ 65
THE SOUTH ARMING FOR THE WAR........ 67
MURDER OF REV. JAMES PHELAN........... 70
RETURN TO TISHOMINGO COUNTY........... 73
   Events by the Way..................... 74
BATTLE IN GOOD SPRINGS GLEN........... 79
MURDER OF PAYSON AND MURCHISON BY THE
   VIGLANTES............................ 84
MISS SILVERTHORN'S LETTER.............. 85
SUMMONS TO ATTEND COURT MARTIAL...... 86
   Escape to Rienzi...................... 87
   Return to Paden's Mills................. 90
THE ARREST BY HILL'S CAVALRY.......... 94
   Examination by Col. Bradfute........... 96

Gen. Pfeiffer and Gen. Jordan Enter the Dungeon at Tupelo...................... 100
Cruel Treatment of Prisoners.............. 109
Murder of Poole and Harbaugh............ 111
Songs of Incarcerated Slaves.............. 115
Visited by Col. Mark Lowry and Others.... 116
Miss Daisy Carson's Visit................ 118
Witherspoon's Escape.................... 121
Pursued by Cavalry with Bloodhounds...... 122
Witherspoon and Denver Overtaken........ 123
Condemned to Death.................... 124
Death of their Captors.................. 124
Miss Witherspoon's Letter................ 125
OLD PIRGARLIC AND HIS SON OSCAR........ 126
His Trial before Gen. P. G. T. Beauregard. 127
Gen. Braxton Bragg Orders Prof. Yarbrough's Execution 130
He is Shot.............................. 130
Restored to Consciousness by his Friends.... 131
His Final Escape........................ 131
Death of Rebel Capt. Pender.............. 134
ESCAPE OF AUGHEY AND MALONE........... 135
Separate in the Encampment.............. 143
Set out Alone.......................... 144
Concealed in the Chaparral............... 144
The Booming Cannon and Passing Soldiers.. 145
Soldier's Conversation about the Escaped Prisoners Overhead.................... 146
Crosses an Affluent of the Tombigbee River 148
David Hough's Cabin.................... 149
The Re-arrest.......................... 150

Running the Gauntlet amid Rebel Camps. 152
Again at Gen. Jordan's Headquarters.... 153
Examined and Shackled................. 153
Returned to Tupelo..................... 153
Examined by the Rebel Generals.......... 154
To be Shot in an Hour................. 155
Letter to My Wife..................... 156
The Reprieve.......................... 157
Remanded to Prison.................... 158
Reception by the Prisoners.............. 159
Floor Spiked Down..................... 160
BENJAMIN CLARK'S STORY................. 160
Pursuit by Cavalry with Bloodhounds...... 161
Capture of the Bear.................... 162
Death of Snediker and Rucker at the Bagnio
  in Fulton............................ 163
Death of Downs........................ 163
Clark's Wife and Children.............. 164
Arrive at Paden's Mills................. 164
The Search of the House, Mills and Negro
  Quarters............................ 165
The Minorcans 165
Louis Las Cassas Lornette.............. 166
COL. FEULLEVERT......................... 169
His Interview with His Nephew Louis...... 169
The Rescue............................ 170
Interview with Col. Walter, the Judge Ad-
  vocate.............................. 173
Charges Preferred..................... 174
Bailie and Childress Shot.............. 177
Second Visit of Col. H. W. Walter....... 178
PERSONAL APPEARANCE OF GEN. BRAGG.... 186

CHAMPE AND BRAXTON.................... 186

    Murder of Chenault, Vedder, Bynum and
        other Unionist........................ 187

    Hymns................................. 188

FOREORDINATION.......................... 190

HERMON BLEDSOE, THE EAST TENNESSEE
    UNIONIST............................. 191

    Bledsoe's Arrest......................... 191

    Escape from Death by Fire.............. 198

    His Travels, Re-arrest and Incarceration in
        Tupelo............................. 199

ESCAPE OF BOVARD WILLIS................. 203

    Pursuit by Cavalry with Hounds......... 204

    Narrow Escape........................ 204

TROVER ANDERSON'S REMARKABLE DREAM... 206

LETTER TO MY WIFE..................... 209

    Obituary 212

THE PRISONERS' PETITION TO ABRAHAM LIN-
    COLN AND WILLIAM H. SEWARD........ 217

MURDER OF STREET AND MAYNARD......... 220

RESOLVE TO ESCAPE....................... 229

    Plan Adopted.......................... 230

    Under the Prison...................... 236

    Among the Guards..................... 238

    In the Forest.......................... 240

    Meet a Negro.......................... 240

    Perishing from Hunger and Thirst........ 241

    Find Water............................ 244

    The Ethiopian Charley.................. 246

    The Unionist, Israel Nelson.............. 247

    Col. Barry and his Son Volney Torn to
        Pieces by the Bloodhounds.............. 247

Traveling in a Circle.................... 248
Pursued by Bloodhounds................ 249
Death Iminent......................... 250
Ascent of the Oak...................... 251
The Hounds Baffled.................... 252
Jingo Dick............................ 253
Under the Juniper..................... 253
I Plod My Weary Way................. 254
Perishing from Hunger and Thrist........ 555
The Presentiment...................... 255
Find Water, Bright Sparkling Water....... 256
The Bear Hunt........................ 257
In at the Death........................ 258
Bloodhounds 259
Meet the Videttes..................... 262
Find Friends.......................... 266
The Midnight Ride.................... 271
Meet many Unionist................... 272
Death of Newson...................... 272
Daughter of Gen. Nathaniel Green....... 273
Meet Rebels.......................... 274
Thrilling Adventure and Escape.......... 274
Halted by Guerrillas................... 274
Fired at and Guide Wounded............ 275
Reach the Union Lines at Rienzi......... 279
Kind Reception....................... 281
Serenade 282
Speech 282
Wife and Child....................... 283
MELVIN ESTILL'S LETTER................ 289
The Escape from Saltillo............... 290
Pursuit with Bloodhounds 290

Tragic Fate.................................. 290
Their Scalps Taken........................ 291
Reach the Unions Lines 294
"The Bones of the Dead.".................. 295
Letter found in Gideon's Tent after his Burial 296
From a Soldier's Letter.................... 301
The Southern Barbecue.................... 301
"Strike for the Right.".................... 307
The Death of Slavery 308
"Cover them Over.".......................... 310
How Sleep the Brave...................... 314
Decoration Day............................ 314
The Blue and the Gray.................... 316
The Answer to the "Blue and Gray.".... 317
The Nation's Dead......................... 319
Sleep, Comrades, Sleep.................... 320
The Veteran's Request..................... 322
The Soldier's Reprieve.................... 323
"Fear Not Ye."............................. 326
John J. DeGrummond's Letter 327
The Mustering............................. 330
Battle of Corinth 332
Battle of Tupelo 333
Thomas Grimke............................ 337
The Southern Unionist 353
Prisoner's Hope........................... 354
John Brown, of Osawatomie, Kansas....... 355
Marching Through Georgia............... 356
The Colored Philosopher................... 357
"Better than the Bayonet."............... 359
My Country................................ 359
The Ship of State......................... 360

John H. Aughey.

From a photograph taken in the year 1860.

FIGHTING THE PREACHER

CHAPTER I.

At the breaking out of the rebellion, I was engaged in the work of an Evangelist in the counties of Choctaw and Attala in Central Mississippi. My congregations were large, and my duties onerous. Being constantly employed in ministerial labors, I had no time to intermeddle with politics, leaving all such questions to statesmen, giving the complex issues of the day only sufficient attention to enable me to vote intelligently. Thus was I engaged when the great political campaign of 1860 commenced—a campaign conducted with greater virulence and asperity than any I have ever witnessed. During my casual detention at a store, Colonel Drane arrived according to appointment, to address the people of Choctaw. He was a member of one of my congregations, and as he had long been a leading statesman in Mississippi, having for many years presided over the state senate, I expected to hear a speech of marked ability, unfolding the true issues before the people, with all the dignity, suavity, and earnestness of a gentleman and patriot; but I found his whole speech to be a tirade of abuse of the North, commingled with the bold avowal of treasonable sentiments. The Colonel thus addressed the people:

"My Fellow-Citizens—I appear before you to urge anew resistance against the encroachments and aggressions of the Yankees. If the Black Republicans carry their ticket, and Old Abe is elected, our right to carry our slaves into the territories will be denied us; and who dare say that he would be a base, craven submissionist, when our God-given and constitutional right to carry slavery into the common domain is wickedly taken from the South. The Yankees cheated us out of Kansas by their infernal Emigrant Aid Societies. They cheated us out of California, which our blood and treasure purchased, for the South sent ten men to one that was sent by the North to the Mexican war, and thus we have no foothold on the Pacific coast; and even now we pay five dollars' for the support of the general Government where the North pays one. We help to pay bounties to the Yankee fishermen in New England; indeed *we are always paying, paying, paying, and yet the North is always crying, give, give, give.* The South has made the North rich, and what thanks do we receive? Our rights are trampled on, our slaves are spirited by thousands over their underground railroad to Canada, our citizens are insulted while traveling in the North, and their servants are tampered with, and by false representations, and often by mob violence, forced from them. Douglas, knowing the power of Emigrant Aid Societies, proposes squatter sovereignty, with the positive certainty that the scum of Europe and the mudsills of Yankeedom can be shipped in, in numbers sufficient to control the destiny of the embryo state. Since the admission of Texas in 1845, there has not been a single foot of slave territory secured to the South, while the North has added to their list the extensive states of California, Minnesota, and Oregon, and Kansas is as good as theirs; while, if Lincoln is elected, the Wilmot proviso will be extended over all the common territories, debarring the South forever from her right to share the public domain.

" The hypocrites of the North tell us that slaveholding is sinful. Well, suppose it is. Upon us and our children let the guilt of this sin rest; we are willing to bear it, and it is none of their business. We are a more moral people than they are. Who originated Mormonism, Millerism, Spirit-rappings, Abolitionism, Free-lovism, and all other abominable *isms* which curse the world. The reply is, the North. Their puritanical fanaticism and hypocrisy is patent to all. Talk to us of the sin of slavery, when the only difference between us is that our slaves are black and theirs white. They treat their white slaves, the Irish and Dutch, in a cruel manner, giving them during health just enough to purchase coarse clothing, and when they become sick they are turned off to starve, as they do by hundreds every year. A female servant in the North must have a testimonial of good character before she will be employed; those with whom she is laboring will not give her this so long as they desire her services; she therefore cannot leave them, whatever may be her treatment, so that she is as much compelled to remain with her employer as the slave with his master.

"Their servants hate them; our's love us. My niggers would fight for me and my family. They have been treated well, and they know it. And I don't treat my slaves any better than my neighbors. If ever there comes a war between the North and the South, let us do as Abraham did—arm our trained servants and go forth with them to battle. They hate the Yankees as intensely as we do, and nothing could please our slaves better than to fight them. Ah, the perfidious Yankees. I cordially hate a Yankee. We have all suffered much at their hands; they will not keep faith with us. Have they complied with the provisions of the Fugitive Slave Law? The thousands and ten of thousands of slaves aided in their escape to Canada, is a sufficient answer. We *have* lost millions and *are* losing millions every year, by the operation of the underground railroad. How deep the perfidy of a people, thus to violate every article of compromise we have made with them! The Yankees are an inferior race, descended from the old Puritan stock, who enacted the Blue Laws. They are desirous of compelling us to submit to laws more iniquitous than ever were the Blue Laws. I have traveled in the North, and have seen the depth of their depravity. Now, my fellow-citizens, what shall we do to resist Northern aggression? Why simply this: If Lincoln or Douglas is elected

THE CAVALIER.

(as to the Bell-Everett ticket, it stands no sort of chance), let us secede. This remedy will be effectual. I am in favor of no more compromises. Let us have Breckenridge, or immediate, complete, and eternal separation."

The speaker then retired amid the cheers of his audience.

Soon after this there came a day of rejoicing to many in Mississippi. The booming of cannon, the joyous greeting, the soul-stirring music, indicated that no ordinary intelligence had been received. The lightnings had brought the tidings that Abraham Lincoln was President-elect of the United States, and the South was wild with excitement. Those who had been long desirous of a pretext for secession now boldly advocated their sentiments, and joyfully hailed the election of Mr. Lincoln as affording that pretext. The conservative men were filled with gloom. They regarded the election of Mr. Lincoln by the majority of the people of the United States in a constitutional way as affording no cause for secession. Secession they regarded as fraught with all the evils of Pandora's box, and that war, famine, pestilence, and moral and physical desolation would follow in its train. A call was made by Governor Pettus for a convention to assemble early in January, at Jackson, to determine what course Mississippi should pursue, whether her policy should be submission or secession.

Candidates, Union and Secession, were nominated for the convention in every county. The speeches of

two whom I heard will serve as a specimen of the
arguments used *pro* and *con*.   Captain Love, of
Choctaw, thus addressed the people:

"MY FELLOW CITIZENS—I appear before you to
advocate the Union—the union of the states under
whose favoring auspices we have long prospered.
No nation so great, so prosperous, so happy, or so
much respected by earth's thousand kingdoms as the
Great Republic, by which name the United States is
known from the rivers to the ends of the earth.   Our
flag, the star-spangled banner, is respected on every sea,
and affords protection to the citizens of every state,
whether amid the pyramids of Egypt, the jungles of
Asia, or the mighty cities of Europe.   Our Repub-
lican Constitution, framed by the wisdom of our
Revolutionary fathers, is as free from imperfection
as any document drawn up by uninspired men.
God presided over the councils of that convention
which framed our glorious Constitution.   They
asked wisdom from on high, and their prayers were
answered.   Free speech, a free press, and freedom to
worship God as our conscience dictates, under our
own vine and fig tree, none daring to molest or make
us afraid, are some of the blessings which our Constitution guarantees; and these prerogatives which
we enjoy are features which bless and distinguish us
from the other nations of the earth.   Freedom of
speech is unknown amongst them; among them a
censorship of the press and a national church are
established.

"Our country by its physical features seems fitted for but one nation. What ceaseless troubles would be caused by having the source of our rivers in one country and the mouth in another. There are no natural boundaries to divide us into separate nations. We are all descended from the same common parentage, we all speak the same language, and we have really no conflicting interests, the statements of our opponents to the contrary notwithstanding. Our opponents advocate separate state secession. Would not Mississippi cut a sorry figure among the nations of the earth? With no harbor, she would be dependent on a foreign nation for an outlet. Custom-house duties would be ruinous, and the republic of Mississippi would find herself compelled to return to the Union. Mississippi, you remember, repudiated a large foreign debt some years ago; if she became an independent nation, her creditors would influence their government to demand payment, which could not be refused by the weak, defenceless, navyless, armyless, moneyless, repudiating republic of Mississippi. To pay this debt, with the accumulated interest, would ruin the new republic, and bankruptcy would stare us in the face.

"It is true, Abraham Lincoln is elected President of the United States. My plan is to wait till Mr. Lincoln does something unconstitutional. Then let the South unanimously seek redress in a constitutional manner. The conservatives of the North will join us. If no redress is made, let us present our ultimatum. If this, too, is rejected, I for one will not advocate submission; and by the co-operation of all the slave states, we will, in the event of the perpetration of wrong, and a refusal to redress our grievances, be much abler to secure our rights, or to defend them at the cannon's mouth and the point of the bayonet. The Supreme Court favors the South. In the Dred Scott case the Supreme Court decided that the negro was not a citizen, and that the slave was a chattel as we regard him. The majority of Congress on joint ballot is still with the South. Although we have something to fear from the views of the President-elect and the Chicago platform, let us wait till some overt act, trespassing upon our rights, is committed and all redress denied; then, and not till then, will I advocate extreme measures.

"Let our opponents remember that secession and civil war are synonymous. Who ever heard of a government breaking to pieces without an arduous struggle for its preservation? I admit the right of revolution when a people's rights cannot otherwise be maintained, but deny the right of secession. We are told that it is a reserved right. The constitution declares that all rights not specified in it are reserved to the people of the respective states; but who ever heard of the right of total destruction of the government being a reserved right in any constitution? The fallacy is evident at a glance. Nine millions of people can afford to wait for some overt act. Let us not follow the precipitate course which the ultra politi-

cians indicate. Let W. L. Yancey urge his treasonable policy of firing the Southern heart and precipita-
ting a revolution, but let us follow no such wicked
advice. Let us follow the things which make for
peace.

" We are often told that the North will not return
fugitive slaves. Will secession remedy this grievance?
Will secession give us any more slave territory? No
free government ever makes a treaty for the rendition
of fugitive slaves—thus recognizing the rights of the
citizens of a foreign nation to a species of property
which it denies to its own citizens. Even little
Mexico will not do it. Mexico and Canada return no fugitives. In the event of secession the
United States would return no fugitives, and our peculiar institution would, along our vast border, become very insecure; we would hold our slaves by a
very slight tenure. Instead of extending the great
Southern institution it would be contracting daily.
Our slaves would be held to service at their own
option throughout the whole border, and our gulf
states would soon become border states; and the
great insecurity of this species of property would
work, before twenty years, the extinction of slavery,
and, in consequence, the ruin of the South. Are we
prepared for such a result? Are we prepared for
civil war? Are we prepared for all the evils attendant upon a fratricidal contest—for bloodshed, famine,
and political and moral desolation? I reply, we are
not; therefore let us look before we leap, and avoiding the heresy of secession—

> "'Rather bear the ills we have,
> Than fly to others that we know not of.'"

A secession speaker was introduced, and thus addressed the people:

"LADIES AND GENTLEMEN—Fellow citizens, I am a secessionist out and out; voted for Jeff Davis for Governor in 1850, when the same issue was before the people; and I have always felt a grudge against the *free state* of Tishomingo for giving H. S. Foote, the Union candidate, a majority so great as to elect him, and thus retain the state in this accursed Union ten years longer. Who would be a craven-hearted, cowardly, villainous submissionist? Lincoln, the abominable, white-livered abolitionist, is President-elect of the United States; shall he be permitted to take his seat on Southern soil? No, never! I will volunteer as one of thirty thousand to butcher the villain if ever he sets foot on slave territory. Secession or submission! What patriot would hesitate for a moment which to choose? No true son of Mississippi would brook the idea of submission to the rule of the baboon, Abe Lincoln—a fifth-rate lawyer, a broken-down hack of a politician, a fanatic, an abolitionist. I, for one, would prefer an hour of virtuous liberty to a whole eternity of bondage under Northern, Yankee, wooden-nutmeg rule. The halter is the only argument that should be used against the submissionists, and I predict that it will soon, very soon, be in force.

"We have glorious news from Tallahatchie. Seven

tory-submissionists were hanged there in one day, and the so-called Union candidates, having the wholesome dread of hemp before their eyes, are not canvassing the county; therefore the heretical dogma of submission, under any circumstances, disgraces not their county. Compromise! let us have no such word in our vocabulary. Compromise with the Yankees, after the election of Lincoln, is treason against the South; and still its syren voice is listened to by the demagogue submissionists. We should never have made any compromise, for in every case we surrendered rights for the sake of peace. No concession of the scared Yankees will now prevent secession. They now understand that the South is in earnest, and in their alarm they are proposing to yield us much; but the die is cast, the Rubicon is crossed, and our determination shall ever be, no union with the flat-headed, nigger-stealing, fanatical Yankees.

"We are now threatened with internecine war. The Yankees are an inferior race; they are cowardly in the extreme. They are descended from the Puritan stock, who never bore rule in any nation. We, the descendants of the Cavaliers, are the Patricians, they the Plebeians. The Cavaliers have always been the rulers, the Puritans the ruled. The dastardly Yankees will never fight us; but if they, in their presumption and audacity, venture to attack us, let the war come—I repeat it—let it come! The conflagration of their burning cities, the desolation of their country, and the slaughter of their inhabitants, will

strike the nations of the earth dumb with astonish-
ment, and serve as a warning to future ages, that the
slaveholding Cavaliers of the sunny South are terrible in their vengeance. I am in favor of immediate,
independent, and eternal separation from the vile
Union which has so long oppressed us. After separation, I am in favor of non-intercourse with the
United States so long as time endures. We will
raise the tariff, to the point of prohibition, on all
Yankee manufactures, including wooden-nutmegs,
wooden clocks, quack nostrums, etc. We will drive
back to their own inhospitable clime every Yankee
who dares to pollute our shores with his cloven feet.
Go he must, and if necessary, with the blood-hounds
on his track. The scum of Europe and mudsills of
Yankeedom shall never be permitted to advance a step
south of 36° 30'. South of that latitude is ours—
westward to the Pacific. With my heart of hearts I
hate a Yankee, and I will make my children swear
eternal hatred to the whole Yankee race. A mongrel
breed—Irish, Dutch, Puritans, Jews, free niggers,
etc.—they scarce deserve the notice of the descendants
of the Huguenots, the old Castilians, and the Cavaliers. Cursed be the day when the South consented
to this iniquitous league—the Federal Union—which
has long dimmed her nascent glory.

"In battle, one southron is equivalent to ten northern hirelings; but I regard it a waste of time to speak
of Yankees—they deserve not our attention. It
matters not to us what they think of secession, and

THE PURITAN.

ticket; and their children, and their children's children, will owe them a debt of gratitude which they can never repay. The day of our separation and vindication of states' rights, will be the happiest day of our lives. Yankee domination will have ceased forever, and the haughty southron will spurn them from all association, both governmental and social. So mote it be!"

This address was received with great eclat.

On the next Sabbath after this meeting, I preached in the Poplar Creek Presbyterian church, in Choctaw, now Montgomery county, from Romans xiii. 1: "Let every soul be subject unto the higher powers. For there is no power but of God: the powers that be, are ordained of God."

Previous to the sermon a prayer was offered, of which the following is the conclusion:

"Almighty God—we would present our country, the United States of America, before thee. When our political horizon is overcast with clouds and darkness, when the strong-hearted are becoming fearful for the permanence of our free institutions, and the prosperity, yea, the very existence of our great Republic, we pray thee, O God, when flesh and heart fail, when no human arm is able to save us from the fearful vortex of disunion and revolution, that thou wouldst interpose and save us. We confess our national sins, for we have, as a nation, sinned grievously. We have been highly favored, we have been greatly prospered, and have taken our place amongst the leading powers of the earth. A gospel-enlightened nation, our sins are therefore more heinous in thy sight. They are sins of deep ingratitude and presumption. We confess that drunkenness has abounded amongst all classes of our citizens. Rulers and ruled have been alike guilty; and because of its wide spreading prevalence, and because our legislators have enacted no sufficient laws for its suppression, it is a national sin. Profanity abounds amongst us; Sabbath-breaking is rife; and we have elevated unworthy men to high positions of honor and trust. We are not, as a people, free from the crime of tyranny and oppression. For these great and aggravated offences, we pray thee to give us repentance and godly sorrow, and then, O God, avert the threatened and imminent judgments which impend over our beloved country. Teach our senators wisdom. Grant them that wisdom which is able to make them wise unto salvation; and grant also that wisdom which is profitable to direct, so that they may steer the ship of state safely through the troubled waters which seem ready to engulf it on every side. Lord, hear us, and answer in mercy, for the sake of Jesus Christ our Lord. Amen and Amen!"

The following is a synopsis of my sermon:

Israel had been greatly favored as a nation. No weapon formed against them prospered, so long as they loved and served the Lord their God. They were blessed in their basket and their store. They were set on high above all the nations of the earth. * * * * When all Israel assembled, ostensibly to make Rehoboam king, they were ripe for rebellion. Jeroboam and other wicked men had fomented and cherished the spark of treason, till, on this occasion, it broke out into the flame of open rebellion. The severity of Solomon's rule was the pretext, but it was only a pretext, for during his reign the nation prospered, grew rich and powerful. Jeroboam wished a disruption of the kingdom, that he might bear rule; and although God permitted it as a punishment of Israel's idolatry, yet he frowned upon the wicked men who were instrumental in bringing this great evil upon his chosen people.

"The loyal division took the name of Judah, though composed of the two tribes, Judah and Benjamin. The revolted ten tribes took the name of their leading tribe, Ephraim. Ephraim continued to wax weaker and weaker. Filled with envy against Judah, they often warred against that loyal kingdom, until they themselves were greatly reduced. At last, after various vicissitudes, the ten tribes were carried away, and scattered and lost. We often hear of the lost ten tribes. What became of them is a mystery. Their secession ended in their being blotted out of existence or lost amidst the heathen. God alone knows what did become of them. They resisted the powers that be—the ordinance of God—and received to themselves damnation and annihilation.

"As God dealt with Israel, so will he deal with us. If we are exalted by righteousness, we will prosper; if we, as the ten tribes, resist the ordinance of God,

"No, Never! I will volunteer as one of thirty thousand to butcher the villian if ever he sets foot on slave territory."   Page 30

we will perish. At this time many are advocating the course of the ten tribes. Secession is a word of frequent occurrence. It is openly advocated by many. Nullification and rebellion, secession and treason, are convertible terms, and no good citizen will mention them with approval. Secession is resisting the powers that be, and therefore it is a violation of God's command. Where do we obtain the right of secession? Clearly not from the word of God, which enjoins obedience to all that are in authority, to whom we must be subject, not only for wrath, but also for conscience's sake.

"There is no provision made in the Constitution of the United States for secession. The wisest statesmen, who made politics their study, regarded secession as a political heresy, dangerous in its tendencies, and destructive of all government in its practical application. Mississippi, purchased from France with United States gold, fostered by the nurturing care, and made prosperous by the wise administration of the general government, proposes to secede. Her political status would then be anomalous. Would her territory revert to France? Does she propose to refund the purchase money? Would she become a territory under the jurisdiction of the United States Congress?

"Henry Clay, the great statesman, Daniel Webster, the expounder of the constitution, General Jackson, George Washington, and a mighty host, whose names would fill a volume, regarded secession as treason.

One of our smallest states, which swarmed with tories in the Revolution, whose descendants still live, invented the doctrine of nullification, the first treasonable step, which soon culminated in the advocacy of secession. Why should we secede, and thus destroy the best, the freest, and most prosperous government on the face of the earth, the government which our patriot fathers fought and bled to secure? What has Mississippi lost by the Union? I have resided seven years in this state, and have an extensive personal acquaintance, and yet I know not a single individual who has lost a slave through northern influence. I have, it is true, known of some ten slaves who have run away, and have not been found. They may have been aided in their escape to Canada by northern and southern citizens, for there are many in the South who have given aid and comfort to the fugitive; but the probability is that they perished in the swamps, or were destroyed by the blood-hounds.

"The complaint is made that the North regards slavery as a moral, social, and political evil, and that many of them denounce, in no measured terms, both slavery and slaveholders. To be thus denounced is regarded as a great grievance. Secession would not remedy this evil. In order to cure it effectually, we must seize and gag all who thus denounce our peculiar institution. We must also muzzle their press. As this is impracticable, it would be well to come to this conclusion: If we are verily guilty of the evils charged upon us, let us set about rectifying those

evils ; if not, the denunciations of slanderers should
not affect us so deeply. If our northern brethren
are honest in their convictions of the sin of slavery,
as no doubt many of them are, let us listen to their
arguments without the dire hostility so frequently
manifested. They take the position that slavery is
opposed to the inalienable rights of the human race;
that it originated in piracy and robbery; that mani-
fold cruelties and barbarities are inflicted upon the
defenceless slaves ; that they are debarred from intellectual culture by state laws, which send to the penitentiary those who are guilty of instructing them;
that they are put upon the block and sold, parent and
child, husband and wife being separated, so that they
never again see each other's face in the flesh; that
the law of chastity cannot be observed, as there are
no laws punishing rape on the person of a female
slave; that when they escape from the threatened
cat-o'nine-tails, or overseer's whip, they are hunted
down by blood-hounds and bloodier men ; that often
they are half starved and half clad, and are furnished
with mere hovels to live in ; that they are often murdered by cruel overseers, who whip them to death, or
overtask them until disease is induced which results
in death; that masters practically ignore the marriage relation among slaves, inasmuch as they frequently separate husband and wife, by sale or re-
moval; that they discourage the formation of that
relation, preferring that the offspring of their female
slaves should be illegitimate, from the mistaken notion

that it would be more numerous. They charge, also, that slavery induces in the masters, pride, arrogance, tyranny, laziness, profligacy, and every form of vice.

"The South takes the position that if slavery is sinful, the North is not responsible for that sin; that it is a state institution, and that to interfere with slavery in the states in any way, even by censure, is a violation of the rights of the states. The language of our politicians is, upon us and our children rest the evil! We are willing to take the responsibility and to risk the penalty! You will find evil and misery enough in the North to excite your philanthropy and employ your beneficence. You have purchased our cotton; you have used our sugar; you have eaten our rice; you have smoked and chewed our tobacco—all of which are the products of slave labor. You have grown rich by traffic in these articles; you have monopolized the carrying trade and borne our slave-produced products to your shores. Your northern ships, manned by northern men, brought from Africa the greater part of the slaves which came to our continent, and they are still smuggling them in. When, finding slavery unprofitable, the northern states passed laws for gradual emancipation, but few obtained their freedom, the majority of them being shipped South and sold, so that but few, comparatively, were manumitted. If the slave trade and slavery are great sins, the North is *particeps criminis*, and has been from the beginning.

"These bitter accusations are hurled back and forth

through the newspapers, and in Congress crimination
and recrimination occur every day of the session.
Instead of endeavoring to calm the troubled waters,
politicians are striving to render them turbid and
boisterous. Sectional bitterness and animosity prevail to a fearful extent, but secession is not the proper
remedy. To cure one evil by perpetrating a greater
renders a double cure necessary. In order to cure a
disease, the cause should be known, that we may treat
it intelligently and apply a proper remedy. Having
observed, during the last eleven years, that sectional
strife and bitterness were increasing with fearful ra-
pidity, I have endeavored to stem the torrent, so far
as it was possible for individual effort to do so. I
deem it the imperative duty of all patriots, of all
Christians, to throw oil upon the troubled waters,
and thus save the ship of state from wreck among
the vertiginous billows.

"Most of our politicians are demagogues. They
care not for the people, so that they accomplish their
own selfish and ambitious schemes. Give them
power, give them money, and they are satisfied.
Deprive them of these, and they are ready to sacrifice the best interests of the nation to secure them.
They excite sectional animosity and party strife, and
are willing to kindle the flames of civil war to accomplish their unhallowed purposes. They tell us
that there is a conflict of interest between the free and
slave states, and endeavor to precipitate a revolution,
that they may be leaders and obtain positions of trust

and profit in the new government which they hope
to establish. The people would be dupes indeed to
abet these wicked demagogues in their nefarious designs. Let us not break God's command, by resisting the ordinance of God—the powers that be. I
am not discussing the right of revolution, which I
deem a sacred right. When human rights are in-
vaded, when life is endangered, when liberty is taken
away, when we are not left free to pursue our own
happiness in our own chosen way—so far as we do
not trespass upon the rights of others—we have a
right, and it becomes our imperative duty to resist
to the bitter end the tyranny which would deprive
us and our children of our inalienable rights. Our
lives are secure; we have freedom to worship God.
Our liberty is sacred; we may pursue happiness to
our hearts' content. We do not even charge upon
the general Government that it has infringed these
rights. Whose life has been endangered, or who has
lost his liberty by the action of the Government? If
that man lives, in all this fair domain of ours, he has
a right to complain. But neither you nor I have
ever heard of or seen the individual who has thus
suffered. We have therefore clearly no right of
revolution.

"Treason is no light offence. God, who rules the
nations, and who has established governments, will
punish severely those who attempt to overthrow them.
Damnation is stated to be the punishment which
those who resist the powers that be, will suffer. Who

wishes to endure it? I hope none of my charge will incur this penalty by the perpetration of treason. You yourselves can bear me witness that I have not heretofore introduced political issues into the pulpit, but at this time I could not acquit my conscience were I not to warn you against the great sin some of you, I fear, are ready to commit.

"Were I to discuss the policy of a high or low tariff, or descant upon the various merits attached to one or another form of banking, I should be justly obnoxious to censure. Politics and religion, however, are not always separate. When the political issue is made, shall we, or shall we not, grant license to sell intoxicating liquors as a beverage? the minister's duty is plain; he must urge his people to use their influence against granting any such license. The minister must enforce every moral and religious obligation, and point out the path of truth and duty, even though the principles he advocates are by statesmen introduced into the arena of political strife, and made issues by the great parties of the day. I see the sword coming, and would be derelict in duty not to give you faithful warning. I must reveal the whole counsel of God. I have a message from God unto you, which I must deliver, whether you will hear, or whether you will forbear. If the sword come, and you perish, I shall then be guiltless of your blood. As to the great question at issue, my honest conviction is (and I think I have the Spirit of God,) that you should with your whole heart, and soul, and mind, and strength, oppose secession. You should talk against it, you should write against it, you should vote against it, and, if need be, you should fight against it.

"I have now declared what I believe to be your high duty in this emergency. Do not destroy the government which has so long protected you, and which has never in a single instance oppressed you. Pull not down the fair fabric which our patriot fathers reared at vast expense of blood and treasure. Do not, like the blind Samson, pull down the pillars of our glorious edifice, and cause death, desolation, and ruin. Perish the hand that would thus destroy the source of all our political prosperity and happiness. Let the parricide who attempts it receive the just retribution which a loyal people demand, even his execution on a gallows high as Haman's. Let us also set about rectifying the causes which threaten the overthrow of our government. As we are proud, let us pray for the grace of humility. As a state, and as individuals, we too lightly regard its most solemn obligations; let us, therefore, pray for the grace of repentance and godly sorrow, and hereafter in this respect sin no more. As many transgressions have been committed by us, let the time past of our lives suffice us to have wrought the will of the flesh, and now let us break off our sins by righteousness, and our transgressions by turning unto the Lord, and he will avert his threatened judgments, and save us from dissolution, anarchy, and desolation.

"If our souls are filled with hatred against the people of any section of our common country, let us ask from the Great Giver the grace of charity, which suffereth long and is kind, which envieth not, which vaunteth not itself, is not puffed up, does not behave itself unseemly, seeketh not her own, is not easily provoked, thinketh no evil; rejoiceth not in iniquity, but rejoiceth in the truth; beareth all things, believeth all things, hopeth all things, endureth all things, and which never faileth; then shall we be in a suitable frame for an amicable adjustment of every difficulty; oil will soon be thrown upon the troubled waters, and peace, harmony, and prosperity would ever attend us; and our children, and our children's children will rejoice in the possession of a beneficent and stable government, securing to them all the natural and inalienable rights of man."

CHAPTER II.

VIGILANCE COMMITTEE AND COURT-MARTIAL.

Soon after this sermon was preached, the election was held. Approaching the polls, I asked for a Union ticket, and was informed that none had been printed, and that it would be advisable to vote the secession ticket. I thought otherwise, and going to a desk, wrote out a Union ticket, and voted it amidst the frowns, murmurs, and threats of the judges and by-standers, and, as the result proved, I had the honor of depositing the only vote in favor of the Union which was polled in that precinct. I knew of many who were in favor of the Union, who were intimi-dated by threats, and by the odium attending it, from voting at all. A majority of the secession candidates were elected. The convention assembled, and on the 9th of January, 1861, Mississippi had the unenviable reputation of being the first to follow her twin sister, South Carolina, into the maelstrom of secession and treason. Being the only states in which the slaves were more numerous than the whites, it became them to lead the van in the slave-holders' rebellion. Be-fore the 4th of March, Florida, Georgia, Louisiana, and Texas had followed in the wake, and were en-gulfed in the whirlpool of secession.

It was now dangerous to utter a word in favor of

the Union. Many suspected of Union sentiments were lynched. An old gentleman in Winston county was arrested for an act committed twenty years before, which was construed as a proof of his abolition proclivities. The old gentleman had several daughters, and his mother-in-law had given him a negro girl. Observing that his daughters were becoming lazy, and were imposing all the labor upon the slave, he sent her back to the donor, with a statement of the cause for returning her. This was now the ground of his arrest, but escaping from their clutches, a precipitate flight alone saved his life.

Self-constituted vigilance committees sprang up all over the country, and a reign of terror began ; all who had been Union men, and who had not given in their adhesion to the new order of things by some public proclamation, were supposed to be disaffected. The so-called Confederate States, the new power, organized for the avowed purpose of extending and perpetuating African slavery, was now in full blast. These *soi-disant* vigilance committees professed to carry out the will of Jeff. Davis. All who were considered disaffected were regarded as being tinctured with abolitionism. My opposition to the disruption of the Union being notorious, I was summoned to appear before one of these august tribunals to answer the charge of being an abolitionist and a Unionist. My wife was very much alarmed, knowing that were I found guilty of the charge, there was no hope for mercy.

On the evening before the session of the vigilance committee, I walked out in the gloaming for meditation and prayer. When a short distance from my residence, I encountered an old colored man who belonged to a planter named Major F. M. Henderson. The old man, who was known as Uncle Simon Peter, embraced every opportunity of hearing me preach. He approached me with his hat under his arm, and in a very deferential manner. Said he, "Master, I is in great trouble."

"What troubles you, Uncle Peter?"

"Master, I brings a note to you, and I'se 'feared it bodes no good to you. Master and Gus Mecklin and some more folks what I didn't know fixed it up las' night, and de way dey talked dey's ready to 'sassinate you."

"Give me the note, Uncle Peter."

"Here it am."

The paper was unique. A skull and cross-bones illuminated one corner, a coffin and newly-made grave were rudely drawn in another corner, a gallows was conspicuous, a victim whose hands were bound behind his back and a cap drawn over his face, stood upon the trap ready for execution. In bold letters was written, "Such be the doom of all traitors." Within was the following citation:

"Parson John H. Aughey, your treasonable proclivities are known. You have been reported to us as one of the disaffected whose presence is a standing menace to the perpetuity and prosperity of our newly-organized government—the Confederate States of America. Your name heads the proscribed list. You are ordered to appear on to-morrow afternoon at 2 o'clock before our vigilance committee, in W. H. Simpson's carriage shop, to answer to the charges of treason and abolitionism.

"BY ORDER OF THE VIGILANTES.

"K. K. K. & K. G. C."

Flight was now impossible, and I deemed it the safest plan to appear before the committee. I found it to consist of twelve persons, five of whom I knew, viz., Rev. John Locke, Armstrong, Cartledge, Simpson, and Wilbanks. Parson Locke, the chief speaker, or rather the inquisitor-general, was a Methodist minister, though he had fallen into disrepute among his brethren, and was engaged in a tedious strife with the church which he left in Holmes county. The parson was a real Nimrod. He boasted that in five months he had killed forty-eight raccoons, two hundred squirrels, and ten deer; he had followed the blood-hounds, and assisted in the capture of twelve runaway negroes. W. H. Simpson was a ruling elder in my church. Wilbanks was a clever sort of old gentleman, who had little to say in the matter. Armstrong was a monocular Hardshell-Baptist. Cartledge was an illiterate, conceited individual. The rest were a motley crew, not one of whom, I feel confident, knew a letter in the alphabet. The committee assembled in an old carriage shop. Parson Locke acted as chairman, and conducted the trial, as follows:

4

"Parson Aughey, you have been reported to us as holding abolition sentiments, and as being disloyal to the Confederate States."

"Who reported me, and where are your witnesses?"

"Any one has a right to report, and it is optional whether he confronts the accused or not. The proceedings of vigilance committees are somewhat informal."

"Proceed, then, with the trial, in your own way."

"We propose to ask you a few questions, and in your answers you may defend yourself, or admit your guilt. In the first place, did you ever say that you did not believe that God ordained the institution of slavery?"

"I believe that God did not ordain the institution of slavery."

"Did not God command the Israelites to buy slaves from the Canaanitish nations, and to hold them as their property for ever?"

"The Canaanites had filled their cup of iniquity to overflowing, and God commanded the Israelites to exterminate them; this, in violation of God's command, they failed to do. God afterwards permitted the Hebrews to reduce them to a state of servitude; but the punishment visited upon those seven wicked nations by the command of God, does not justify war or the slave trade."

"Did you say that you were opposed to the slavery which existed in the time of Christ?"

"I did, because the system of slavery prevailing in Christ's day was cruel in the extreme; it conferred the power of life and death upon the master, and was attended with innumerable evils. The slave had the same complexion as his master; and by changing his servile garb for the citizen dress, he could not be recognized as a slave. You yourself profess to be opposed to white slavery."

"Did you state that you believed Paul, when he sent Onesimus back to Philemon, had no idea that he would be regarded as a slave, and treated as such after his return?"

"I did. My proof is in Philemon, verses 15 and 16, where the apostle asks that Onesimus be received, not as a servant, but as a brother beloved?"

"Did you tell Mr. Creath that you knew some negroes who were better, in every respect, than some white men?"

"I said that I knew some negroes who were better classical scholars than any white men I had as yet met in Choctaw county, and that I had known some who were pre-eminent for virtue and holiness. As to natural rights, I made no comparison; nor did I say anything about superiority or inferiority of race. I also stated my belief in the unity of the races."

"Have you any abolition works in your library, and a poem in your scrap-book, entitled 'The Fugitive Slave,' with this couplet as a refrain,

'The hounds are baying on my track;
Christian, will you send me back?' "

"I have not Mrs. Stowe's nor Helper's work; they are contraband in this region, and I could not get them if I wished. I have many works in my library containing sentiments adverse to the institution of slavery. All the works in common use amongst us, on law, physic, and divinity, all the text-books in our schools—in a word, all the works on every subject read and studied by us, were, almost without exception, written by men opposed to the peculiar institution. I am not alone in this matter."

"Parson, I saw Cowper's works in your library, and Cowper says:

'I would not have a slave to fan me when I sleep,
And tremble when I wake, for all the wealth
That sinews bought and sold have ever earned.'"

"You have Wesley's writings, and Wesley says that 'Human slavery is the sum of all villainy.' You have a work which has this couplet:

' Two deep, dark stains, mar all our country's bliss:
Foul slavery one, and one, loathed drunkenness.'

You have the work of an English writer of high repute, who says, 'Forty years ago, some in England doubted whether slavery were a sin, and regarded adultery as a venial offence; but behold the progress of truth! Who now doubts that he who enslaves his fellow-man is guilty of a fearful crime, and that he who violates the seventh commandment is a great sinner in the sight of God?'"

"You are known to be an adept in phonography, and you are reported to be a correspondent of an abolition phonographic journal."

I Encountered An Old Colored Man.　　　　　Page 48

They Lived in a Cave on the Banks of that Stream.   Page 57

"I understand the science of phonography, and I am a correspondent of a phonographic journal, but the journal eschews politics."

Another member of the committee then interrogated me.

"Parson Aughey, what is funnyography?"

"Phonography, sir, is a system of writing by means of a philosophic alphabet, composed of the simplest geometrical signs, in which one mark is used to represent one and invariably the same sound."

"Kin you talk funnyography? and where does them folks live what talks it?"

"Yes, sir, I converse fluently in phonography, and those who speak the language live in Columbia."

"In the Deestrict?"

"No, sir, in the poetical Columbia."

I was next interrogated by another member of the committee.

"Parson Aughey, is phonography a abolition fixin'?"

"No, sir; phonography, abstractly considered, has no political complexion; it may be used to promote either side of any question, sacred or profane, mental, moral, physical, or political."

"Well, you ought to write and talk plain English, what common folks can understand, or we'll have to say of you, what Agrippa said of Paul, 'Much learning hath made thee mad.' Suppose you was to preach in phonography, who'd understand it?—who'd know what was piped or harped? I'll bet high some

Yankee invented it to spread his abolition notions underhandedly. I, for one, would be in favor of makin' the parson promise to write and talk no more in phonography. I'll bet phonography is agin slavery, tho' I never hearn tell of it before. I'm agin all secret societies. I'm agin the Odd-fellers, Freemasons, Sons of Temperance, Good Templars, and phonography. I want to know what's writ and what's talked. You can't throw dust in my eyes. Phonography, from what I've found out about it to-day, is agin the Confederate States, and we ought to be agin it."

Parson Locke then resumed:

"I must stop this digression. Parson Aughey, are you in favor of the South?"

"I am in favor of the South, and have always endeavored to promote the best interests of the South. However, I never deemed it for the best interests of the South to secede. I talked against secession, and voted against secession, because I thought that the best interests of the South would be put in jeopardy by the secession of the Southern States. I was honest in my convictions, and acted accordingly. Could the sacrifice of my life have stayed the swelling tide of secession, it would gladly have been made."

"It is said that you have never prayed for the Southern Confederacy."

"I have prayed for the whole world, though it is true that I have never named the Confederate States in prayer."

"Where and by whom were you educated?"

"In my childhood I attended the free schools in New York state and also in Steubenville, O. I was a student of Grove Academy, in Steubenville, O., 1844-5. Rev. J. W. Scott, D.D., was the principal. I was a student of Richmond College, Richmond, Jefferson Co., Ohio, three years. Rev. J. R. W. Sloane, D.D., was the president. Prior to this I studied classics two years with Rev. John Knox, of Springfield, Jefferson Co., O. I am an alumnus of Franklin College, New Athens, Harrison Co., O., was graduated during the presidency of Rev. A. D. Clark, D.D."

"Did you ever attend Oberlin College, O.?" said the presiding officer.

"I never had that honor, sir."

"What were the views of your educators on the slavery question?"

"They all believed that human slavery was a moral, social, and political evil—a cancer on the body politic, to be eradicated as soon as possible by mild means, or by heroic treatment as the exigencies of the case might demand, in order to the preservation of the national life. Since I came South I have taught in Winchester, Ky., Baton Rouge, La., Memphis, Tenn., Holly Springs and Rienzi, Miss., and have been acting pastor of the churches of Waterford and Spring Creek, in the Presbytery of Chickasaw, near Holly Springs, Miss.; and of Bethany Church in North Mississippi Presbytery."

"Are you a Mason or Odd Fellow?" said Parson Locke.

" I object to that question," said Mr. Armstrong, who belonged to a church that refused to fellowship any members of secret societies.

"I will not press the question," said the parson. " You may retire."

As I wended my way home I saw a large concourse in front of the shop, in the garb or rather guise of hunters. They had guns upon their shoulders and pistols in their belts. I recognized the majority of them as Unionists who had come, doubtless, to see that no harm befell me. There were a few virulent secessionists in the post-office, who, as I passed through it to the street, looked fiercely at me, and with horrid blasphemy gave their views as to what fate should befall traitors, tories, submissionists, and unionists. These remarks were intended for my ears.

After I had retired, Parson Locke said: "Mr. Cartledge, what is your opinion? Is Parson Aughey guilty or not guilty of the crimes charged against him in the indictment?"

"Guilty, sir, guilty. I node that afore I come here to-day. I node it after I hearn him preach that sermon agin secession, an' when I seed him rite out an' vote the Union ticket I didont need no more evidence of his a being guilty of all that is charged agin him, an' more too. Put me down in favor of hangin'."

ALEXANDER KNEELING AT THE SHRINE OF ACHILLES.

"Very well said, Mr. Cartledge. An honest, un-
equivocal, straightforward expression of your convictions. General Bolivar, let us hear from you."

Bolivar was a foundling. The gentleman at
whose gate the babe was abandoned gave him to the
colored women to raise. He was a great admirer of
the South American patriot and liberator, General
Simon Bolivar, so he named the waif, Simon Bolivar.
The gentleman lived in Boyle Co., Ky., on Rock
Creek, near Danville. Bolivar, when grown, married a poor white girl, and they lived in a cave on
the banks of that stream. He joined his fortunes
to a class of poverty-stricken people who were known
as rock angels, from their habitation amid the clefts
of the rocks. They procured a precarious livelihood
by hunting and fishing, often eking out their meagre
supply of life's necessaries by predatory excursions
to the sheep-folds and hen-roosts of the neighboring
gentry. Bolivar came to Mississippi in the employ
of a man who brought a drove of mules for sale, and
liking the climate he returned and brought his family.

Bolivar, when addressed, started suddenly as from
an apparent revery, and ejecting a quantity of ambier
from his filthy mouth, replied: "I agrees with my
neighbor Cartledge. Better men nor him hez been
hung in this county lately, an' it has done good. I
can't see no reason why he shouldent hang, an' that's
the way I votes."

"Major Wilbanks, how do you vote in regard to
the guilt or innocence of the prisoner?"

"You wish my candid opinion?"

"Yes, we do."

"Well, then, I will give it for what it is worth. I am in favor of a free country, a free press, free speech—free men, a free ballot and fair count."

"You might have added free niggers and completed your free catalogue," said Parson Locke. "Bro. Simpson, please give us your opinion and advice."

"Parson, I am halting between two opinions. I do not approve the views of my pastor, but he has never committed any overt act of treason. We can afford to wait for that. It may be possible—should the sentiments of those who have spoken prevail—that civil war would be inaugurated in our midst. The assembled crowd in front of this building is ominous of evil. I have looked out upon them, and I know that many of the men out there have been far more outspoken in the expression of opinions adverse to the Southern Confederacy than him whom we have had before us to-day, and they are armed to the teeth."

Parson Locke turned pale, and said if Bro. Simpson thought there was any immediate danger of exciting a riot, he would adjourn the session till some time in the near future, when, it was hoped, the excitement would have subsided.

Mr. John Mecklin arose and said, "I am but a spectator, but I would advise you to adjourn at once. Many of our best people think this to be an un-

warranted and illegal proceeding. Civil law is still
in force, and even if it were superseded by military
law that fact would not justify the arbitrary course
of this committee, who have acted without any
proper or competent authority, civil or military.
This man ·is not under your jurisdiction, and you
may have to answer for this day's proceedings."

Parson Locke, who was an arrant coward, replied
that he could not fully agree with the last two speak-
ers, but in the interests of peace and harmony he
would adjourn this meeting to a time in the near
future, when it would be convened at the call of the
president.

The committee then hastily adjourned. Parson
Locke made his exit by a door in the rear of the
building, and, making a circuit through the woods,
reached his home without observation.

The crowd was informed that an adjournment had
taken place, and that no formal verdict had been rendered. In a short time the crowd had dispersed.
Some of the more violent secessionists were greatly
exasperated when they learned that the vigilance
committee had not rendered a verdict of guilty and
ordered my execution. They determined to take the
matter into their own hands. I was speedily advised
of their threats. My friends provided me with arms,
and I resolved to defend myself to the best of my
ability. One evening I had gone over to a neighbor's,
Mr. Pickens Mecklin's. It was the dark of the
moon. As I returned, at. a late hour, I heard the

trampling of steeds. I concealed myself as they approached me. When they had come quite near, the men dismounted and tied their horses to trees. One said, "Do you think he's at home?" Another, "Well, boys, the tory parson's got to sup with Pluto to-night." Another said, "All I'm afeard of is that some of us will have to sup with him in Pluto's dominions. He's got fight in him, an' no mistake."

I had heard enough. I hastened home. My wife had retired. I quickly armed myself, after barricading the doors. After awhile there came a knock. No notice was taken of it. Soon a voice said, "Halloo!" Within the house all was silent as the grave. I had cocked both barrels of a gun heavily loaded with buckshot. I sat on a chair and aimed at the door, resolved to shoot the first that entered, should they succeed in breaking in the door. Soon there was a noisy demonstration. At length two of the men volunteered to go to the rear of the building, to the woodpile, and get a log to use as a battering-ram to break down the door. In their hot haste they ran against a clothes-line. I had eked the line with a piece of telegraph wire that some one in Vaiden had given me a short time before. Both of these men, John Cook and a Mr. Tower, were prostrated by the recoil, and quite severely injured. Cook was rendered unconscious, and Tower howled like a beaten hound. Several ran to their assistance. At this juncture two volleys of firearms were heard in quick succession. My would-be assassins ran and cried and fled.

A Mr. Denman had just finished digging a well for me. The structure at the surface, to guard against the danger of falling into the well, had not been completed. Some of the fugitives fell into the well, descending with the bucket. How they succeeded in getting out, I know not. Dr. Le Grand told me of one man, who was his patient, who died of the injuries received on that eventful night. How I had been so opportunely delivered was a mystery I could not fathom. My little daughter said to her mother, in the lull of the storm, "Ma, may I pray those verses you taught me?" Upon receiving permission, she arose in bed, knelt upon the pillow, and folding her little hands, said: "The angel of the Lord encampeth round about them that fear him, and he deivereth them. The righteous cry, and the Lord heareth them and delivereth them out of all their troubles. They cry unto the Lord in their trouble, and he bringeth them out of their distresses. Oh, that men would praise the Lord for his goodness and for his wonderful works to the children of men. Deliver us, O our God, out of the hand of the wicked, out of the hand of the unrighteous and cruel men. Oh, God! be not far from us. Oh, God! make haste for our help. For Christ our Redeemer's sake. Amen." Then she lay down, and was soon lost in innocent and unconscious slumber.

In an hour after the flight of these midnight marauders I heard a knock, which I recognized as a preconcerted signal of recognition among Unionists.

I went to the back door, whence the knock sounded, and signaled a reply. A low voice then uttered in a distinct tone the sentence, "Liberty and union, now and forever, one and inseparable." I opened the door; half a dozen friends entered. They and others, who remained on duty, had been guarding my house unknown to me. They remained an hour, uttering words of comfort, and gave me the assurance of all the assistance I should need, though at the peril of their lives. After parting salutations, I opened the door, and my friends disappeared in the darkness. We named this the battle of Wyandoue, the name of my home. Probably the first blood of the war was shed in this *rencontre.*

> "War is dread when battle shock and fierce affray
> Perpetuate a tyrant's name;
> But guarding freedom's holy fane, .
> Confided to her valiant keeping,
> The sword from scabbard leaping
> Flashes a heavenly light."

In the afternoon of the next day Elder John Mecklin and his estimable wife came to visit us, bringing their young son Reemer with them. Mr. Mecklin advised us to say nothing about this attempt upon my life, as reticence in war time was a virtue. The perpetrators of the dastardly attack would conceal their participation in it, even though some of their number should die of their wounds. Excitement must be allayed as much as possible. He feared that this assault would be followed by others, till they had accomplished their nefarious purpose. He said that my public position and avowed sentiments, and the fact that I was of northern birth and education, had concentrated upon me the malice of all those of secession proclivities, but he assured me that my friends would defend me at the risk of their lives. I advised him of my intention of removing into Attala county, near Nazareth church, which was also in my field of labor. He approved this course, since the excitement here ran very high, but affirmed that there was no place within the seceded states very safe for one whose Unionism was of so pronounced a type.

At this time there was a man named Dr. Smith who resided in Canton, Mississippi. He frequently visited friends in Choctaw county. He was a violent secessionist. Having learned of the failure of the attempt upon my life, he resolved to take charge of the matter himself, and execute summary vengeance upon one who had too long been suffered to live.

I had the charge of three churches — Poplar Creek and French Camp, in Choctaw county, and Nazareth, in Attala county. French Camp was twelve miles from my home, and Nazareth twenty-eight miles distant. Dr. Smith determined to come to French Camp on the Sabbath I preached in that church, and kill me there. He ordered his fast trotter, Bucephalus, to be attached to the buggy, and preparing his pistols, he started in hot haste to effect his murderous purpose. He reached French Camp about one o'clock P.M. He learned that after service I had gone to dine with Major Garrard. This was a mistake; I dined with Col. Hemphill. Dr. Smith dined with Dr. John Hemphill. He made known to Dr. Hemphill the object of his visit. The doctor tried in vain to dissuade him from his purpose. He now determined to follow me to my home and murder me there. He called at Col. Hemphill's and learned that I had dined with the colonel, and had left *en-route* for my home an hour before. I called at Esquire Pilcher's to see his daughter, Miss Belle, who was quite ill of malarial fever. After administering to her spiritual need, I pursued my journey homeward. Dr. Smith had just passed, driving Jehu-like (furiously). I followed rapidly, as a storm seemed imminent. I heard the vehicle in advance and tried to overtake it, as I desired company on this lonely road, but my horse was no match for the doctor's swift steed, so I providentially failed to overtake him.

About three miles from my home Dr. Smith left the main road for one that led to a Methodist chapel. He drove up to the chapel, descended from his buggy and ordered a colored boy to hold his horse. He approached a group of men, and noticing one who was quite well dressed and had a ministerial look and bearing, addressed him thus:

"Are you, sir, a messenger of the Lord of Hosts?"

The gentleman smiled and made no reply. The doctor then presented a pistol and fired. The ball passed through the lungs of his victim. Reason had left her throne. The doctor was a raving maniac.

DAVID AND GOLIATH.

"I COME TO THEE IN THE NAME OF THE LORD OF HOSTS."

The congregation rushed out of the chapel, took the doctor into custody, and resolved to administer summary vengeance according to the code of Judge Lynch. While they were waiting for a halter for which they had sent, Dr. Smith's brother and other friends arrived. They rescued him with difficulty from the infuriated crowd, conveyed him to his home in Canton, an alienist pronounced him hopelessly insane, and he soon after became an inmate of the insane asylum at Jackson. Deacon Colclough (pro. kokely), the doctor's victim, lingered for months on the border of the spirit land. The latest information I had indicated a fatal termination. Thus in the providence of God I was once more delivered from the wrath of man.

A rumor found its way into the papers that I had been fatally shot by Dr. Smith, of Canton. A friend residing in Carthage, Leake county, sent me a paper containing this notice:

" Rev. John H. Aughey, a Presbyterian minister, who has been doing evangelistic work in Attala and Choctaw counties, was fatally shot last week by Dr. Smith, of Canton. The doctor was a monomaniac. He believed himself to be commissioned by heaven to exterminate all who were not friendly to the Confederate States of America. He had been informed that Mr. Aughey had expressed disloyal sentiments, and was a leader of the disaffected. He left home with the avowed intention of killing him on sight. The doctor's brother, learning the nature of his mis-

5

sion, followed, but was unable to overtake him till he had committed the fatal deed. The particulars we have not learned. Mr. Aughey had the reputation of being an able minister, and very faithful in the discharge of his ministerial duties. That he was one of the disaffe ted is true. The extent of his opposition we have not learned. In times of great excitement rash acts are committed which are not warranted or required for the public safety. We regret Mr. Aughey's tragic end, and if justifiable we regret the necessity that required it. He leaves a widow and one child. *Requiescat in pace.*"

Commodore Spiva, a planter and leading member of my church in Attala county, offered myself and family a home as members of his family upon condition that I would superintend the studies of his son and daughter. They had entered upon a course of private study supplementary to the finished education they had received at the college and seminary. We were now domiciled in his spacious mansion on the banks of the meandering Yockanookany. We enjoyed comparative quiet for a time. My students were very much enamored of belles-lettres, and we took delightful rambles in the higher walks of literature. We enjoyed a continuous feast of reason and flow of soul. In my absence my wife became my vicegerent, and their rapid advance was not retarded.

The battle of Manassas had been fought and the boastful spirit of the secessionists was almost unendurable. The whole confederacy did nothing but brag

of what had been done and what would be done if
the Yankees persisted in their futile attempts to sub-
jugate the South. The South was arming for the
war. Joyfully and with alacrity the young chivalric
sons of the slave-holding aristocracy responded to
the call for volunteers. The young ladies presented
company and regimental flags of costly material,
deftly embroidered by their own fair fingers with rare
and significant designs, to every regiment as it left
for the theater of war. Upon their departure to the
seat of war, they were given an ovation, barbecues
were held, grandiloquent orations were pronounced,
in which the superiority of the South over the North
in valor, military skill, and chivalric spirit was an-
nounced in terms that admitted no contrary opinion.
They were assured that when they returned victorious—of which result there was not the least shadow
of doubt—and had secured the independence of a
glorious slave-holding confederacy, they would be
honored living, and when dead their memory
would be embalmed in the hearts of a grateful posterity and remembered with veneration, even until
the last moment of recorded time. Sax-horn bands
discoursed delicious music. "The Bonnie Blue
Flag that Boasts a Single Star," "Maryland, my
Maryland," and pre-eminently, "Dixie," were played
and sung by band and orchestra and choir. The
South had donned her holiday attire, and wine-cup,
dance, and song ruled the hour.

"Oh! that the Yankees would come," cried they,

"we would welcome them with bloody hands to hospitable graves. One of our companies is equivalent to a regiment of Yankees, and a southern regiment more than a match for ten thousand northern mudsills."

One evening Commodore Spiva met me as I walked museful in a grove. He joined me in a walk, and shortly drew me to a seat beneath a fig tree and thus began:

"Are you aware that your life is in danger?"

"Whence the danger?"

"There are men in our neighborhood that would have made the attempt to assassinate you ere this, but they know you are under my protection. I fear that as you travel about in the discharge of your pastoral duty they may waylay and murder you."

"I am prepared, if attacked, to defend myself."

"Your pistols would avail nothing at long range against men armed with rifles."

"Well, what would you advise?"

"Dr. Hughes will call upon you to-morrow and inform you of the decision arrived at at an informal meeting attended by the leading members and supporters of Nazareth Church."

On the next day Dr. Hughes called to inform me that if I wished to live long on the earth I must declare my adhesion unequivocally to the government of our nation, the sovereign state of Mississippi, and also my good-will toward the subordinate Confederate States of America, and my approval of their constitutions.

INSTANTLY THEY ALL THREE FIRED UPON THEIR WOUNDED AND
DEFENCELESS VICTIM. Page 70

"Declare my adhesion unequivocally to the government of our nation, the sovereign state of Mississippi, and also my good-will toward the subordinate Confederate States of America, and my approval of their constitutions? Doctor, is there any virtue in such a political creed to promote long life?"

"Yes, we all think so, and we believe the time has come when we cannot longer tolerate any sentiments in conflict with the views of the dominant class in our country. We like you as a man and as a minister, but we deprecate your treasonable opinions, and we cannot much longer, if we would, save you from the vengeance of the soldiers and the vigilantes. I will call to-morrow for your decision."

On the morrow he called, and I told him that I had decided to return to Tishomingo county. He expressed his approval. I removed my household goods to Goodman, a town on the Mississippi Central R. R., ordering their shipment to Iuka. I conveyed my wife and child by private conveyance. We spent one night in Macon, Noxubee Co. Rev. James Pelan had been called to the pastorate of the Presbyterian church of Macon. He was a Unionist. A committee was appointed by the citizens to examine his library. Many of his books were condemned by this committee as containing abolition sentiments. Rev. James Pelan was a man of excellent spirit—a ripe scholar and a worthy christian gentleman. His life was being embittered by his political enemies. Every sermon was misconstrued and tortured into teaching something contrary to the interests of the sovereign state of Mississippi and the Confederate States of America. Threats of lynching were freely made. The Unionists often conveyed secret information of plots against the life of this good man. Often his foes endeavored to impair his reputation by slander and calumny, but these as often recoiled upon their fabricators. Wearied of such a life of turmoil, he resigned his charge and removed to the country, but the malice of his enemies pursued him to his rural retreat. One evening, when walking on the lawn near his home, concealed assassins fired upon him, wounding him severely. For a long time he lingered between life and death, but a naturally strong constitution, together with good nursing, triumphed, and he began to convalesce. But his enemies were on the alert, and ascertaining that he was likely to recover, three devils incarnate came armed to his house. Mr. Pelan was sitting in a chair eating some delicacy that his wife had prepared for him. These demons in human form asked Mrs. Pelan if they could have supper. She replied, "Certainly, I will order my servants to prepare supper for you.' She left the room to give the order These men then arose and one of them said, "All the supper we want is to kill you, you infernal Unionist and abolitionist." Instantly they all three fired upon their wounded and defenseless victim. Mrs. Pelan, hearing the report, rushed in and caught her husband in her arms. In ten minutes he was a corpse. Before losing consciousness the dying martyr said, "Father, forgive them, they know not what they do." He also said, "Farewell, dear wife, I die, but the government still lives and will eventually subvert rebellion, for God is just." His last utterance was, "Lord Jesus, receive my spirit." Rev. James Pelan was of English birth and parentage. His brother, Rev. Wm. Pelan, was pastor of the Presbyterian church in Connorsville, Ind., for twenty years, now of Wells, Faribault Co., Minn.

Thus died one of my co-presbyters and dear friends. When our presbytery—the presbytery of Tombeckbee—convened at Aberdeen, we lodged and roomed together at the female seminary, of which Rev. R. S. Gladney was principal. Rev. R. S. Gladney was a violent secessionist. He had just written a poetical defense of slavery, and was woefully vexed that the blockade had prevented his publishers, the Lippencotts, of Philadelphia, from sending him the books. A young licentiate named Gallaudet was ordained at this session of presbytery to the full work of the gospel ministry. Mr. Gladney rebuked him quite severely in open presbytery because he had given a negative answer to the question, "Will slavery exist during the millennium?" Mr. Gladney affirmed that it would exist during the millennium, and would also exist in a modified form in heaven. The necessity of the marriage relation would terminate with earth, but he thought the southern people would require slaves in heaven in order to promote their highest happiness.

Rev. Gallaudet became pastor of the Presbyterian church in Aberdeen. Being a Unionist, the secessionists bitterly opposed him. At length to save his life he was compelled to abandon his field of labor. He made good his escape to the North. But poor Pelan was not so fortunate. The villain most prominent in his murder was killed in battle just three days after his diabolical crime. The righteous retribution of Divine Providence was not long delayed. Near this Judge Chisholm and his lovely daughter were murdered by the Ku Klux Klan.

We spent one night in Okolona, lodging at a hotel. A friend whom I had long known lived here. His name was Col. Carothers. He was a strong secessionist. He met me just as I had given my horse and buggy into the care of the proprietor of the hotel. He advised me to register under an assumed name, as the vigilantes had my name on their list of proscribed persons, and if recognized my fate would be sealed. He said: "On the morrow a regiment will leave for the seat of war in Virginia, and if your presence should become known they will surely take your life. Colin McIvor was hanged last Monday as a Unionist, although I and several others exerted our utmost influence to save his life. But it was without avail. We pleaded, but in vain, for a respite of two hours that he might make his will and bid his family farewell."

I demurred and declared that I was not ashamed of my name, that I had not done anything to disgrace it. He assured me that I must take his advice or pay the penalty of my temerity with my life. I walked up to the register and made this record: "George Bushrod Washington, wife, and daughter, Mt. Vernon, Va." After supper we entered the ladies parlor. Mrs. Des Lande, a lady boarder at the hotel, called our child to her, took her into her lap and said: " What is your name, my dear?"

" Anna Kate Aughey," she lisped.

"Where do you live?"

" Near Kosciusko, Attala Co., Mississippi."

" Where are you traveling?"

"To grandpa's, Mr. Alexander Paden's, at Iuka. But I think my pa is going to 'scape Norf from the bad people that tried to kill him. I heard him tell ma so. I ask God every day to take care of my dear pa, and ma does too. We are good people and love God; what do they want to shoot my poor pa for?"

The ladies present gave each other significant glances. Soon after Col. Carothers called me out. Said he: "You should not have registered by a name so renowned. It has attracted the attention of all the loungers at the hotel, and your little daughter, Major Linden informs me, has betrayed your secret. You should have registered your *nom de guerre* as John Smith, of Pontotoc, or some obscure town. Now do you and family retire to your room at once. I will arrange for your safety with Major Linden. He will order an early breakfast, and you can start by daylight or a little before. Drive rapidly to avoid pursuit, if it should be made, and it would be well to start southward and make a circuit as a blind."

We took his advice, and left ere the shades of night had lifted from the magnolia-embowered streets of Okolona. We started in a southern direction, made a circuit of several squares, and left the town *via* the northern suburbs. My good horse, Bellerophon, assumed a gait that led us to fear no pursuers.

"They will have swift steeds that follow with any prospect of success," said my wife.

Our horse slackened not his speed for several hours, and our babe slept sweetly and calmly. While the guests were at breakfast that morning in Okolona the chief of the vigilantes called to ascertain the antecedents and business in their city of the traveler who had registered as George Bushrod Washington. He learned, to his surprise and regret, that he had left at an early hour. The landlord disclaimed all knowledge of him or of his destination. At a meeting of the vigilantes that morning this matter was brought to their attention, but no definite action was taken, for lack of testimony, except that this telegram was sent to Tupelo: "Look sharp for a suspicious character traveling in a buggy with a lady and child. He travels *incognito*, or rather, under the assumed name of George Bushrod Washington. If he visits Tupelo, arrest him and send us word. He evaded us by leaving in the night. All charges will be paid out

of our secret service fund." Similar messages were
sent southward to the vigilantes in Columbus,
Lowndes county, and Meridian, Lauderdale county.

Upon reaching Marietta, Prentiss county, we met
Misses Bettie Greene and Josephine Young, my former
pupils at the Rienzi Female College. At their urgent
solicitation, we spent the night with their parents.
These families were Unionists. They informed us
that Messrs. Wroten and Nowlin, Unionists, had
been abducted by the vigilantes a month ago, and
had not been heard of since. They were either languishing in prison, or had been murdered. Their
families were in great distress because of their ominous absence. We reached the residence of Mr. Alexander Paden, my wife's father, the next afternoon, at
four o'clock, without further incident of interest, except that when we reached Mackey's creek we met
Major Stephen Davenport and Dr. Orton Choate, two
virulent secessionists, who hurrahed for Jeff Davis
and the Southern Confederacy. They asked me how
that suited me. I replied, "I am in favor of the
Union, the Constitution, and the enforcement of the
laws." They produced a flask of liquor and drank
confusion and death to all Yankees, tories, traitors,
submissionists, renegades, and abolitionists, North
and South. Saying, "We will see you later," they
rode off, brandishing their sword-canes and singing
"Dixie" in maudlin tones.

Upon our arrival in Tishomingo county I found
that the great heart of the county still beat true to

the music of the Union. At the last election they were permitted to hold the Union delegates received 1,400 majority. Union sentiments could be expressed with entire safety in many localities. Corinth, Iuka, and Rienzi had been from the commencement of the war camps of instruction for the training of Confederate soldiers. These three towns in the county being thus occupied, Unionists found it necessary, in their vicinity, to be more cautious, as the cavalry made frequent raids throughout the county, arresting and maltreating those suspected of disaffection. Corinth is a very important strategical point, situated in a semi-mountainous country, a branch of the Appalachian range which diverges from the Allegheny mountains and forms the mountains and gold-bearing regions of Georgia and Alabama. Here, also, is the junction of the Memphis and Charleston with the Mobile and Ohio railroads, which form the means of communication between the Atlantic and Gulf seaboards. After the reduction of Forts Henry and Donelson, and the surrender of Nashville, the Confederates made the Memphis and Charleston railroad the base of their operations, their armies extending from Memphis to Chattanooga. Soon, however, they were all concentrated at Corinth, in Tishomingo county.

Tishomingo and Iuka were two Indian chieftains. The town of Iuka was named for one and Tishomingo Co. for the other. After the battle of Shiloh, which was fought on the 6th and 7th of April, 1862, the Federal army advanced to Farmington, four miles north of Corinth, while the Confederates occupied Corinth, their rear extending to Rienzi, twelve miles south on the Mobile & Ohio railroad. Thus there were two vast armies encamped in Tishomingo Co. Being within the Confederate lines, I, in common with many other loyalists, found it difficult to evade the rigorously enforced conscript law. Believing that in a multitude of counselors there is wisdom, we held secret meetings in order to devise the best methods for evading the law. We met at midnight's weird and solemn hour. Often our wives, sisters, and daughters met with us. Our meeting place was some ravine or secluded glen, or by some mountain mere, as far as possible from the haunts of the secessionists. All were armed; even the ladies carried concealed revolvers which they knew well how to use. We had countersigns so as to recognize friends and discern enemies. *Taisez vous* was the countersign known by loyalists from the Ohio river to the Gulf of Mexico. The recognition of it was *Oui, Oui* (pronounced we, we). It was never discovered by the disloyal during the war. The nefarious crime of treason we were resolved not to commit. Our counsels were somewhat divided. We did not coincide in opinion upon the question whether we should attend the militia musters. Some advocating as a matter of policy the propriety of attending them; others, myself among the number, opposing it for conscience's sake, and for the purpose of avoiding every appearance of evil. Many who would not muster nor be enrolled as conscripts resolved to escape to the Federal lines, and making the attempt in squads, under skillful guides who could course it from point to point through the densest forests, with the unerring instinct of the panther or catamount or aborigines, at length reached the Union army, enlisted under the old flag, and have since done good service as patriot warriors.

The vigilantes became very troublesome. They arrested and murdered Unionists wherever they could be found. Few loyalists dared sleep at home, but seeking out some jungle or copse they improvised a rude arbor or den in which they spent the night, and to which they betook themselves when an alarm was given by their families or friends. Late one evening I saw the beacon fires burning. Mt. Sinai was all ablaze, the flames ascending high. The moon was obscured by dark dismal clouds. Mt. Nebo was lurid. The lambent flames from Pisgah had enveloped a stately pine—long since dead—standing on the lofty summit far above all other trees. Hermon and Horeb were dark as Erebus. Unless these two were illuminated it was but a call to an ordinary meeting. We gave these peaks those names to designate them so that by the fires kindled upon them they might serve as danger signals or call together in solemn assemblage the scattered Unionists. At 10 o'clock P.M. Horeb and Hermon blazed out from their lofty summits. The fierce and spiral flames recalled the pictures of Etna and Vesuvius in the geographies of my school days, where the mighty waves of glittering fire, through some internal convulsion, shot from their craters far upward into the midnight sky. These indicated a special call, either some impending danger was to be guarded against or some Unionist had been wounded or slain. I was just returning from a visit to Josselyn, Amos, Petrie, Aaron, and Morrow, who were in hiding and were awaiting the return of the guides who had gone with a squad to the Federal lines. As soon as I ascertained that Hermon and Horeb were blazing I returned to the lair of these hidden ones, and when from the summit of a hill they had seen the signal fires blazing, they at once started to the place of rendezvous. I did the same after I had secreted my horse in the stable of a friend.

THE MIDNIGHT MEETING, AND BATTLE IN GOOD SPRINGS GLEN.

Dark hills frowned on every side; the waters of a crystal spring bubbled up and in mournful cadence murmured a sad refrain, then swiftly glided away adown the glen; the midnight moon gazed wistfully down from the zenith; fitful clouds and the over-arching branches of the lofty forest trees, stately monarchs of the woods, obscured her light. I reached the place of rendezvous just at the noon of night. Quietly approaching from all possible points, human forms appeared, gliding noiselessly into the narrow arena around the spring. The numbers increasing, this place was tacitly surrendered to the women, the men retreating to the hillsides adjacent. John Beck received in a whisper from each the countersign, "The Union Forever." He reported ninety-four present, sixty-five men and twenty-nine ladies. I was the presiding officer, supported by two vice presidents, Henry Spence and Byron Hall.

Washington Gortney arose and said: "Mr. President—We are here assembled to determine what is the best method of evading the conscript law and keeping out of the rebel army. I favor enlisting in the Federal army. We will then be far more efficient in defending our government from subversion by traitors. James Reece, who is seated by yonder linden tree, and I have proved our faith by our works. We are soldiers in the Federal army. We fought at Shiloh and are with the army at Farmington assisting in the siege of Corinth, and soon we hope to capture that stronghold and bring deliverance to the persecuted Unionists in North Mississippi. If you stay here you will be forced into the rebel army, or you will be shot or hung, as too many of our loyal fellow citizens have been. There are already three hundred from this county in the Federal army, and four hundred from Franklin, the county contiguous to this in North Alabama. Leave your families; it will be only for a short time. Corinth will fall and before the Fourth of July this county, and probably the whole state, will be delivered from rebel

domination. I will make this motion: Be it resolved, that we believe it to be conducive to the best
interests of ourselves personally, and the Union
cause, to which we will ever adhere, for all of suitable
military age to escape to the Federal army now besieging Corinth and to enlist in that army."

Carle Ritter arose and said: "With all my heart
I second this motion, and I hope that it may be
adopted with entire unanimity. Our numbers have
been more than decimated by rebel violence within
the last month, and I firmly believe that this resolu-
tion presents the best method of securing our own
safety and overthrowing this ungodly rebellion
against the best government that ever existed on
earth—a rebellion inaugurated by slave holders in
the interests of an institution we detest."

The president called for remarks. Several made
brief addresses in favor of its passage. It was then
passed with entire unanimity.

At this juncture ominous sounds were heard.
Dark forms were seen on the hillside to the south.
Soon a line of battle was formed by our foes. We
quietly formed in line on the north hillside. They
dispatched a messenger who crossed the ravine to inform us that they were friends. John Beck hurried
over and found that they had a former countersign,
but he saw Bill Robinson and Major Ham at the
head of the line. Then we knew that we had been
betrayed and must fight for our lives without hope
of quarter if defeated. We told them not to ap-

6

proach a step nearer as we knew their character.
Major Ham was in command of this force sent to destroy us. He crossed the ravine and informed us
that he had been within twenty feet of the president
of the meeting, had heard the speeches and resolutions passed, was cognizant of our traitorous designs
against the Southern Confederacy, and informed us
that we must surrender unconditionally, give up our
arms, and be sent as prisoners to Corinth. He would
give us ten minutes for consultation. Should we re-
fuse he would not hold himself responsible for the
consequences. He feared that we would all be put
to death. We replied that we would not surrender
but would stand for our lives and do the best we
could, if attacked. He retired, deprecating our
course. They were startled at our apparent numbers.
They were led to believe that there were but few of
us, and that our disparity of force compared with
theirs would lead us to surrender at once. Had we
surrendered not one of us would have left that glen
alive. The gathering clouds indicated the near approach of a storm. The lightning flashed, the thunder rolled, the rain commenced to fall in torrents.
In the midst of the storm Ham's men advanced and
delivered a volley. James Brown fell dead at my side.
Smith Burgess was shot through the left hand. We
returned the fire with effect. The women crowded
round the spring in terror, all except Sadie Beck
and Sallie Ritter, who from behind two trees kept
up an incessant fire with navy repeaters. This in-

decisive contest had continued for an hour. The storm had passed and the moon shone brightly, no cloud intervening. John Beck detached nineteen men, passed down the glen, and making a circuit approached from the summit of the hill in the rear of Ham's men. Our fire slacking somewhat, Ham resolved on a charge across the ravine. As they crossed the ravine we fired rapidly; one man approaching me I emptied all the chambers of my revolver. He did the same with his. I was now without any means of defense. He approached and raised his revolver to strike me with it. I struck first and he fell unconscious at my feet. At that moment I received a blow on my head and fell unconscious on my prostrate foe. The last sounds I heard were the cheers of Beck and his men coming down the hill in the rear of Ham. When consciousness returned I was lying on a bed in a cabin surrounded by forest trees. Two ladies were the only persons present in the cabin, one of whom was seated at my bedside. On the green-sward in front of the door lay a man bound with cords. Gortney and Reece were seated on the ground near him. Gortney had recognized him as the guerilla who had murdered his brother only a week before because of his Unionism, and for this crime declared that he must die. At the moment of my fall Ham and his force, finding themselves assaulted in front and rear, precipitately retreated, leaving the Unionists masters of the field. Six were killed outright, two Unionists and four rebels. The dead were buried in separate graves on the hillside. I pleaded for the life of Bill Hodge, but Gortney was inexorable. I told him that I forgave Hodge for the wound he had inflicted upon me. Gortney and Reece went to procure me some water. After considerable persuasion I secured the consent of the ladies and after receiving a solemn oath from Hodge that he would not reveal the whereabouts of the cabin or anything to our injury I severed the cords that bound him and let him loose. He sprang away nimbly, and was ascending a knoll fifty yards distant when the sharp report of a rifle rang out on the morning air and I saw Hodge fall. When Gortney reached him he was dead. He and Reece buried him where he fell.

On the evening preceding this the vigilantes had tried and immediately hung George Payson and Rhoderick Murchison. They compelled them to dig their own graves, and then hung them and buried them in the graves they had dug. They had insisted upon being buried. The vigilantes said, "Yes, we'll bury you, but you shall dig your graves."

Payson said that he was a citizen of Bay Minette, Baldwin Co., Ala., and Murchison claimed his residence in Citronelle, Mobile Co., in the same state. He had removed from Multona Springs, Miss., a few months before. They said when arrested that they were *en route* to Enola, Butler Co., Ky., to visit friends. Upon searching them a letter was found on the person of Payson which read thus:

SADIE BECK AND SALLIE RITTER FROM BEHIND TREES KEPT
UP AN INCESSANT FIRE. Page 82

ALPHARETTA, MILTON CO., GA.,
Jan. 28, 1862.

Dear Geo.:

The Confederate authorities are becoming very cruel. They have incarcerated a number of our neighbors in a filthy prison, and forced several into their army. They say traitors to their Confederacy must die the death of dogs. My brothers, Leonidas and Perceval, have not slept at home for a month. More than fifty Unionists are in hiding. Good guides are difficult to procure. Two are expected from Selma soon, and we trust they will be successful in conducting to the Federal lines a large company. Gillam, Gilson, and Gillette, three Unionists of Seguin, Guadalupe Co., Texas, arrived here yesterday. They had many hairbreadth adventures in reaching this place. They were pursued by hounds, but succeeded in poisoning the dogs. They were compelled to leave Lee Ayler, who started with them, sick at the house of that staunch Unionist, Hornbrook Gradwohl. O, the troublous times we have fallen upon. I hear while I write the howling of the hounds in search of my brothers and other Unionists, led by those terrible vigilantes. But I feel sure that they will not be able to find them, thanks to the swamp, Little Dismal, and their knowledge of all the successful methods of destroying the scent and of evading or killing the dogs. I must close. I have to prepare food for the hidden ones. It will be taken to them to-night. Dear cousin, the loyal people will never be satisfied till the cruel perpetrators of so great outrages upon them are adequately punished. They deserve a severe penalty for the crimes committed to promote the interests of a usurpation organized to destroy the best government˙ this world has ever known, and to perpetuate an institution subversive of the rights of man.

Your affectionate Cousin,

JENNIE SILVERTHORN.

This letter led the vigilantes to infer that Payson and Murchison were endeavoring to escape to the Federal lines. They were convicted and hanged, and buried in the grave they were compelled to dig.

I received three citations to appear on a certain day to be enrolled to attend muster as a conscript. I paid no attention to the citations. At length I received this summons to attend court-martial:

Ma. the 22, 1862.

Parson John H. Awhay:

You havent tended nun of our mustters as a konskrip. Now you is herby summenzd to atend a kort marshal at Jim Mocks. June the furst.

BLOUNT.

When I received this summons I called a meeting of the Unionists. Several had on the same day received similar official notices to attend the court-martial. We spent a whole night in consultation. We were one hundred strong, and I advocated attending in a body, properly armed, and, if necessary, to accept the gage of battle, but McElhinny and Scotland's wives had learned that a large force of cavalry from Corinth would be sent to assist the vigilantes. The majority refused to credit this report till a note was read from Miss May Coe, who was a spy in our interest. We could not doubt the authenticity of her information, corroborative of Mesdames McElhinny and Scotland's report. We then resolved as a dernier resort to make the attempt to reach Farmington, where the Federal army was encamped besieging Corinth. When I reached Rienzi it was evident that the Confederates were evacuating Corinth. On the 1st day of June (the day appointed for the convening of the court-martial) I had the pleasure of once more beholding the star spangled banner, as it was borne in front of General Gordon Granger's command, which led the van of the pursuing army. Thus for the present I escaped death at the hands of the rebels.

General W. S. Rosecrans upon his arrival made his head-quarters at the house of my brother, David H. Aughey, where I had the pleasure of forming his acquaintance, and that of Generals Ammen, Smith, Pope, and others. Tishomingo county was now measurably in possession of the Federal army. Col. Elliott, in his successful raid upon Booneville, passed Jim Mock's, at whose house the court-martial was to convene, scaring him so greatly that he dared not sleep in his house for several weeks. The Union cavalry scoured the country in all directions, and we

were rejoicing in the prospect of continuous safety
and freedom from outrage.

The rebels in their retreat had burned all the cotton which was accessible to their cavalry on their route.
At night the flames of the burning cotton lighted up
the horizon for miles around. These baleful pyres
with their lurid glare bore sad testimony to the horrors of war. In this wanton destruction of the great
southern staple, many families lost their whole staff
of bread, and starvation stared them in the face.
Many would have perished had it not been for the
liberal contributions of the North, for learning of the
sufferings of the poor of the South, whose whole supply had been destroyed by pretended friends, they
sent provisions and money, and thus many who were
left in utter destitution were rescued from perishing by
this timely succor. I have often heard the rejoicings
and benedictions of the poor, who, abandoned by their
supposed friends, were saved with their children from
death by the beneficence of those whom they had been
taught to regard as enemies—the most bitter, implacable, and unmerciful. Their prayer might well be,
"Save us from our friends, whose tender mercies are
cruel." I have never known a man to burn his own
cotton, and I have heard bitter anathemas and fierce
invective hurled at those who thus robbed them, and
their denunciations were loud and deep against the
government which authorized such cruelty. It is true
those who lose their cotton, if secessionists, receive a
promise to pay, which all regard as not worth the

"Noah got tight too, and cussed his nigger boy Ham."

paper upon which it is written.) Ere pay day those
who are dependent upon their cotton for the necessaries of life would have passed that bourne whence
no traveler returns.

'Tis like the Confederate bonds—at first they were
made payable two years after date, and they were
printed upon paper so worthless that it would be en-
tirely worn out in six months, and the promise to
pay would have become illegible in half that time.
The succeeding issues were made payable six months
after the ratification of a treaty of peace between the
United States and the Confederate States. Though
not a prophet, nor a prophet's son, I venture the
prediction that those bonds will never become due.
The war of elements, the wreck of matter, and
the crash of worlds announcing the final consum-
mation of all things will be heard sooner.

As the prospect was so favorable that this whole
region of country would soon be in the hands of the
Federal troops and occupied by them, I deemed it
safe to return to my father-in-law's, in the south-east-
ern part of Tishomingo Co. I applied to Gen. Rosecrans for a pass through the lines for myself, wife,
and child. Gen. Rosecrans went with me to see
General Pope, and after introducing me and vouching
for my loyalty, asked him for the pass I desired.
Gen. Pope said that he had issued orders to the effect
that no passes through the lines should be granted
for a specified time. Gen. Rosecrans then proffered
to send Captain Gilbert, one of his staff officers, with

us beyond the lines. This he said was done in consideration of the kindness I had shown him and staff
upon his arrival in Rienzi. He told me that the
rebels were over there in the woods not more than a
fourth of a mile distant, and that they were about to
move upon them. He advised me to return to Rienzi
till the rebels were driven farther south. We were
then near Mr. McClaren's, seven miles from Rienzi,
on the road to Booneville. I resolved to run the risk,
as Mrs. Aughey was anxious to return to her father's.
We started and had not gone far when the screaming
shells and bursting bombs came howling through the
valley. Then followed the rattle of musketry, and
presently the impinging of steel. The din of battle
sounded in our ears. Suddenly a shell, screeching like
a howling demon, passed over us. The pomp and
circumstance of glorious war were displayed to our
startled gaze. A retrograde was as dangerous as a
forward movement, and we persistently followed our
leader, Captain Gilbert. Our child, not realizing the
danger, laughed merrily at the grand panorama.
Soon a charge was sounded and the rebels fled pell-
mell, pursued vigorously by the victorious boys in
blue. I had no fear for my own personal safety because of the excitement, but feared greatly that some
of the missiles might injure wife or child. But they
seemed to bear a charmed life, for though the air was
full of messengers of death, and many whistled by in
close proximity, none did us the least injury. Several
times when a shell exploded near, our horse reared

and plunged, to the imminent peril of the occupants of
the vehicle.   Before the noise of the battle had wholly
ceased my wife pointed to a navy repeater lying on
the ground.   I descended from the buggy and secured
it.

At this time all marketable commodities were commanding fabulous prices.   Flour sold at $30 per bar-
rel, bacon 40 cents per pound, coffee one dollar per
pound; salt was nominally one hundred dollars per
sack of one hundred pounds, but there was none to
be obtained even at that high price.   All manufactured
goods were very costly.   Upon the occupation of the
country by Federal troops goods could be obtained
at reasonable prices, but our money was all expended
except Confederate bonds, which were worthless.
Planters who lived beyond the lines of the retreating
rebel army had cotton, but they feared to sell it as
the rebels called it treason to trade with the invaders,
and threatened to inflict the penalty in every case.
As there was no penalty attached to the selling of
cotton by one Mississippian to another, my Unionist
friends offered to sell their cotton to me for whatever
price I could afford to pay.   I was also solicited to
act as their agent in the purchase of commodities.   I
agreed to this risk because of the urgent need of my
friends, many of whose families were destitute of the
indispensable necessaries of life.   I thought it was
better that one should take a great risk than that
many people should perish.   By this arrangement
my Unionist friends would escape the punishment

meted out to those who were found guilty of trading
with the Yankees; if discovered I alone would be
amenable to their unjust and, under the appalling
environment, extremely cruel and vindictive law, and
my friends would thus save their cotton liable to be
destroyed at any moment by a dash of rebel cavalry.
I sold their cotton, procured supplies for the famishing, and thus relieved the wants of many. I did not
charge one cent for commission fees, and expended
one hundred dollars of my own money to furnish
provisions for families utterly destitute, some of whom
had not tasted food for days. One day I rode into
Iuka to the head-quarters of Gen. Wm. Nelson. The
Gen. told me that he learned that Norman's bridge
over Bear creek was held by a force of rebels. He
asked me if I could send one or two Union men to
that place to ascertain the number and position of the
troops holding that point. I replied that I could.
I secured the services of Wm. and John Thompson,
who were brothers and staunch Unionists, to accomplish this hazardous undertaking. Only one of them
succeeded. He got through on the pretext that he
was desirous of getting medicine for his sick wife.
He gave the diagnosis, procured the medicine at a
cost of three dollars, and returned. During his brief
stay he learned the probable number and disposition
of the troops stationed at the bridge, and discovered
the vulnerable point and recommended a plan of attack. I conveyed his report to Gen. Nelson. The
next night the attack was made and not a rebel sol-

dier escaped death or capture. Thus was Norman's bridge captured and destroyed.

One day I rode over to Mr. Holland Lindsay's on business. I had learned that he was a rabid secessionist, but supposed that no rebel cavalry had come so far north as his house since the evacuation of Corinth. Mr. Lindsay had gone to a neighbor's. His wife was engaged in weaving. She was a coarse, masculine woman, and withal possessed of a strong prejudice against all whom she did not like, but an especial hatred of the Yankees rankled in her bosom. I sat down to await the return of her husband. Soon Mrs. Lindsay broached the exciting topic of the day, the war. She thus vented her spleen against the Yankees:

"There wur a Yankee critter company (cavalry) come along here last week. They hearn a noise an' thought our troops waz a comin' so they drawed up in two streaks of fight right in front ov our house. Arter a while they axed me ef I haddent seen no rebels scoutin' round here lately. I jes' tole 'em it warnt none ov their bizness. Them nasty, no-account scamps callin' our men rebels. Them triflin', nigger-stealin' scoundrels. They runs off our niggers an' won't let us take 'em to Mexico an' the other territories."

I ventured to remark, "The Yankees are mean indeed, not to let *us* take *our* negroes to the territories and not help catch them for *us* when they run off."

The emphatic us and our nettled her, as none of

the Lindsays had ever owned a negro, being classed
by the white nabobs as poor white trash, nor did I
ever own a slave.

She replied: "I've hearn that you is a tory." She
became reticent, indeed quite morose.   I concluded
to ride over to Mr. Spigener's, to whose house Mrs.
Lindsay had informed me her husband had gone.
On the way I met Hill's cavalry.   One of them
halted me, inquired my name and business, which I
gave.   He informed me that Mr. Lindsay had gone
across the fields home and that he was on his way to
Mr. Lindsay's.   When we reached Mr. Lindsay's
house we saw him in the yard.   I transacted my business with him as quickly as possible.   Some soldiers
had gone into the house.   Mrs. Lindsay told them
that I was a double-dyed tory and advised my arrest.
The cavalrymen were all around me.   Davis, Lindsay's nephew, came out and ordered my arrest.   He
sent my horse to the stable.   After supper my horse
was brought and I was taken to camp.   I was now
a prisoner in the hands of my own and my country's
enemies.   Four men were detached to guard me during the night.   They ordered me to lie down on the
ground and sleep.   The ground was wet and I had
no blanket, so I insisted upon going to Mr. Spigener's, about one hundred yards distant, to secure a
bed.   They would not consent, but I started without
permission.   The guards followed me.   Mr. Spigener gave me a bed, the guards remaining in the room
watched me while I slept.   The next morning I

asked permission to see their captain, whose name
was Hill. I asked to be allowed to return home, in-
forming him that I had been arbitrarily arrested by
some of his men. I said that I was a civilian and
not amenable to military law. Capt. Hill replied:

"Are you a Unionist?"

"I voted the Union ticket, sir."

"That is not a fair answer. I voted the Union
ticket myself. Now I am warring against the
Union."

"I have seen no valid reason for changing my
sentiments."

"You confess, then, that you are a Unionist?"

"I do. I regard the union of these states as of
paramount importance to the people inhabiting them."

"You must go to head-quarters, where you will be
dealt with as we are accustomed to deal with all the
abettors of an abolition government."

A guard numbering fifteen were detached to take
charge of me. The apparent leader was a soldier
named Saccapee Vaudreuil, who claimed that he was
a descendant of Pocahontas in the 10th generation.
They then started to convey me to Fulton, the county
seat of Itawamba Co., Miss. When we reached a
cross-roads about 12 miles from the point of starting,
we found a company in charge of a Unionist prisoner
named Benjamin Clarke. We were then placed in
charge of two men, Dr. Crossland, of Burnsville, and
Ferdinand Woodruff. They were under the influence
of liquor and were very insulting in their denuncia-

tions of all traitors to the Southern Confederacy.
They detailed to each other a history of their licen-
tious amours. Dr. Crossland was the father of a
very pretty little girl whose mother was a poor white
woman. We halted for dinner. They asked me to
pay for it, which I did, they promising to refund the
money when we reached Fulton. This they forgot
to do.

On our arrival at Fulton we were taken to the
head-quarters of Col. Bradfute, the commander of the
post. My fellow-prisoner was examined first. Woodruff stated that they had played off on Clarke. They
had visited him as he was plowing in his field, telling him that they were Federal soldiers—they were
disguised as such—Clarke assured them that he was
a Unionist, and that he hoped soon to enlist in the
Federal army. Bradfute became very angry upon
hearing this, swearing that Clarke ought to be taken
out and shot then, but he said a few days' respite
would make but little difference, as Gen. Beauregard
would not allow such a tory to live long. Said he,
addressing the guards, "Had you hung Clarke you
would have saved us some trouble and have done
your country good service." The colonel, turning
round, glared upon me with eyes inflamed with passion and liquor, and thus addressed me: "Are you
a Unionist, too?"

"I am, sir. I have never denied it."

"Where do you reside?"

"My home is Rienzi, Tishomingo Co., Miss."

THE BEGGAR.

"What is your profession?"

"I am a minister of the Gospel."

"I suppose, then, that you go to the Bible for your politics, and that you are a sort of higher law man?."

"My Bible teaches, let every soul be subject to the higher powers, for there is no power but of God. The powers that be are ordained of God. Whosoever, therefore, resisteth the power, resisteth the ordinance of God, and they that resist shall receive to themselves damnation. I have seen no valid reason for resistance to the government under which as a nation we have so long prospered."

"I command you to hush; you shan't preach treason to me, and if you were to get your deserts you would be hanged immediately. Have you ever been within the Federal lines?"

"I have, sir."

"At what points?"

"Rienzi and Iuka."

"When were you at Iuka?"

"On last Saturday."

"Had the Federals a large force at that place, and who was in command?"

"They have a large force, and Generals Thomas and Steedman were in command."

"That is contrary to the report of our scouts, who say that there are but two regiments in the town. I fear you are purposely trying to mislead us."

"Gen. Steedman has but two regiments in the town, but Gen. Geo. H. Thomas is within striking distance with a large force."

7

"What was your business at Iuka?"

"I went there to pay a debt of fifty dollars which a widow—Mrs. Nixon Paden—owed. She wished it to be paid in Confederate money before it became worthless."

"Have you a Federal pass?"

"I have none with me, but have one at home."

"How does it read?"

"It was given by Gen. Wm. Nelson, and reads thus: 'The bearer, Rev. John H. Aughey, has permission to pass backward and forward through the lines of this division at will.'"

"Where were you born?"

"In New Hartford, Oneida Co., New York."

"Yankee born," said the colonel, with a sneer, "you deserve death at the rope's end, and if I had the power I would hang all Yankees who are among us, for they are all tories, whatever their pretensions may be."

"My being born north of the nigger line, Col., if a crime worthy of death, was certainly my misfortune, not my fault, but the fault of my parents. They did not so much as consult me as to any preference I might have as to the place of my nativity."

Woodruff, one of the guards, now informed Col. Bradfute that I was a spy, and while the Confederates were at Corinth had, to his certain knowledge, visited Nashville, Tenn., carrying information.

I told Woodruff that his statement was false, and that he knew that it was utterly without foundation in fact.

At the close of the examination, Col. Bradfute and an officer, whom the guards told us was Gen. Chalmers, spent fifteen or twenty minutes in bitterly cursing and denouncing all traitors, Yankees, and tories, as they termed us.

Gen. Chalmers wrote me from Washington City, while he was a member of congress, that he was not the officer who was present with Col. Bradfute. That on that day he was eight miles east of Fulton, busily engaged in making preparations for a battle with Gen. Philip Sheridan, which was fought on the next day; and he asserted that he would not have treated prisoners with so great insolence and severity. He also denied any complicity in the Fort Pillow massacre. This officer, at the instance of Col. Bradfute, wrote to Gen. Pfeiffer. He absented himself for a short time, and I, from my position behind his chair, could read the letter. The following sentences occurred in the document: "An avowed Unionist. Has done our cause much harm. Advocates reconstruction at this late day. A pestilent fellow. Has in our presence uttered treasonable sentiments, and seems to take pleasure in doing so. He has held treasonable correspondence with the enemy, and has more than once enacted the spy. We can furnish testimony to establish all the above charges." We were then placed under guard and sent to the head-quarters of Gen. Pfeiffer, in Saltillo. We were brought into the august presence of this redoubtable general. When he read the letter handed him by the guards, he soundly berated us, and then sent us out a mile and a half from town, where we were placed under guard for the night in a small plat of ground surrounded by a chain. Quite a number of prisoners were there under guard; it was a sort of guard house, except that there was no house. No supper was furnished us, and the bare, cold ground was our bed and the blue canopy of heaven our covering.

The next morning we were brought into the presence of Gen. Pfeiffer. I asked for breakfast. This was refused. I offered to pay a dollar for a meal, as I was very hungry. To this he deigned no reply. I then offered three dollars for a lunch for myself and Clarke. This offer was arrogantly refused. He said he had no supplies for traitors at any price.

Said he, "I learn that you were born in New Hartford, New York, brought up in Steubenville, Ohio. How long have you lived in the South?"

"I have lived in the South eleven years."

"Where have you lived?"

"In Winchester, Clark county, Ky., Baton Rouge, La., Memphis, Tennessee, Holly Springs, Miss. My home at present is Rienzi, Miss."

"Are you a slave-holder?"

"I am not."

"Will you take the oath of allegiance to the Confederate States of America?"

"I will not."

"Have you recently taken the oath of allegiance to the United States of America?"

WE WERE BROUGHT INTO THE PRESENCE OF GEN. THOS. JORDAN.   102

"I have."

"Where and when?"

"Gen. Wm. Nelson administered to me the oath June 8th, 1862, at his head-quarters in Iuka, Miss."

"Do you regard that oath of any binding force?"

"I do, most assuredly."

"Did you take it voluntarily?"

"I certainly did."

"Do you know that in taking that oath you became guilty of treason against the Confederate States of America, and the Republic of Mississippi?"

"I could not be a traitor to a cause I never espoused, nor betray the interests of a government which I have always denounced as a usurpation. I profess to be a loyal citizen of the state of Mississippi and of the United States of America, and I hope to see this state, whose true interests I have ever endeavored to promote, return to her allegiance to the Federal Union which she has for the present endeavored to repudiate. I hope the sober second thought will lead her to see and repent her folly. Had the secession ordinance been submitted to the people and a free ballot and a fair count allowed, then we would have voted it down by a majority of more than two to one."

"Are you a higher law man?"

"Yes, I believe in the command, 'Let every soul be subject unto the higher power,' the powers that be."

"Well, the Confederate authorities are the higher

powers, and the powers that be. The Confederate government is the government *de facto*, and by the Bible rule you ought to submit to it as a good citizen."

"Any insurrectionary faction usurping temporarily the reins of government, may have a *de facto* power to compel obedience to its behests by those who are willing to acquiesce rather than endure the penalty for resistance of its illegal and tyrannical exactions. Mobs in cities are often the powers that be, and a horde of bandits have often been the *de facto* rulers, terrorizing the people of a wide district, and for a time defying the civil authorities. I regard the Federal government engaged in quelling rebellion as the *de jure* government to which I owe allegiance. Those who are engaged in rebellion against this government are traitors to their God, recreant to their own best interests, and are guilty of treason against the best government the world has ever known."

"Do you know, sir, that all you have uttered has been recorded, and that you have spoken these words against your own life?"

We were then delivered to the guards, fourteen in number, and conducted to a hamlet near Verona, where were the head-quarters of Gen. Sterling Price. We were brought into the presence of Gen. Thomas Jordan, Gen. Beauregard's chief of staff. When he read the letter from Gen. Pfeiffer, handed him by one of the guards, he said, looking at me sternly: "You, sir, are charged with sedition."

" What does sedition mean ? "

" It means enough to hang you, you villainous tory. Where were you born."

"In New Hartford, near Utica, Oneida county, New York."

" Born in an abolition state, you doubly deserve to die, and no mercy or pity should be shown you."

".As to the guilt attached to my first seeing the light in the Empire state, if sin, it is not mine, but the sin of my parents. But you talk as a veritable son of folly, and in so doing you reproach God. Parents, native place, and clime. All appointed were by Him. But I glory in my native state. New York has never done anything to stain her fair escutcheon. She has never repudiated her just debts. She has never nullified Federal laws. She has never attempted to secede from the Union. Permit me, General, to ask you where you were born and educated ? "

"I was born in Georgia, and graduated from the military academy at West Point, in your native state."

"New York may have, in some degree, tarnished her fair fame by nourishing in her bosom and allowing to be educated within her borders, a few traitors to the Federal government, but it is some palliation that it was not wittingly done."

" Do you call me a traitor to my face ? "

" I make no personal application, but allow each one for himself to draw the inference his own conduct justifies."

"If you were so enamored of New York, why did you not stay there or return when Mississippi seceded, or when an act was passed by the congress of the Confederate States of America, entitled 'An act respecting alien enemies,' warning and requiring every male citizen of the United States, fourteen years old and upward, to depart from the Confederate States of America within forty days from the date of the president's proclamation, which was issued August 14, 1861, this proclamation excepting from its operation Delaware, Maryland, Kentucky, Missouri, District of Columbia, and the territories of New Mexico, Arizona, and Indian Territory."

"I regard Mississippi as still a member of the Federal Union, and the act of secession illegal and unconstitutional, and therefore void. I am a citizen of the United States of America. If the proclamation issued August 14, 1861, was aimed at and included the Unionists, we were recognized as citizens of the United States at that date, many months after the passage of the secession ordinance, and as we have as often as it has been offered, firmly refused to take the oath of allegiance to the Confederate States of America, and thereby become citizens of the Southern Confederacy, we are still, as you must acknowledge, citizens of the United States of America. If we are citizens of the Confederate States of America, why so persistently offer us the oath of allegiance. Many citizens of Germany, Great Britain and Ireland, and other foreign countries, have long resided in our country and have never taken the oath of allegiance, or become naturalized. Why not allow us to remain as residents within, but not as citizens of, the Confederate States of America?"

"By your own statement you are an alien enemy of our Confederacy, and have no rights that we are bound to respect. You clearly come within the scope of the law and proclamation. My plan would have been to suffer all alien enemies to depart in peace who were willing to accept the offer, and hang those who desired to stay and do us all the harm they could."

"The Unionists are a mighty host. In forty days they could not dispose of their property."

"No, they would not be allowed to take with them any of their property. Our congress passed a law to the effect that the property of all in the South who have a domicile in the North shall escheat to the Confederate States, and that any of our citizens who are indebted to citizens of the United States shall, upon payment of three-fourths of their indebtedness to the treasury of the Confederate States of America, be liberated from any claim upon them by their alien creditors."

"Perfidy personified! Now, sir, suppose the cause of the Union should triumph, what will become of those like you who have taken a solemn oath to support the government at whose expense you have been educated, and then in violation of that oath, and forgetful of her fostering care, as base ingrates have rebelled and with malice prepense are endeavoring to subvert the best government on earth, a government which has never in person or property inflicted upon you a single injury, but has bestowed many favors, and superabundant blessings?"

"I will never ask clemency from a government I detest. There is no danger of abolitionism and puritanism triumphing. Should they do so I would make my home in Brazil or Cuba. I will hear no more of your detestable palaver. Jefferson Davis, in clemency and mercy to the misguided, issued his proclamation; those who have not availed themselves of it must bear the terrible and just consequences."

"My friends who expressed their willingness to accept Jeff Davis' permission to leave, are either dead or languishing in gloomy prisons. It was only a piece of treachery on the part of your *honorable* president and his *most honorable* congress. But just give me a pass to go north and I will go instanter."

"The first pass you will get will be a free ticket to hell, where you would have been long ago if the devil had his due, or the Confederate officers had done their duty."

"Thanks, for your kind offer to give me a free ticket to the infernal regions. I was not aware before that you were the devil's ticket agent. You have me in your power and may take my life, but you cannot destroy the government. It will live long after you and I are dead. But what right, may I ask, have you, who believe in state sovereignty, you, a citizen of what you term the republic of

Georgia, to leave your own nation, and crossing the foreign republic of Alabama, enter the republic of Mississippi, and interfere with me, one of its humble citizens, who has never breathed the air of your august republic to do you or any of the citizens of your foreign government any harm. This is an unwarranted and unlawful act, and evinces a high degree of presumption upon the part of an alien—a foreigner who has not, I opine, been naturalized since his advent into our nation, the independent, sovereign republic of Mississippi."

"Did you oppose the secession of Mississippi?"

"I did, but I now favor it. I trust that she will soon become convinced of her folly and secede from this confederation and resume her allegiance to the Federal union."

"That tongue of yours will not long give utterance to such vile and treasonable sentiments, you ought upon your capture to have been sent to hell from the lowest lateral limb of the nearest tree. Corporal of the guard, take charge of the prisoners."

We were soon under way to Tupelo. When we reached this town we were conducted to the office of the provost marshal. We underwent an examination here in presence of officers of high rank, Gen. Braxton Bragg, Gen. Hardee, and Gen. Sterling Price being among the number. Their insignia of high rank, their dignified bearing, their resolute demeanor, their searching and subtle questions, wisely put to elicit the desired information to secure our condemnation, awed me into reticence. I perceived that my life hung in a balance, and realized as never before the necessity of exercising great discretion in giving answers so as not to provoke these officers (who had the authority to order my immediate execution), and thus avoid the doom which a single incautious word would doubtless precipitate.

I told General Bragg, in reply to one of his leading questions, evidently designed to force from my lips a confession of my guilt, that it was an admitted principle in law, that no one is required to criminate himself.

General Sterling Price, who had just completed a dispatch which he handed to a courier, ordering him to convey it as speedily as possible to some subaltern in Verona, with a sharp look and an air of triumph said, "Your answer, by implication, admits your guilt. You would, it seems, shelter yourself behind a provision of the common law, which is suspended in its operation by martial law, which supersedes civil law during the continuance of the war. Will you take the oath of allegiance?"

"I will not make any admission nor confession, nor will I take the oath of allegiance."

"Well," said General Bragg, "we will await the testimony. From the tenor of this paper which I hold in my hands, there seems to be an abundance of it. We have too long been lenient with this dangerous class in our midst. I am inclined to punish them hereafter to the extent of my authority and the demerit of their treasonable conduct."

Clarke trembled like an aspen, and utterly refused to make any statement. I felt greatly depressed. I was hungry, thirsty, greatly fatigued, and mentally disquieted, knowing that my wife would be much distressed because of my ominous absence, the cause of which she could only conjecture.

We were then taken into the presence of the commander of the post. The provost marshal's name was Paden—the name of the commander was Clare. Gen. Thomas Jordan was now present, as well as the former named officers of distinguished rank. General Jordan made a statement. I feared from the interjected utterances of Gen. Bragg that we would be shot or hung at once. He was very angry, and several times declared that we deserved immediate execution. At length, in apparently great excitement and indignation, he called the officer of the guard, and I feared the worst, but he only ordered him to take us to the dungeon. We were speedily committed to prison. When we entered, two men, Capt. Bruce and Lieut. Richard Malone, men who had been elected to these positions by their fellow prisoners, received us with a cordial greeting. We told them that we were perishing from hunger and thirst. Bruce and Malone set two of the prisoners at work to prepare something for us to eat. Bruce, addressing us, said, "Our bill of fare is not very extensive nor inviting. We have no coffee, nor molasses, nor sugar, nor salt, nor beef, nor vegetables. In these war times we must not be epicures nor expect the luxuries

of life, but be content with what we can get, just
what is indispensable in prolonging existence. We
are allowed to do our own cooking, but that, in the
kindness of heart of the Confederate authorities, is
accorded as a favor, an indispensable sanitary regulation. We have but little exercise, they say, and exercise being conducive to health, cooking promotes
that object. We will soon have ready for you some
corn-bread and a little meat. The meat makes up in
strength and odor what it lacks in quantity, and the
parasites will impart a freshness to it so that you will
think of fresh meat while chewing it." The prison
was filthy in the extreme, and full of vermin, even
our food was infested. No brooms were furnished
us, and we could not sweep the floor. No beds or
bedding were provided, and we were compelled to sleep
upon the floor without covering and nothing but the
hard planks underneath us. When night came a
space on the floor was assigned to Clarke and myself.
We lay down on our hard bed and tried to sleep,
but our slumbers were sadly disquieted by the cold
and filth and hardness of the floor, and the graybacks, with which our clothing was already infested.
The building had been an old grocery. Now it was
metamorphosed into a prison. Where we lay the
floor was saturated with molasses. When I tried to
rise in the morning I could not. My coat was apparently hermetically fastened to the floor. Clarke
was in the same condition. He, through the aid of
a fellow prisoner, succeeded in freeing himself from

the adhesive floor. He then assisted in extricating me, but a part of my coat remained attached to my wooden couch.

The crimes charged upon the prisoners were desertion, trading with the Yankees, adhesion to the Federal Government or Unionism, enacting the spy, refusing Confederate bonds and money, piloting the Yankees, the utterance of treasonable language, etc. The crime of the negroes, mulattoes, quadroons, and octoroons was endeavoring to escape from Dixie-land and the Iron Furnace of slavery, via the underground railroad. These remained till their masters, learning of their arrest, came for and released them. On the evening succeeding our incarceration two prisoners had been led out and shot. I soon learned that this was not an unusual occurrence. Nearly every day one or more suffered death as the punishment of their patriotism. Many of the prisoners wore heavy fetters. Some were handcuffed, had fetters on their ankles, and were chained to bolts in the floor. Often, without previous warning, the guards came, accompanied by an officer or two, usually two officers, and marched the poor prisoners to the fatal spot and shot them to death or ended their existence by suspension from the gallows. The two prisoners who were shot a few hours after we entered the prison were named Jerome B. Poole and Calvin Harbaugh. Being Unionists, they refused to take the arms offered them, when they were arrested and brought in as conscripts. Poole was from Brazella, and Harbaugh from Shuqualak, Noxubee Co., Miss. They were then suspended by the thumbs till they begged the officers to order them to be shot, as they preferred death to such excruciating torture. After the endurance of every refinement of cruel torture, they were at length brought to Tupelo, tried, and condemned to be shot to death. They inferred by a remark made by one of the officers who brought us into prison that I was a minister. Poole came to me and told me that they would be shot at sunset, and wished me to explain to Harbaugh more fully the way of salvation. He had tried to do so in a feeble way, but feared that he had not made it sufficiently plain to the mind of his friend. Harbaugh then asked me what he must do to be saved. I replied, "Believe on the Lord Jesus Christ and thou shalt be saved. You must exercise faith in Jesus Christ. Come to Jesus just as you are, not waiting to cleanse your soul from one dark blot. Do not tarry till you are better. Away from Christ you will only become more guilty. Come with all your guilt and fear oppressed, and say God be merciful to me a sinner. Ask him to receive you and forgive you, and adopt you into his family and make you one of his dear children by adopting love and grace for Christ's sake."

Harbaugh asked, "What is faith in Jesus Christ?"

"Faith in Jesus Christ is a saving grace whereby we receive and rest upon him alone for salvation as he is offered to us in the gospel."

"But Poole says I must be born again—that I must have a change of heart."

"The bible tells us that whosoever believeth that Jesus is the Christ, is born of God. Ye are all the children of God by faith in Jesus Christ. Therefore if a man be in Christ he is a new creature. He is born again. And as Moses lifted up the serpent in the wilderness, even so must the Son of Man be lifted up, that whosoever believeth in Him should not perish but have eternal life. Whosoever believeth then has eternal life, and whosoever has eternal life surely sees and enters the kingdom of God, so that whosoever believeth is born again. For God so loved the world that he gave his only begotten Son, that whosoever believeth in Him should not perish but have everlasting life. God loved and gave, we believe and have, and this is all of it to attain life and experience the new birth."

"I do believe on Jesus Christ and accept him as my Savior. I have never been baptized. Will you baptize me?"

"Yes, I will, gladly."

Capt. Bruce asked one of the guards to call an officer. When the officer came he sent a prisoner under guard for water. Harbaugh now told me that his father was a Baptist minister, and that he had taught him that the true scriptural mode of baptism was by immersion. An officer was called to whom the request was preferred that I should be allowed to immerse the prisoner in Old Town creek near by. Old Town creek is a tributary of the Tombigbee river. The officer returned stating that the military

8

authorities absolutely refused to grant this request, believing it a ruse to secure an opportunity to effect an escape. Harbaugh said that he would submit to baptism by pouring or sprinkling, though he did not believe it to be the scriptural mode. He trusted that the good Lord would look upon the sincerity of his intentions to obey his command, which he was doing to the extent of his ability and opportunity. He did not think the Lord would require an impossibility.

In the presence of the prisoners and in the most solemn manner possible (the circumstances enhanced the solemnity), the ordinance was administered. Just at its close food prepared by the prisoners was brought and offered these men. They took it in their hands, but ere it was tasted the sun began to dip his disk beneath the western horizon, the dreaded squad appeared before the door. These men, putting away the food untasted, said, " We go to eat bread in the kingdom of God. Pray for us that we may have grace to deport ourselves with becoming dignity and propriety in our last moments. Farewell till we meet before the great white throne. You will probably come soon, for our foes are cruel as the grave."

The officers unlocked their gyves, led them out, and we saw them no more. A half dozen captured slaves seated in a corner of the prison, led by a young octoroon, sang some hymns. They called them spiritual songs. The following, to the tune,

Old Folks at Home, was very melodiously and sweetly rendered :

OUR FATHER'S HOME.

Far over Jordan's rolling river,
   Eternal day.
There's where my eyes are turning ever,
   There's where the angels stay.
All through this vale of sin and sorrow,
   Patient we roam,
Still trusting for the happy morrow,
   Bright in our Father's home.

Chorus.
   All our heavy load sits lighter
     Every storm we bide.
   Oh ! brothers, how the way grows brighter,
     Near to the Savior's side.

Far from his tender arms benighted,
   Dark was our way.
Still every precious promise lightened,
   Where could the spirit stay.
Down at the foot of Calvary's mountain,
   Pilgrims we come,
Oh, may we through that crimson fountain,
   Come to our Father's home.
    Chorus.

One lovely form among the sainted,
   Heaven within,
Stands on my vision ever painted,
   Stretched on the cross for sin.
When shall we hear his voice commanding,
   Come, higher, come,
When in his golden courts be standing,
   With our beloved ones at home.
    Chorus.

The Southern Slave's Song.

Oh, poor negro, he will go.
　　Some one day.
Over the water and the snow,
　　Far away.
Over the mountain big and high,
　　Some one day.
To that country in the sky,
　　Far away.

Jesus, Massa, bring me home,
　　Some one day.
Then I'll live with the Holy One,
　　Far away.
Sin no more my heart make sore,
　　Some one day.
I praise my Jesus evermore,
　　Far away.

Our privations were so great from a lack of good, wholesome food and pure water—for the scanty supply of water allowed us was tepid and foul—and from a want of beds, cots, couches, or something better than a filthy floor whereon to sleep, that I resolved upon an attempt to escape at the risk of my life. I felt sure that I could not long survive the horrors of this prison-pen. As soon as my arrest became known to the 32d Mississippi regiment, encamped in the suburbs of Tupelo, the officers called upon me. Col. Mark Lowrey, Capt. L. A. Lowrey, the Col.'s brother, Major Arnold, and Adjutant Irion. This regiment was raised in Tishomingo Co. One of its companies, the Zollicoffer Avengers, having been raised in Rienzi, where I had been for years

I GOT MY BACK AGAINST A TREE, AND WITH A KNOTTY CLUB
I KILLED SIX HOUNDS.   Page 120

the proprietor and president of the Rienzi Female
College. The daughters of many of the officers of
this regiment had been educated at this college during my connection with it. Owing me a debt of gratitude as they professed, could I expect less than the
manifestation of deep sympathy with me in my sad
condition—confined in a gloomy dungeon, deprived
of the comforts, yea, even the necessaries, of life, and
menaced and insulted by the officers in whose power
I was? Some of these officers had publicly expressed
themselves under great obligations to me for the
thorough moral, mental, and physical training their
daughters had received while under my care. In
proof of this I have their own statements published
in the public journals of the day. Whatever may
have been my hopes, they were doomed to disappointment. These summer friends, so obsequious in my
prosperity, conversed for a time upon indifferent top-
ics, never alluding to my condition, and I did not
obtrude it upon their attention, except that Capt.
Lowrey, looking around upon the prisoners clanking
their chains as they moved uneasily, trying to secure
a less painful posture, said this is war—grim-visaged
war with all its attendant horrors. When they left
they said, "We will call soon again." I replied,
"Do so, gentlemen, you will always find me at home,"
yet I was hoping they would not—my mind was
bent upon and occupied with the high resolve of escaping or dying in the attempt, and even then I was
maturing a plan to compass that end.

A young gentleman and his sister, by virtue of a pass, entered our prison. They conversed with the prisoners freely. An officer escorted the young lady to the part of the prison which I occupied. She enquired naively: "What is the charge against this prisoner?" The officer replied that I was an avowed Unionist. She said to me, "Are you a merchant?" I replied that I was a minister.

"Of what church?"

"Of the Presbyterian church."

"We are Presbyterians," said she.

She then made inquiries about Reverends Wm. A. Gray, of Ripley, Jno. II. Miller, of Pontotoc, Jas. Stafford, of Danville, Dr. E. T. Baird, of Crawfordsville, J. N. Carothers, of Okólona, R. Henderson, of Danville, and others. While she conversed with me the officer visited another part of the prison. She then said *taisez vous*, and slipped into my hand a note. She gave me her name as Miss Daisy Carson.

The note was written with a pencil, and read: "We sympathize deeply with you. We will aid you in any way you may suggest. We live two miles from Tupelo due —— [the cardinal point indicated was so defaced that it was illegible]. If you could reach our house you would find all possible assistance. We are true blue. Ambrose Kavanaugh will visit the prison soon, if he can secure a pass. Ernest Travis, of Verona, informed us of your imprisonment. I met you at Mr. Price's, in Ripley, but you may not remember me. My friend, Miss

Jane Kendrick, often speaks of you. Chew and swallow this as soon as you have read it. I take a great risk in this matter, but I am of a romantic turn and love adventure. After the war and the triumph of the government it will be pleasant to recount our exploits in behalf of the suffering patriots. *Taisez vous,*
Votre amie.

"CHARLOTTE CORDAY,

"My *nom de guerre.*

"P. S.—Prof. Yarbrough lodged with us one night. We sincerely hope that he has safely reached his destination ere this. Do not become dispirited, you have hosts of friends and are doubtless under the kind protecting care of Jesus.

"'Tis late before
The brave despair.
        Stand
Firm for your country,
        It were a noble life,
To be found dead embracing her.
        There is strength,
Deep bedded in our hearts, of which we reck
But little.

"Very respectfully,

"C. C."

A prisoner came to me and said, "Chaplain, I have been informed that I will be shot to-morrow, and I am not prepared to die."

"What was your offense?"

"I was a Unionist—was forced into the army. I deserted, they followed me with blood-hounds. When the hounds came near I got my back against a tree, and with a knotty club of pecan wood I killed six hounds. The cavalry came up and fired upon me. I fell, wounded in the head and left arm. The wounds were not very severe. They brought me to Tupelo, and I had my trial yesterday by court-martial. My captain, who just now left, informed me that on to-morrow I would be shot as a deserter."

"What is your name?"

"My name is John R. Witherspoon. I was born in Sumter, South Carolina, but have lived in Bolivar, Tennessee, for ten years. I have a wife and seven children, six are girls. The baby, John R. Wither-spoon, Jr., is my only boy. My oldest daughter, Gertrude Maud, named for her mother, is fifteen years old. She is a good scholar, has a talent for music and painting. All my children are devotedly attached to their parents. What will become of them God only knows. I own one hundred acres of land in McNairy Co., Tennessee. My wife's mother gave her a colored girl. I am a poor man and will leave my family dependent. I am a member of the Presbyterian church, but have been living in the neg-lect of duty for some time, and now I must die unprepared."

"What caused your neglect?"

"I became a candidate for office, and as it was cus-tomary to treat a great deal when canvassing the dis-trict, I did so. I formed convivial habits that were disastrous to devotional duties. I became negligent and absented myself from the church. My wife and family are faithful, and many prayers are sent up to heaven in my behalf. O, if I were rescued from this impending doom I would, by the grace of God, no longer neglect duty."

I pointed him as well as I could to the Lamb of God that taketh away the sin of the world. We went up into a corner of the prison and knelt down. I prayed God to heal his back-sliding and restore to him the joy of His salvation, then asked him to offer up a prayer in his own behalf. He did so in language and with an unction that surprised me. At the close he earnestly implored God to spare his life for the sake of his dear family. He asked to be longer spared that he might atone in some degree for his past remissness in duty by devoting all the days of his allotted time to faithful service in his heavenly father's vineyard. I asked him if he entertained any hope. He replied that he did, and wished he could live to test its genuineness, but he had some fear.

And now came still evening on. Mr. Witherspoon volunteered to go for water. He took two buckets, one in each hand. Two guards accompanied him, one on each side. He drew the water and started back. It was now dark; when he reached a clump of bushes he dropped one bucket and raising the other he dashed it in the faces of the guards, and sprang for the bushes. The guards speedily brought their muskets to bear, fired in the direction of the fugitive, and instead of pursuing at once, ran to the tents of some officers and gave the alarm. The whole camp was soon intensely excited and hundreds joined in the pursuit. A cry would be heard, "Here he goes." A few minutes later in an opposite direction the same cry would be taken up. Unionists impressed into the service did this to contribute to the escape of the prisoner. He made good his escape, and succeeded after some time in getting his family conveyed to the North, through the kindness of Major General Hatch. An account of his escape has been published. He encountered much difficulty in avoiding the bloodhounds. At one time he heard their howling in his rear, and not more than a mile distant. He came to a field in which cattle were grazing. He sprang upon the back of an ox, and using a goad he compelled the ox to carry him across the field in a direction that broke the trail and baffled pursuit.

His final adventure, his last peril before his safety was insured, may be worth narrating. One day as he lay concealed in a ditch he heard in the remote distance in the direction whence he came the faint howling of hounds. The sound became more and more distinct, till he became convinced that they were pursuing him and had found his track. He arose from his moist bed, and hastened onward with all the speed his enfeebled condition would permit. He had not gone far till he descried another fugitive a short distance in advance. He called upon him to halt. The man obeyed. He gave his name as John Denver. The vigilantes of the vendetta, as they called themselves, had attacked his house last night. He had defended himself. They fired through a window, wounded him and killed his l:ttle daughter Nellie. He rushed out, slew the murderer of his child, and wounded two others. They beat a hasty retreat. He had lost an ear, and had a flesh wound in the left thigh which made travel difficult. He was on his way to Corinth to get assistance from the Federal commander, so that he and his family might go North. The howling of the hounds indicated to him that the vigilantes had been reinforced and were in pursuit of him. As rapidly as possible these panting fugitives made their way toward Corinth. The hounds gained upon them. Mr. Denver had two revolvers. He gave his companion one of them, and they both resolved to sell their lives as dearly as possible. The hounds were but a mile distant, when, to their joy, they suddenly met a regiment of Federal cavalry on a scouting expedition. They as quickly as possible explained the situation of affairs. The colonel ordered the regiment to fall back out of sight. He ordered a company to dismount and conceal themselves in the chaparral, he sending their horses back. He requested Witherspoon and Denver to climb two small trees and await their pursuers. He then joined the company in ambush. When the pursuers came up they ordered the fugitives to come down from the trees. There were twenty of the vigilantes. They asked Witherspoon who he was. He replied, " A prisoner from Tupelo, escaping to the Federal lines." After a few moments' consultation, they told these men that they had but five minutes to live, and if they wished to say their prayers they might spend the time in that way. They had but one rope, which they had brought to use in hanging Denver, but one of their number furnished a halter, taking it from his horse's neck. Two men approached, threw the nooses over the heads of their victims and adjusted them. They then selected two lateral limbs projecting from a tree near by, threw the ends of the ropes over them and were awaiting the order of Jack Clinkskales, their leader, to consummate their murderous purpose, when a volley from the ambushed Federal troopers made sixteen of them bite the dust. The four survivors rushed to their horses, but a second volley caused them to fall bereft of life. The bodies were scrutinized closely to be sure that life was extinct. They were then piled up in the chaparral, and the hounds killed. Upon the return of the regiment a few hours after a drove of wild hogs were found feeding upon them. Thus perished a band of desperadoes not fit to live, less fit to die. Mr. Denver's family were brought into Corinth in an ambulance, and soon after came North to Evansville, Indiana. Mr. Denver enlisted in the Federal army, and did effective service in his country's cause. Mr. Witherspoon also enlisted in the Federal service. He died on the field of honor. He was instantly killed on the 1st day of the battle of Gettysburg. Mrs. Witherspoon thus wrote me:

"My dear husband often spoke of you, and had hoped to meet you again, but Providence otherwise ordered it. His death is a sad bereavement to me and the dear children. But God makes no mistakes, and I bow submissively to His will. He has promised to be the husband of the widow and the father of the fatherless. I trust implicitly in the promises of a covenant-keeping God. The tone of my dear husband's piety was very different after his imprisonment in Tupelo. He seemed to think that he could not do too much to show his gratitude to the God who in his providence delivered him from the execution of the death sentence already pronounced by the court-martial, and which only lacked a few hours of fulfillment at the time of his escape. Pray for me and my dear children, that we may be enabled to bear with becoming resignation this afflictive dispensation of Divine Providence, and that it may be sanctified to the highest and holiest interests of our souls, work in us the peaceable fruits of righteousness, and while looking to things unseen and above a far more exceeding and eternal weight of glory. We will, Providence permitting, move soon to Cincinnati. My daughter Gertrude has secured a position as teacher in one of the public schools of that city. We would be happy to have you visit us at your earliest convenience.

Your friend,

MRS. G. M. WITHERSPOON.

OLD PILGARLIC.

An elderly gentleman was ushered into prison on the morning of the 2d of July, 1862. He seemed anxious to convince the officer who accompanied the guard that he was mistaken in regard to some abstruse question. As soon as the officer left, I approached the prisoner, and after gaining his confidence, drew from him his sad history. His true name was Prof. Lorimer Vickroy Yarbrough, a native of Fincastle, Va. He had resided in Austin, Texas, and New Orleans, La. He loved the old flag, and resolved to reach the North, in company with his son Oscar. By some means suspicion was aroused, and they were taken from the steamboat at Vicksburg, Miss., and thrown into prison, where they languished for months. At length, through the aid of Unionist friends they escaped from prison, and in due time from the city of Vicksburg.

Prof. Yarbrough had a friend named Leroy Paden, living in Hazelhurst, Miss., upon whom he could depend for aid. He also held a note overdue for two thousand dollars, upon a gentleman who resided in Brookhaven, in Lincoln county, Miss. Could he collect the money due on this note it would assist him materially in making his way to the North. On the border of Copiah county, they were arrested by a committee of vigilantes, and thrown into an extemporized prison. Here they were immured six weeks and fed on corn bread and water. At length, Oscar enlisted in a company bound for the scat of war in Virginia, with the intention of deserting upon the first favorable opportunity. His father was still held a prisoner. Now malarial fever of a malignant type supervened. During its progress reason left her throne, but a naturally vigorous constitution triumphed, and the prisoner began to convalesce. Hearing the attendants say he had known nothing for three weeks, Prof. Yarbrough resolved upon a ruse which he hoped would give him an opportunity to escape. He would, by the use of incoherent expressions and singular conduct, feign madness. In the course of time, health returned, and the military authorities sent him to Gen. Beauregard at Tupelo. Gen. Beauregard believed him to be a malingerer, and sent for two alienists to decide upon his sanity. On the 12th of June, 1862, the commission to determine the sanity of the prisoner convened. A number of officers of high rank were present.

I will give the account of the examination in Yarbrough's language :

" I was brought in under guard, a seat furnished me, and the farce commenced.

" Gen. Beauregard enquired, ' What is your name?'

" ' My name, Capting, air old Pilgarlic.'

" Gen. B.—'What does that mean?'

" ' It means old Baldhead. You see, Capting, I hain't got no har on the top of my head. I was born so, and when some growed on, a nigger girl spilled some rusma on my crown, and I hain't hed no har sence.'

"Gen. B.—'Well, old Pilgarlic, you are in a bad fix.'

"'Yes, Capting, and ef I hed as soft a skull us sum of these here young chaps, I could raze har to sell.'

"Gen. B.—'Where do you live?'

"'I live in a cabin with a stick chimly, in Arkansaw.'

"Gen. B.—'Does your chimney draw well?'

"Yes, Capting, it draws the 'tention of every fool that passes on that trail.'

"Gen. B.—'Are you a married man?'

"'Not now, I ain't, but I spect to be before long, fur you see, Capting, I hev the refusal of mor'n half a dozen widders.'

"Gen. B.—'Where did you say you were from?'

"'From every place but this, an' ef you'll jis send them fellers away with the guns an' bayonets I'll be away from this in a giffy, that is, providin' you takes this jewelry off'n my legs an' wrists.'

"Gen. B.—'Pilgarlic, what's your opinion about this war?'

"'I thinks, Capting, that no Southerner ort to fight agin liberty, nor no Yankee agin his country.'

"Gen. B.—'Where's your son?'

"'Well, Capting, I duzzent know. He give me the slip. I spec he went off ter the war.'

"Gen. B.—'Well, sir, your son attempted to desert to the enemy, and he now lies in prison with a ball and chain attached to his ankle.'

"I then commenced to sing as loudly as I could:

> Spread all her canvas to the breeze,
>   Set every threadbare sail,
> And give her to the god of storms,
>   The lightning and the gale.

"The General ordered me to cease. I heeded him not, and sang:

> When a deed is done for freedom,
>   Through the broad earth's aching breast
> Runs a thrill of joy prophetic, trembling on
>   From east to west;
> And the slave, where'er he cowers,
> . Feels the soul within him climb
> To the awful verge of manhood,
>   As the energy sublime,
> Of a century bursts full blossomed
>   On the stormy stem of time.

"The alienists felt my pulse and inserted a thermometer into my mouth, which I crushed between my teeth. I then sang, or rather shouted vociferously:

> Oh! for an hour of youthful joy,
>   Give me back my twentieth spring,
> I'd rather laugh a bright-haired boy,
>   Than reign a gray-haired king.

"At this juncture Gen. Beauregard ordered the guards to make me hush. I then yelled, for it could not be called singing:

> Prudent on the council train,
>   Dauntless on the battle plain,
> Ready at the country's need
>   For her glorious cause to bleed.

9

"By the general's order the guards bound and gagged me. The alienists differed in opinion as to my sanity. One regarded me as a malingerer, the other declared that I was in a state of mental aberration which bid fair to culminate in incurable insanity. I was confined under guard in a room in a hotel in Tupelo till yesterday, when I was incarcerated in this dungeon."

Gen. Beauregard was now superseded by Gen. Braxton Bragg. Gen. Bragg had been but a short time in supreme command when he reviewed the testimony in the case of Prof. Yarbrough. On the 11th of July, 1862, the order came for his execution. He was taken from our prison to the fatal spot where so many brave Unionists had ended their lives. His request that they would not blindfold him was granted. He faced the muskets with an unblanched countenance. A volley rang out upon the evening air, and the professor fell pierced by the bullets of the squad. When his struggles ceased and he was pronounced dead by the sergeant, the corpse was given into the custody of Billingsly and Kaiser, conscripts, from near Tallaloosa, Miss., and relatives, they claimed, of the professor. They bore the body tenderly to a house in the suburbs of Tupelo. These men were Unionists, and had been forced into the Confederate service. This family, whose name was Montreal, were pronounced Unionists. When the putative corpse was laid upon the couch prepared for its reception, an examination revealed that one ball had shattered the left arm so that amputation would have been required had no other wound caused death. A ball had glanced from the ribs, another ball had passed through his clothing. The limbs had not assumed rigidity, and it was evident that the professor was not dead, but only in a state of syncope. From this condition he slowly rallied. Billingsly understood surgery, and with the aid of some Unionist neighbors Prof. Yarbrough's arm was amputated, and upon his recovery, which was rapid, he was conducted by night from one Union neighborhood to another, till at length he reached La Grange, Tenn., which was in the possession of the Federal troops. Among the first to visit him were his son Oscar, now a captain of a company in a Federal regiment, and a nephew, Charles Barry, formerly of D'Arbonne, La., now an officer in the Union army, Gen. Beauregard's statement in regard to the capture of Oscar Yarbrough being false.

The following letter will unfold some of the more thrilling incidents of his final escape:

Rev. John H. Aughey:

DEAR FRIEND—Having learned through John H. Stanton that you are chaplain of Gen. Benjamin Grierson's old regiment, the 6th Ill. cavalry, I send you by him this short letter. Please inform me how you escaped from Tupelo. I heard Gen. Bragg tell Major Grosvenor, when he tried to say something in your defense, that you would be hanged on Tuesday of the next week as sure as there was a God in heaven.

He said you deserved to suffer a hundred deaths for your disloyal speeches and your many treasonable acts.   That there was a ghost of a chance for you seemed incredible, chained as you were, and so vigilantly guarded, far away from the Federal lines and surrounded by the great rebel army.   Do write me at once and tell me all about your escape.   It must have been well-nigh miraculous.   The first intimation I had of your escape was an extract from the New York *Tribune* of an address delivered by you in Cooper Institute in that city, from which I learned that you had succeeded in effecting an escape, but the particulars were not given.

After I was able to travel I was conducted from one neighborhood to another, till at length I reached the Federal lines.   At one time we thought it best to travel in daylight.   There were ten of us in company, eight of us Unionists endeavoring to reach the Federal lines.   Two were guides, Paden Pickens and Paul Paden.   We called at the house of a widow named Mrs. Violetta Markle.   Her husband had been tried by a vigilance committee and shot, April 19, 1861, as a Unionist.   We gave her the countersign *taisez vous.*   She replied *oui, oui,* all right, and then after preparing a meal for us, she informed us that we were near a rebel camp, and advised us to take the route traveled by the guide, Solomon Frierson, who had called at her house yesterday on his return from a trip to the Federal lines, to which he had conveyed twenty Unionists from Oktibbeha

PENDER FELL PIERCED BY TWO BALLS.   Page 134

and Pontotoc counties. After leaving Mrs. Markle's, Pickens climbed a tree and made an observation of the surrounding country. Two rebel encampments were visible, one to the north-east, another to the north-west. He thought that we might pass between them without much danger. We started on our way. At one point it became necessary to travel on a road a short distance so as to obviate the necessity of ascending a lofty and precipitous hill. We had just entered upon the road when we saw a company of rebel cavalry about half a mile distant. They had just appeared on the summit of a hill behind which they had been concealed from view. They descried us, and putting spurs to their horses came rapidly toward us. We gave up all for lost, and were about to break for the woods, when Paden, taking ropes from his pockets, told Bryson and Birney to put their hands behind them, when he securely bound them with the ropes. As soon as the cavalry reached us we went to one side of the road to let them pass. The captain, whose name was Pender, wished to know what this cavalcade meant. Paden replied that they had in charge these two tories, and were taking them to camp to surrender them to the general in command, that they might get their just deserts. "Good," said the captain, "I'll go back with you. Sergeant Buford, take command, and go on; I'll go back to camp with these men."

On the way back Paden proposed to the captain that we try these men now, and if they are found

guilty shoot them.　Capt. Pender agreed to this at
once.　He said that was the object of his expedition
at this time—to quell the disaffected traitors to the
Confederacy.　He declared that it was he that had
ordered the shooting of ten tory devils in the Poplar Springs neighborhood, led by one Methuselah
Knight, as arrant a tory as ever lived.　We then left
the road, and coming to a copse of dwarf tamaracks,
we held a trial, and upon their own confession convicted Bryson and Birney of treason against the
Confederate States of America.　Paden and Pickens
asked the privilege of shooting the prisoners.　This
Capt. Pender granted.　Upon the pretense that they
had no pistols, Pender drew his pistols from their
holsters and presented them to Paden.　Paden
handed one to Pickens.　The prisoners were then
bound to two saplings.　Paden asked Pender to
give the command.　The captain told the prisoners
that, in compassion to their souls, he would grant
them five minutes to make their peace with God.

Birney said, "Captain, we have long ago made our
peace with our God.　Have you done the same?"
Pender replied, "I have killed Union traitors
enough to save me."

He then gave the command, "*Make ready*, TAKE
AIM, FIRE.　Pickens and Paden fired simultane-
ously, but not at the prisoners.　Pender fell pierced
by two balls, and in five minutes his soul had taken
its flight to the bar of God.　As Pender fell he said,
"D—n the traitors," and without uttering another

word his spirit left its clay tenement. It became
necessary to kill the horse, as his presence would en-
danger our safety. Bryson and Birney were un-
bound, and we pursued our journey rejoicing, leaving Pender where he fell. Without further incident
of importance we reached the Union lines, and
received a cordial welcome.

Let me hear from you at your very earliest convenience.

Yours truly,

L. V. YARBROUGH,

Alias, OLD PILGARLIC.

Having determined to attempt an escape at all
hazards, I thought it would be well to secure a
companion who would undertake with me the perilous adventure. Two are better than one. After
due deliberation, I selected Richard Malone, his
piercing eye and his intellectual physiognomy led me
to believe that if he should consent to make the
attempt with me, our prospect for success would be
enhanced. Upon broaching the matter to him, he
drew from his pocket a paper containing the proper
route to pursue, mapped out clearly. A Unionist
friend had covertly conveyed it to him. Gray Wal-
ton was his name. For some days Malone had
resolved to escape or perish in the attempt. With
all the ardor imparted by a new born hope, we entered upon the formation of a plan of escape. We
went out now upon every possible pretext. We no
longer tried to avoid the guard that came to obtain

detachments of prisoners to do servile labor. We
were the first to present ourselves, our object being to
reconnoitre, in order to learn where guards were
stationed, so as to determine the best method of escaping through the town after leaving the prison, and
of passing through the great army that environed us.
During the day we made these observations, that two
guards stationed on the western enclosure attached to
the prison were very communicative and very verdant, that after relief they would come on duty
again at midnight, that there was a building on the
south side of the prison, sixteen feet distant from it,
which extended beyond our prison, and beyond the
enclosure in the rear of the prison in which the
guards were stationed. We learned that the moon
would set about 11 P.M., and we ascertained that
there were no guards upon the south side of the
prison during the day. I learned this by vol-
unteering to go for water. Two guards accompanied me; as I neared the prison, having drawn
the soft hat I was wearing down pretty well, I
peered from under it and scanned the surroundings as
closely as possible, observing where every vidette
was stationed, and gaining by close scrutiny all possible information. We learned that one of the planks
in the floor was in a condition to be readily removed.
The building was placed on blocks, and the planks
were nailed on perpendicularly, and the ragged edges
did not in some places reach the ground. Apertures
were thus formed by which we hoped, if once under

the prison, egress might be secured. We then hoped
to reach the building which was about sixteen feet
distant, on the south side, and by crawling along
close to it pass the enclosure on the western end of
our prison in which the guards were stationed.
Troyer Anderson, and De'Grummond, Federal
prisoners, assisted by Hermon Bonar, Prince Shelby,
and Gaither Breckenridge, Unionists, managed to
raise the plank from the floor and replace it loosely,
so that it could be removed at the opportune moment.

Benjamin Clarke came to me and said, " Take me
along with you." I referred him to Malone, who refused. Clarke came back, and told me that Malone
would not consent, and begged me to try to prevail
upon Malone to agree to take him with us. Said
he, " I have been tried and condemned, and should I
be shot my poor wife and eight children will perish."
I went to Malone and asked him to consent to take
Clarke along. Said he, " No, Clarke has not nerve
sufficient to face the glittering bayonet, which we
may have to do, nor has he the tact necessary to make
his way through this great army without detection.
He would do something that would betray us, not
intentionally, of course." As Malone was inexorable,
I told Clarke that he and Robinson must come half
an hour after us. This they failed to do. They
dared not make the attempt, which was indeed perilous. This was July 4, 1862. We improvised a
4th of July celebration. I was the orator of the
day, and delivered a eulogy of our patriot fathers

who had fought and bled to secure our country's liberty.

We may say of these noble men as was said of the cathedral builder:

> The hand that rounded Peter's dome,
> And groined the aisles of Ancient Rome,
> Wrought with a sad sincerity;
> Himself from God he could not free,
> He builded better than he knew—
> The conscious stone to beauty grew.

Yes, they builded better than they knew. They erected a temple of freedom which we trust shall be lasting as time. No weapon formed against it shall prosper. In the providence of God no parricidal hand shall be permitted to succeed in overthrowing this grand edifice, this glorious temple of our country's liberties. Let us endeavor to be worthy sons of these noble sires, imitate their virtues, prize the heritage bequeathed to us by them, and preserve it unimpaired as a blessing to our posterity forever.

> Breathes there a man with soul so dead,
> Who never to himself hath said,
> This is my own, my native land,
> Whose heart hath ne'er within him burned;
> As home his footsteps he has turned
> From wandering on a foreign strand?
> If such there be, go mark him well,
> For him no minstrel raptures swell.
> High though his titles, proud his name,
> Boundless his wealth as wish can claim;
> Despite these titles, power, and pelf,
> The wretch concentered all in self,

Living, shall forfeit fair renown,
And doubly dying shall go down
To the vile dust from whence he sprung,
Unwept, unhonored, and unsung.

Perish the hand that with parricidal intent would apply the torch of the incendiary to the fair fabric erected at so great a cost by our revered ancestors.

Ah, never shall the land forget
   How gushed the life-blood of the brave,
Gushed warm with hope and courage yet
   Upon the soil they fought to save.

Oh, is there not some chosen curse,
   Some hidden thunder in the store of heaven
Red with uncommon wrath to blast the man
   Who would compass our loved country's ruin?

A dishonored grave and a hell of torment will be the final fate of every traitor, and while he lives remorse will haunt the impious wretch.

Not sharp revenge, nor hell itself, can find
A fiercer torment than a guilty mind,
Which, day and night, doth dreadfully accuse,
Condemns the wretch, and still the charge renews.

Such be the doom of all traitors. May Jehovah, God of nations, blast all treasonable designs against the best of governments, a government founded upon justice and equity, and promotive of all the holiest interests dear to the heart of every true patriot, and philanthropist, and only subversive of despotic principles which would impair human rights and overthrow constitutional liberty.

> Yes, my native land, I love thee,
> All thy scenes I love full well.—
> Land of every land the pride.

It is your high prerogative and mine to be able to say, I am an American citizen.

Our glorious government will live and flourish and dispense innumerable blessings broadcast over a smiling land long after treason has been consigned to an infamous and gory grave.

We may not live to see this prediction verified, but

> "It is sweet to die for our country,"

and to know that although we perish as patriot martyrs, our children and the millions yet unborn who are to come into the possession of this glorious heritage, will enjoy during the coming cycles of the future the perennial sweets of liberty, equality, and fraternity. May God speed the day when the enemies of our Lord and of our country's liberty shall be overthrown.

I see officers approaching who may not be able to appreciate and approve sentiments such as I am enunciating. Permit me, therefore, to close somewhat abruptly with this sentiment:

> Our Banner: Now wave in strength its pennons fair,
> In peerless grandeur round the world,
> Proclaiming far that freemen dare
> Defend the right with flag unfurled.

We then sang with a will,

> My country, 'tis of thee,
> Sweet land of liberty, etc.

J. A. H. Spear, of Ellisville, Ill., or Troyer Anderson, sang a patriotic song. I remember but one couplet:

We've lofty hills and lovely vales,
And streams that roll to either sea.

It was well received. Some of the Federal prisoners started,

Rally round the flag, boys,
Rally once again,
Shouting the battle cry of freedom.

The officers who had entered, now in great anger forbáde any further patriotic demonstration. They carried off our flag which we had improvised, and told the guards to inform them if we disobeyed their orders.

At four o'clock P.M., our plan was fully matured. At midnight (the moon having set and the verdant guards being on duty) we would raise the plank, get under the floor, and, myself in advance, make our exit through one of the apertures upon the south side of the jail, then crawl to the building some ixteen feet distant, and thence continue crawling close to the building till we had passed the sentinels in the western enclosure, then rise and make our way as cautiously as possible to a point in a corn-field in view from the prison, and where was a garment suspended from a fence post. The one who arrived first must await the other. A signal was agreed upon to prevent mistake. The signal was to place the arms akimbo. The countersign, taisez vous, the response, *oui, oui*, (pro.) we, we. If the guards ordered us to halt we resolved to risk their fire, for our firm resolve was liberty or death.

As soon as the prisoners learned that I was a minister, they with entire unanimity and great cordiality chose me chaplain, and I preached to them every evening as long as I remained with them. Night drew on apace. Thick darkness settled upon prison, camp, and town. Murky clouds o'erspread the sky and obscured the stars as we partook of our scanty allowance of corn-bread and water—foul, tepid water. I took this meal with the Federal prisoners who were temporarily incarcerated till after some formalities they would be sent to prison at Camp Oglethorpe, Macon, Ga., and other places. Their names were Jesse L. McHatton, Co. H, 59th Ill. Vols., J. A. H. Spear, Ellisville, Fulton Co., Ill., Brocket and Benedict, 35th Reg. Ill. Vol. Inft., Sullivan, Howell Trogdon, of St. Louis, Mo., M. Troyer Anderson, Foster, Lowery, and a German, who went by the name of Charlie, who wore a saddler's knife sewed on his coat sleeve, Wm. Soper, Co. D, 22d Reg. Ind. Vol. Inft., and DeGrummond, of Galesburg, Ill. The breeches I wore were light colored. McHatton exchanged a pair of brown colored for mine, so that I might better evade the guards.

About ten o'clock Malone raised the plank, and I went under to reconnoitre. I remained under the floor about ten minutes, having learned that there were no guards patroling the south side of the prison, as we feared might be the case after night. I had learned by observation, when returning with water, that there were none during the day. Just at the noon of night we heard the relief called. Malone and I tried to find the prisoners who were to raise the plank, but not being able readily to do so we raised the plank ourselves, and both succeeded in getting under without much difficulty. Malone having gotten under first was compelled, contrary to our arrangements, to take the lead. As he was passing through the aperture he made considerable noise. I patted him upon the back to indicate silence and warn him of danger. He reached back, gave my hand a warm pressure to assure me that all was right, and passed out. I followed. I heard Malone in advance of me, but it was so dark that I could not see him. As I reached the point opposite the sentinels in the rear, one of them, apparently on the alert, and startled by the noise, came to the side of the enclosure nearest me, and leaning over peered into the darkness. He remained a considerable time in that inquisitive attitude. I remained very quiet. At length he walked to the door and looked into the prison. I moved on as noiselessly as possible, passing all the sentinels. It required great presence of mind and vigilant care to pass them without attracting attention or exciting their suspicion. I reached the pre-arranged place of meeting, but Malone was nowhere to be found. I gave the pre-concerted signals, but they elicited no response.

Some mistake had been made, and after waiting a
long time I was compelled to set out alone. Not
being able to rejoin my friend, I regarded as a great
misfortune. He had the chart to guide us, and after
reaching a point fifteen miles north-west of Tupelo
he would be familiar with the topography and
geography of the country. I had frequently passed
through Tupelo in the cars, but knew but little of
the country off the railroad through which I must
pass. Somewhat depressed in spirits by the loss of
my *compagnon de voyage*, I resolved to reach my
family by the safest and most practicable route. I
feared the hounds and the cavalry which would
scour the country in search of us as soon as our escape became known. I was still in the very midst of
the great rebel army, and found great difficulty in
avoiding the videttes that seemed to be well-nigh
omnipresent. I soon found that day was brighten-
ing in the east. I felt glad to think that I was
no longer in the gloomy prison. I could say with
the Psalmist, "I am escaped as a bird out of the
snare of the fowler. The snare is broken and
I am escaped. God hath delivered me out of the
hand of my enemy." I looked to the east, and lo!
the orb of day was peering above the horizon. I
must find a place to hide. I speedily discovered a
small but dense thicket amid a grove of tupelo trees.
This grove gave name to the town of Tupelo. I
secreted myself as covertly as possible. A tree with
low branches was near; I would ascend this if the

hounds should discover my track. After the excitement and consequent mental strain, I tried to woo tired nature's sweet restorer, balmy sleep, and had partially succeeded, when the noise and horrid din of the great encampment sounding in my ears startled me, and drove far hence the winged Somnus. Soon many soldiers passed and repassed me. I was still in the very midst of the great army, and liable to discovery at any moment. I broke off twigs and covered myself with leaves and branches of the underbrush surrounding me. I was within thirty yards of Old Town creek, an affluent of the Tombigbee river, or rather one of the creeks forming the Tombigbee. The soldiers had found a suitable pool for bathing, and they passed and repassed all day; on one side their path or trail ran only six or eight feet distant, on the other the path was but fifteen or twenty feet distant from my lair. About nine o'clock A.M. I heard the booming of cannon all around me, proceeding from the various encampments. The passing soldiers, whose lowest tones were distinctly audible, said that the artillerists were firing salutes in honor of a great victory obtained over General McClellan in the peninsula of Virginia. According to their statements, his whole army, after a succession of losses during eight days' continuous fighting, had been completely annihilated at a place named Malvern, and they were quite sure that Stonewall Jackson would be in Washington City within a week. This sad news depressed me more by far than the

10

thought of my own condition. The hours dragged heavily. At one time two soldiers came within two feet of me in search of blackberries. I feared that one of them would tread upon my feet as they passed out of the copse, but he did not, although he must have missed stepping upon my feet by but a few inches. About noon, judging from the vertical rays of the sun, two soldiers sat down at the point closest to me on the nearer path. They were almost in juxtaposition. Their lowest tones were frightfully audible. One of them informed his companion that he had been in Tupelo in the morning, and that two prisoners had broke jail. They were Parson Aughey and Dick Malone. He said a big reward was offered fur bringin' 'em in dead or alive. He said: "I seed the cavalry start after 'em with two all-fired big packs of dogs. One pack went this away, and the other that away. [I supposed he indicated the directions by pointing.] I'd give my wages fur six month to ketch ary one of 'em. Think uv the honor uv it, Jim, to ketch 'em afore the dogs and cavalry did. Ole Bragg wouldn't stop at a cool thousand or two. Ole Jurdan he were bad flustered. He was a cavortin' aroun' hollerin' out his orders at the top uv his voice, jest a makin' the air blue with his cussin'. I wouldn't be in them prison gards' place for no money. I seed them officers put the irons on 'em, an' they took 'em in ter that same jail thet the tories hed got out on."

The other replied, "It aint no use, Jack Simeral,

fur you to talk about them fellers. I'll bet they's
sharp an' they's safe a hidin' with sum of thar tory
friends hours ago. I'll bet they aint two miles from
town. Jack, you know the Clines an' Kaverners,
they'd die ter save a Union man. They hid Jake
Broome a month, an' your own cousin Tillie Jack,
she carried him grub till the Union fellers got the
thing fixt up an' sent him off ter the Yankees—Bill
Hawkins a giden' a squad of em'.

"Well," said the other, "them dogs'll kum up
with 'em if they hev haf a chance, an' they'll never
make it to the Yankee lines, sure as my name's Jim
Billick."

Soon one of them arose and struck a bush almost
above my head. I thought that he had discovered
me and was about to rise and run, when I heard him
say to his comrade, "Bill, that was the biggest snake
I've seen lately, a regular water moccasin, but it got
off inter the bushes. I reckin' it's makin' fur the
creek, kase they don't git far from water."

I began to feel somewhat uncomfortably situated
when I learned that I was in close proximity to a
large and poisonous snake, but I would have much
preferred meeting an anaconda, boa constrictor, or
even the deadly cobra di capello, rather than those
vile secessionists, thirsting for innocent blood. They,
too, passed on and left me to gloomy rumination.
Presently a large number coming from the creek
were about to enter this thicket in quest of berries,
when one of their number swore that there were no

berries in that thicket. He had been there last evening with a crowd and cleaned them out teetotally.
He then took them to a place where he said there
were plenty of berries, much to my relief. I thought
this 5th of July was the longest day I had ever
known. The sun was so long in reaching the zenith,
and so long in passing down the steep ecliptic way to
the occident. But as all days, however long seem-
ingly, come to an end, so did this. The stars came
glittering one by one. I soon recognized that old,
staunch, and immovable friend of all travelers on
the underground railway, the polar star Rising
from my lair, I was soon homeward bound, guided
by the north star and an oriental constellation.
Plunging into a dense wood, I found my rapid advance impeded by the undergrowth, and had great
difficulty in following my heavenly guides, as the
overarching boughs of the great oaks rendered them
invisible or dimly seen. I came to the creek—Old
Town creek. At that place it was deep and wide. I
found a place where a fallen tree partly spanned it.
I walked on the trunk till I nearly reached its terminus, then I ran and jumped as far as I could. I
alighted near the further shore, in water only up to
my arm-pits. I speedily reached the dry ground
and hastened onward. The water quenched my raging thirst, but I was very hungry, tired, and sleepy.
I at length lay down at the foot of a large water-oak,
resolving to take only a nap, and then rise and pursue my journey. When I awoke the sun was rising.

I Entered, but A Glance Revealed to Me the Character
of the Proprietor.   Page 149

I arose full of regret for the loss of so much precious time. Though somewhat refreshed by my sound sleep, my hunger was almost unendurable, and I was famishing from thirst. At length I descried a small log house by a roadside. In the distance I could see tents. Feeling sick and faint, I resolved to go to the house to obtain water, and if I liked the appearance of the inmates, reveal my condition and ask for aid. I never had much difficulty in discerning between a Unionist and secessionist family. The bile and bitterness of the rabid secessionist was patent, and readily revealed his true character. He gloried in making his proclivities known. The Unionist was ordinarily reticent, unless he was playing the role of a secessionist, and even then his theatrical performance was transparent to one who had himself found it necessary upon occasion to assume that guise, or to one who had mingled with both classes and had studied their idiosyncrasies.

I went to the door of the log edifice and knocked. A gruff voice said, "Come." I entered, but a glance revealed to me the character of the proprietor. I did not like his physiognomy. He looked the villain. A sinister expression, a countenance revealing no intellectuality except a sort of low cunning, bore testimony that it would be the extreme of folly to repose confidence in the possessor of such villainous looks. I asked for water, intending to drink and leave his rude domicile. He pointed to the bucket without speaking. A gourd dipper was floating upon the surface of the water which filled it. I drank and bade him good-bye, and took my departure, glad to escape so easily. I had proceeded but a few steps when I heard the command, halt! uttered in a stentorian tone. Upon looking backward I saw two soldiers within a few steps. One was presenting a double-barreled gun, the other was heavily armed. I asked the soldier who had given the command by what authority he halted me, to which he replied, "I know you, sir, I have heard you preach frequently, you are Parson Aughey, and you were arrested and lodged in prison at Tupelo. I was in Col. Mark Lowrey's regiment yesterday, and learned that you had broken jail, and now, sir, you must return. My name is Dan Barnes. You may have heard of me." I had indeed heard of him. His father had held the office of postmaster. His son had systematically robbed the mail, and for a long time eluded detection. A detective, at length, through a decoy letter, discovered his guilt. When he was arrested the letter with its contents was found upon his person. While being conveyed to prison he escaped from the officer, fled to Napoleon or Helena, Arkansas—was followed, brought back, and incarcerated in jail at Pontotoc. As the evidence against him was positive and admitted no doubt of his guilt, he would have been convicted and sent to the penitentiary, but fortunately for this criminal, at this juncture Mississippi seceded. The jurisdiction of the Federal authorities was regarded at an end—a *nolle prosequi* was entered in the case of Barnes, and he was liberated and soon after joined the Confederate army.

Soon Barnes came to me and said, "Parson, I feel sorry for you, I can sympathize with you for I was once in a tight place myself, and would have been much pleased to have found a friend to lend a helping hand. Now, if you will pay me a reasonable sum I will afford you an opportunity of escaping." I distrusted Barnes' sincerity, but could not make the matter worse by accepting his proffered aid. He named two hundred and fifty dollars as the reasonable sum to secure his connivance at my escape. I proffered two hundred and forty dollars. It was accepted, and I paid it over to him. When he had secured the money, he said, with a sardonic laugh, "I was just playing off on you. You must go back to prison. I have no sympathy for d—d tories, and wish they were all in h—l." They then brought me into the presence of General Jordan, whose headquarters were still at the place where I had the misfortune to meet him at first. The proprietor of the log cabin was named David Hough. He accompanied Barnes and Eph. Hennon, as they returned me to the rebel authorities. Barnes proclaimed, as he passed through the camps, his good fortune, and received the congratulation of the soldiers. He received everywhere an ovation. It was a sort of triumphal march, which he enjoyed greatly.

I became the cynosure of all eyes. As Barnes would stop and recount his heroic and marvelous exploit in arresting me, the soldiers would crowd around me, gazing and hurling at me a torrent of questions. They wanted me to tell them where Malone was, and assured me that old Bragg would be d—d glad to see me. After running this gauntlet for hours, I was ushered into the august presence of Gen. Jordan. He said, "Where is Malone?" I told him that I did not know—that I had not seen him after I had left the prison. He refused to credit any of my statements. He told me that Malone would soon be brought in, dead or alive. He could not evade the hounds and the cavalry. He hoped to heaven that they might catch him speedily, that we might die together. He then ordered a guard to conduct me to a blacksmith's shop. He ordered the blacksmith to forge fetters—bands and chain—so large and strong that I might be so securely manacled as to prevent the least possibility of my giving them the slip till I had expiated my crimes upon the gallows. The blacksmith was ordered to put the bands on while red hot, and my boots were burnt in the process of ironing. It was quite painful, though the blacksmith was as gentle as possible. Gen. Jordan stood by with drawn sword, superintending the execution of his order.

The blacksmith said, "*Taisez vous*." I replied, "*Oui, oui*." He gave me his name, and embraced every opportunity of offering a word of comfort. He was a Unionist. He asked Gen. Jordan to allow me to go to his house and get something to eat, but his request was arrogantly refused. I think his name was Monday or Friday. I remember that it was the name of one of the days of the week. I thus associated it in my mind at the time. He told Gen. Jordan that he had never manacled a man, and was averse to obeying such an order. The General told him to go to work at once, or go to prison. The blacksmith only obeyed upon compulsion.

"Iron him *securely*, SECURELY, *sir*," was the General's oft repeated order. The ironing caused me much pain, my ankles being long discolored from the effects. By wearing shackles so long, ulcers were formed which have left life-long scars. After I was secured by these manacles, they assisted me to remount the horse. I was compelled to ride sidewise. The irons prevented me from riding astride. I told Gen. Jordan that I had been told that iron had become scarce in the Southern Confederacy, but that he had given me an abundant supply. I was conducted under guard to Tupelo. Upon my arrival the provost marshal and commander of the post were much rejoiced to see me. They became hilarious. Barnes, in grandiloquent style, stated that I had attempted to bribe him, that he had listened to my proposition with indignation, and when he had gotten the money did what he regarded was his duty. The commander replied that all of the property of traitors was theirs, and commended Barnes for deceiving me after he had secured the bribe. He also recommended Barnes for promotion for his heroic and patriotic act in arresting me, and for his incorruptible integrity.

The provost marshal said to me: " Why did you attempt to leave us?"

" Because, sir, your prison was so filthy, your fare so meagre and unwholesome, and your treatment so harsh, cruel, and vindictive, that I could not long endure it and survive."

" Parson, you know the bible says, 'the wicked flee when no man pursueth, but the righteous are as bold as a lion.' You must have been guilty of crime or you would not have attempted to escape."

" I confess to the truth of some of the charges made against me, and yet hold that I am innocent of any crime against God or man for which I am amenable to the state or Confederate states. As to pursuit, I think two companies of cavalry with blood-hounds would indicate quite vigorous pursuit."

"You shall never be remanded to the prison you left; rest assured of that. Did any of the prisoners know of or aid you in your escape?"

" No, sir, none of them knew anything about it."

" Are you telling the truth?"

"I am."

"Where is Malone?"

"I know not. I never saw him after I left the prison."

" He cannot escape. He will be brought in, dead or alive. Why did you attempt to bribe Dan Barnes?"

"It was his own offer. I knew that his cupidity was great, and thought it no harm to accept his proffered venal aid. If Barnes had his deserts, he would now be immured in the penitentiary at hard labor."

"Did the jury that tried him acquit him?"

"No, the secession of Mississippi alone saved him. I refer you to Col. Tison. He, being marshal of North Mississippi, arrested Barnes. He found on his person the evidence of his guilt—the money and drafts stolen when he robbed the mail."

I might say here, that after this Barnes was in company with several soldiers, boon companions of his. One of them, named Maness, said to Barnes, in reply to some fanciful story that he had been telling, "Now, Dan, you know that that is a lie." Dan, in anger, said, "If you repeat that I will shoot you." Maness replied, "We all know it isn't true." Barnes immediately shot Maness, and then fled to Chepultepec, Alabama. Was pursued, overtaken, and arrested. On their return, near the place where Barnes had shot Maness, near Paden's mills, the guard, three of whom were brothers of the murdered man, held a consultation, which resulted in a decision to inflict summary punishment upon the murderer. He had escaped the penalty due his crime in robbing the mail, and they feared that if they returned him to the army he might escape merited punishment. They compelled him to dig his own grave, and then they hanged him and buried him in the grave he had dug. His doom was just, and no tears were shed over his tragic fate.

Some of the general officers entered the provost marshal's office. After a short consultation, one of them, approaching me, said, "You will be shot within an hour. If you have any message for your friends you may write it, and I will see to its delivery."

I wrote thus:

TUPELO, MISS., July 7, 1863.

MY DEAR WIFE—I must die within an hour, so General Bragg has this moment informed me. This is the last letter you will ever receive from me. I die because I have pursued unswervingly what I regarded as my duty to my God and my country. I would not, even for the consideration of long life and the endearments of a happy home, prove recreant to duty and swerve from fidelity to a government that has never infringed my rights of person or property.

To the kind protecting care of a covenant-keeping God I commit you and our dear Kate and the unborn babe, whose face in this world I will never see. God has promised to be the husband of the widow and the father of the fatherless, and he is faithful who has promised. I die at the hands of cruel, implacable, and vindictive men, my own and my country's enemies. This is the hour and power of darkness, but it is my time to die. My hour has come. It is appointed unto man once to die. Of man the scriptures say, his days are determined, the number of his months is with thee. There is an appointed bound that he cannot pass. The wicked go when their cup of iniquity is full, the righteous when they have fulfilled the mission appointed them by Jehovah. Our Savior was slain by wicked men carrying out according to the freedom of their own will their own murderous purpose, as Peter declared at Pentecost, Him being delivered by the determinate counsel and foreknowledge of God, ye have taken and by wicked hands have crucified and slain. Kiss our darling Kate for me. I have no fear of death. I go trusting in Jesus. We will meet beyond the river. Farewell, a long farewell.

Your affectionate husband,

JOHN H. AUGHEY.

I wrote within the lines an occasional word in phonography, which read thus: Inform Generals Nelson and Rosecrans of my re-arrest and my sad fate.

I was then placed under guard and conducted to a small room in a hotel till preparations might be made for my death by shooting. Two guards remained in the room with their guns with bayonets fixed, with strict orders to shoot or bayonet me if I made the least show of an attempt at escape. There were two guards also stationed just outside the door, with the same orders, to be enforced if necessary.

I remained in this room an hour or more, supposing that as soon as the necessary arrangements for my execution were completed I would be led to death.

After a time orders came and I was marched into the presence of the officers. General Bragg said, "We have concluded to hang you."

I replied, "I deprecate that mode of execution. Do please shoot me."

He then said, "You will also have a trial, and if it results in conviction, of which there is no doubt, you will be hanged in the presence of the army."

The guards were then ordered to take charge of me. My chain was so short that I could only step about ten inches. I could just set my heel in stepping even with the toe of the opposite foot. They brought me to the same old prison. When I entered it, my old friends, the true, tried, and trusted prisoners who still survived, crowded around me. Captain Bruce addressed me in his facetious manner. In prison his wit had beguiled many a tedious hour. His humor was the pure Attic salt.

"Parson Aughey, you are welcome back to my hotel, though you have played us rather a scurvy trick in leaving without giving me or any of us the least inkling of your intention, or settling your bill."

I replied, "Captain, it was hardly right, but I did not like your fare, and your hotel was sadly infested with chinches, chiggers, ticks, and graybacks."

"Well, you do not seem to have fared better since you left, for you have returned."

"Captain, my return is the result of coercion. Some who oppose this principle when applied to themselves have no scruples in enforcing it upon others.

'No rogue e'er felt the halter draw
'With good opinion of the law,'

is an old saw, and the truth of proverbs is seldom affected by the lapse of time. I am your guest by compulsion, but remember I will leave you upon the first opportunity."

Upon hearing this statement, an officer present, named Cecil Hindman, with a bitter imprecation, said that when I next crossed the threshold of that building it would be to go to cross the railroad to the place of execution.

The prisoners gathered around me upon the exit of the officers, and I related to them my adventures. They then informed me of what had occurred during my absence. At roll call the next morning we were missed. Clarke was taken out to guide a company in search of you. The guards on duty during the night were put under arrest. Your method of escape was speedily discovered and the guards were released, as they were not at fault. The floor was spiked down, the guards increased in number, and greater vigilance enjoined. The prisoners were questioned as to whether they knew of your escape or had in any way contributed to effect it. We all positively denied any knowledge of or complicity in the escape. They asked me if I had given the officers any information about their knowledge of our designs and co-operation in effecting them. I told them that I had positively denied that any except Malone and myself were privy to our plans. Was this right? Is falsehood ever justifiable?

If I had revealed the aid received from my fellow-prisoners they would have been severely punished, perhaps some of them capitally, at once. And my fellow-prisoners would have regarded me as a base ingrate, and would not a second time, as they did, have risked their lives to set me free and save my life. We ought to speak every man truth to his neighbor, but those secessionists, thirsting for innocent blood, were in no true sense our neighbors, though too near neighbors, in regard to physical proximity, for our welfare. In order to save life we may take life, and may we not deceive by words, and be guiltless, those who would use their knowledge to destroy the innocent? I asked Benjamin Clarke, when he was remanded to prison, to give us the particulars of the pursuit of Malone and myself by the cavalry and blood-hounds, to which request he assented.

BENJAMIN CLARKE'S STORY.

"You were not missed till roll-call in the morning. Your name was the first on the roll. This man [laying his hand on the shoulder of a prisoner] is a great mimic. When he tries he can beat a mocking bird. He can mimic any man's voice. He can call up any animal or bird when he wants to shoot it. This man, Will Croghan's his name, sung out, 'Here.' Some of us that knowed you was gone looked round, thinkin' it was your voice. When they got to Malone's name, Jim Benton sung out present, but he wasn't no mimic, and the officer called out agin, Dick Malone, an' nobody answered. He then stopped calling the roll and sent out an orderly. It wasn't long till old Bragg, Hardee, and some other officers come into the prison in a hurry. The officer commenced calling the roll agin. Croghan was afeard to chirp, an' they found that you and Malone was gone. Bragg stormed round a spell, and afore long I was sent for. They told me to mount a horse a nigger was holdin'. I done so, and we all started off. They told me to guide them straight to Paden's mill. We had twenty-five cavalry men and forty dogs. They started with that many, seein' they might have to separate to follow different trails. How the hounds did howl and yelp. To give you a chance, I took 'em round by Bull Mountain, up one hill an' down the same, an' up another. They wanted to find some of your cloze in the prison to let the dogs git a scent. I thought Alex. Spear, that Federal prisoner from Ellisville, Illinois, an' you had traded pants, so you could git a dark pair so as to git by the guards, but they wazent none the wizer for me knowin' that. Well, nigh on to 4 o'clock in the evenin' we struck a trail. The hounds follered it lively. I waz awful feared it waz yourn, still I thought you wouldent be sich a fool as to go off on a straight shoot for Fulton, where they took us on our way here, an' where all the roads waz picketed. The trail was fresh, and the hounds got

11

about a mile ahead.   All at once we knowed they had
treed their game, an' agin I jist trembled in my boots
for fear it waz you.   We loped along as fast as we
could, but the ground got swampy an' the bushes
waz thick, an' drckly we knowed the dogs hed come
up with some big varmint, an' it was givin 'em battle, and they waz gittin' the wust of the skrimmage.
We hed an awful time to git through the chaparral,
an' we had to go out of our way a long trip to git
round a sloo.   But when we did come up with the
dogs they hed killed an awful big bar.   But afore he
knocked under he'd got his work in on the dogs, an'
you may never b'leve me agin ef there wazzent fourteen dogs lyin' dead as herrin's an' some more completely uzed up.   The best sentin' hound waz lyin'
close to the ded bar, and the bar's jaws was clozed
on one of his hind legs like a vise.   We got his jaws
loose, but the dog's leg waz mashed into a jelly, an'
we hed to shoot him to put him out of hiz mizery.
Well, these cavalry fellows swore they wazzent goin'
to leave till they hed tried some of the bar steaks.
They drug the carcass of the bar half a mile to a
hummock, an' rolled up logs till they hed made a big
log-heap, then sot it on fire, skinned the bar, sliced
off the nice steaks, an' jist enjoyed themselves.   'Fore
this waz done it waz very dark, an' the cap'n in
charge of the squad sed he reckoned they'd best go
inter camp fer the night.   'Twazent fur from Fulton.
'Bout midnight ten of these fellers stole off to go to
Madam Dunderberg's, in Fulton.   She kep a bagnio

on the edge of town. They got into a row with some roughs that waz there an' hed monopolized all the girls, and Bill Snediker and Jo Rucker was killed, an' Nath Downs waz hurt bad. They had a tough time gitten back. The cap'n hed to leave Downs at a settler's cabin, an' sent the settler fer a doctor, but before the doctor kum Downs hed gone wher they don't need no doctors, fur as we know. Well, 'twas nigh about noon, an' the cap'n said we'd bury Downs decent afore we left, so we hed dinner fust of 'n the bar, then we dug a grave 'en buried Downs with the honors of war. I thought about escapin', but there wazent the ghost of a chance. The dogs was allowed to tackle the bar, an' there wazent much of bruin, as the cap'n called him, left after they had done satisfied their appetites. The cap'n, Hindman I think waz his name, was purty bad flustered. He'd give me his compass, an' I, hopin' to escape, pertended I'd dropped it accidental in the swamp. The cap'n waz mad as blazes, an' swore wus than old Van Dorn when he foun' out the parson and Malone hed broke jail. He told me I must git them to Paden's mill agin night, or he'd tie me up by the thumbs. I told him that was onpossible. He said onpossible or not it must be did. Well, we started off, bearin' northeast. We passed right by my house. I said, "Cap'n les make some inquiries here." We pulled up before the door, it opened an' my wife an' children come to to the door. I got down of 'n the horse an' they all gathered about me like so many bees. Lilly May,

the baby, nestled her head in my bosom. Jim said,
'Pa, we've been workin' like beavers since you waz
taken away from us. You'll find the crops all right.
Ma helped us, too.' Just then the cap'n ordered me
to mount my horse. 'Oh, pa,' the children shouted,
'Ain't you come home to stay?' but the cap'n hurried on, and the last sight I had of my wife and babes
they waz all weepin' as ef their hearts would break,
an' its the last sight of 'em I ever expect to have in
this world.

He stopped to weep and we all wept in sympathy
with him. "When we got to Mackey's creek," he continued, "near Paden's mill, we camped fur the night.
Next mornin', bright an' early, we rode up to Mr.
Paden's. The cap'n told Mr. Paden he had a dis-
agreeable duty to perform. He had been ordered to
search his premises for a prisoner—a son-in-law of
hizzen that hed broke jail at Tupelo. Mr. Paden
said he might search, but they would find no one,
They searched the house upstairs and down, then
sent a squad to the negro quarters, another to the
mills, but their errand waz a bootless one.

Again he stopped to weep, we all wept with him.
Saying, "Excuse me I could not help it," he continued: "Your wife sat on the sofa in the parlor, pale
as death. Before we left she came to the door and
looked at the hounds and listened to their howling.
Her hands were clasped together. Once I saw her
lips move. I thought she was praying. I stood
near her, but I did not hear her speak. I think she

JUST THEN THE CAP'N ORDERED ME TO MOUNT MY HORSE.   Page 164

couldent speak for sorrow. Oh, how my heart bled for her, an' how much I wanted to tell her that I believed you waz safe in the Federal lines, but I could not git a chance to do so without notice. I got a chance to say to her father, I believed you waz safe in Rienzi by this time, an' I told him to tell his daughter so, which I haint no doubt but what he did. We left an' come back in a hurry. The other company that went due north got back about the time we did. A squad of them reported that they caught Malone, but that he got away from them at a house where they went to git water. They fired on him, and have no doubt that they wounded him bad, an' think he never could make the Federal lines. Our cap'n told everybody he met that a big reward was offered fur you, an' described you the best he could, an' stuck up notices describing you an' offering a reward fur catchin' you. When they got back they put me back in prison, an' I waz very sorry to see you here. Well, we'll have a chance now to go to heaven together. I reckon there aint much show fur either of us."

M. T. Anderson said, "If I am ever exchanged I'll publish this from one end of the North to the other. I'll tell of the heroic endurance of the southern loyalists who prefer death to dishonor, who prefer an ignominious death to the guilt of treason against the best government the sun shines upon."

I approached a prisoner who was heavily fettered. Both hands and feet were bound with iron bands, and he was chained to the floor, the chain being fastened to a bolt. I learned that he was a Minorcan. I said, "You are a Minorcan, I learn." He replied, "I have that honor, sir." After confidence had been established between us, he gave me his history, thus :

"My name is Louis LasCassas Lornette. My father is a native of the island of Minorca. He removed with his family and a large number of Minorcans to a town on the St. John's river, Florida, in the year 1826. There I was born May 8, 1828. My mother gave birth to triplets—all boys—Louis, Pierre, and Philippe. We always dressed alike, and bore a striking resemblance to each other. We were devotedly attached to each other and were inseparable companions. We became mighty hunters before the Lord. We pursued this vocation *con amore*, and the founder of Nineveh himself, the renowned Nimrod, could not have been more successful than we. At length the tocsin of war sounded— civil war. We had all attended the academy of a professor named Nathan Hale, of the state of Vermont. He was a great admirer of the great statesman, Daniel Webster. He had a copy of his speeches which we were permitted to read. We admired them much, especially his debate with Hayne, Calhoun, and others in the U. S. senate in regard to the right of a state to nullify the laws of the national government, or to secede from the Union. We thought those statesmen were like pigmies in the hands of a giant. When the war came, and we were told that the government must be disrupted in the interest of human slavery, my brothers and I resolved, come weal or come woe, we would never, *never* be guilty of treason to subserve an institution we detested. Our parents had taught us to hate slavery with a perfect hatred. Many a poor hunted fugitive have we protected, and taught him how to defend himself from the terrible Siberian blood-hound. We had never entertained for a moment the idea that we ourselves would ever be the object of pursuit by these same horrible dogs. One night a company of cavalry surrounded our father's house, during a re-union of his family. We three brothers were seized, bound, and after various vicissitudes were placed in prison in New Orleans, La., on the charge of treason against the Confederate States of America. We were tried and condemned to be shot. They then offered us a pardon on condition that we would enlist in the Confederate army. They gave us one week's respite for consideration. We were permitted to occupy the same cell in prison. We debated the matter, pro and con. At first we thought it best to send in our decision in the negative at once. Pierre reasoned in this way : ' Would it not be well to accept their terms, take the oath, enter the army, and at the first favorable opportunity desert and make our way to the Federal lines.' ' But what about the oath ? ' said Philippe. ' An oath exacted under such circumstances is much more honored in the breach than in the observance,' replied his brother. In a moment of weakness we sent in an affirmative answer. We begged to be permitted to enter the same regiment and the same company. This request was denied. We were mustered in in different regiments, and thus separated widely. I was put in a Mississippi regiment. I deserted, hoping to reach the Federal lines. A company of cavalry, with a pack of fierce Siberian blood-hounds were sent out in search of me. I came to a planter's quarters. The colored people and I searched all one day, thus losing much precious time, to find some herbs with which I could have compounded a subtle poison, and by means of pieces of meat saturated with it, I could have destroyed a large pack of hounds. But we could not procure the herbs. They are indigenous to a low, swampy country. They abound in the everglades of Florida. The colored people furnished me with cayenne pepper, onions, and matches, and I felt comparatively safe. But one day I heard a pack of hounds behind me. I used every ruse and stratagem I could devise, but just as I felt assured that the trail was broken a company who had gone north in search of you, while returning, came upon me and ordered me to come down from the tree in which I had taken refuge, and here I am."

" What will be your fate ? " I asked.

He replied, " They have discovered the regiment to which I belonged, and I am condemned to death by shooting."

About 11 o'clock A.M., Col. Gustave Feuillevert
came into the prison. He was a planter, a slave-
holder, and a friend of General Sterling Price. He
was of French ancestry. Had formerly lived in
Florida, and was an uncle of Louis Lornette, the
prisoner. He recognized him at once, as Louis a few
years before had visited his uncle and spent the summer with him. Col. Feuillevert, who was an ultra-
secessionist, tried to induce some of the prisoners to
promise to enlist in his regiment in case he secured
their release upon that condition. He was not successful in a single instance. He then approached his
nephew, Louis, who was sitting alone in the corner of
the prison, and informed him that his brothers,
Philippe and Pierre, were at his house in hiding. He
said they had deserted from Florida regiments, and after many remarkable adventures had reached his house
in as ragged and forlorn a condition as it was possible
for men to be found. He detested their treason, but
their aunt would save them at the peril of her life,
and although he would not betray them he felt sorry
and angry at their obstinacy. The colonel urged his
nephew to abjure his allegiance to a government that
made war upon the institutions of the South and refused to keep faith with the Southern states, and had
measurably nullified the provisions of the fugitive
slave law ; but all in vain, Louis refused to swerve
from his loyalty. The colonel bade his nephew
adieu, and departed. The day of Louis' execution
dawned. I conversed with him, prayed with him,

took his last messages to wife and children, promising that if I survived the horrors of this prison I would faithfully deliver them, but of this I had little hope. Louis told me it was clear to his mind that God in His providence had sent me to this prison for such a time as this. Those appointed to die needed the presence of one who could point them to the Savior, and, as a humble instrument in the hand of God, prepare them for a dying hour. It was a source of poignant regret that he had, even for the hope of escape, taken the oath of allegiance to the Confederate States of America. His oath of allegiance to the state of Florida he thought was right and proper, as he understood it.

At noon the guards brought in a prisoner who had voluntarily surrendered himself, declaring that he was Louis Las Cassas Lornette and desired to rejoin his regiment. When confronted with the condemned Louis, they bore such a striking resemblance to each other that the officers were puzzled. Gen. Bragg would be absent from Tupelo for a few days, and Gen. Sterling Price, to whom the case was referred, granted a respite till Gen. Bragg's return. Each prisoner insisted that he was Louis Las Cassas Lornette, and refused to recognize the other. The officers took the matter under advisement, and thought it best to send the two prisoners to Gen. Bragg for his decision. Should they fail to carry out Gen. Bragg's orders promptly they feared the consequences. A regiment was detailed for this purpose.

They went via Paden's Mills. Here they met a regiment of Federal cavalry; a skirmish ensued, several
were killed, and their bodies lie buried in Mr.
Paden's orchard. The Confederates fled and were
pursued four miles. They left their prisoners in the
hands of the Federals.

So Louis and Pierre still live to tell their children
the trials and persecutions of the Southern loyalists.
Philippe soon rejoined them in the North, and enlisting in the same regiment, they served faithfully till
the close of the war. Philippe died May 8, 1866, of
a wound received in the engagement which resulted
in the capture of Fort Fisher. Not till the war was
ended did their families rejoin them. Louis' and
Pierre's and Philippe's families are citizens of California. Pierre had resolved to save his brother or
perish with him. The affection of Damon and
Pythias could not have been stronger. A kind
Providence crowned the scheme to save his brother
Louis with abundant success, and these elderly vet-
erans, still as much alike as in their youth, save the
scar of a sabre thrust which laid open the cheek of
Louis, are still fighting their battles over at the urgent
solicitation of their children and their grand-children
and neighbors.

These brothers are still soldiers, faithful soldiers
of the Cross. Louis dates his conversion from the
time of his incarceration in Tupelo, and when he
writes to me addresses me as his spiritual father, and
speaks of himself as my son in the gospel, begotten

in my bonds. Pierre and Philippe united with the
regimental church at Beaufort, North Carolina,
brought to Jesus by their brother Louis, and their
Christian graces rapidly developed under the faithful
ministrations of that godly pastor, Chaplain LaSalle
Coligny, of Huguenot ancestry.

We are living, we are dwelling,
In a grand and awful time,
In an age on ages telling,
To be living is sublime.

After being remanded to prison, I felt that my
condition was utterly hopeless. For a time, as often
as I approached the door, the guards would order me
back. I preached to my fellow-prisoners every
evening. The best possible order was maintained,
as they stood or sat upon the floor and listened to the
words of eternal life. A deep seriousness prevailed,
and many believed, to the salvation of their souls.
The songs of Zion resounded through the prison
house, and a great concourse of soldiers assembled
outside the guards in front of both doors. Several
officers saw fit to come in during divine service.
Some of them behaved decorously, but on one or two
occasions, officers who neither feared God nor regarded man, nor the proprieties becoming gentlemen,
interrupted the services by talking in a loud and insulting tone, and asking me how I liked my jewelry,
pointing to my fetters. The prisoners protested
against their rude and ungentlemanly conduct, but
without effect; they sent a remonstrance to the com-

mander of the post, but he treated it with silent
contempt.

We were a motley assemblage. All the southern
states and every prominent religious denomination
had representatives among us. The youth in his
nonage, and the gray-haired and very aged man were
there. The learned and the illiterate, the superior
and the subordinate were with us. The descendants
of Shem, Ham, and Japheth, were here on the same
common level, for in our prison were Afric's dark-
browed sons, the descendants of Pocahontas, and the
pure Caucasian. Death is said to be *the* great leveler;
the dungeon at Tupelo was *a* great leveler. A fellow feeling made us wondrous kind; none ate his
morsel alone, and a deep and abiding sympathy for
each other's woes pervaded every bosom. When our
fellow-prisoners were called to die, and were led
through our midst with pallid brows and agony depicted upon their countenances, our heartfelt expressions of sorrow and commiseration were not loud
(through fear) but deep.

An officer entered. My name was called. I arose
from the floor on which I had been reclining. I
recognized him as my old friend, Col. H. W. Walter,
of Holly Springs, Miss. After the ordinary salutations, he informed me that he was judge advocate of
this army, and that he came to inform me of the day
appointed for my trial, and to learn whether I
wished to summon any witnesses, and whom. I
gave him the names and addresses of several wit-

nesses, but he refused to send for them, upon the plea that they lived too near the Federal lines. I replied that the cavalry that had gone in pursuit of me had visited those localities.

He then asked me what I wished to prove by those witnesses. I replied that I wished to prove that the specifications under the charge of enacting the spy are false; that Ferdinand Woodruff is a man of no moral worth; that Barnes is a mail-robber, and therefore not a competent nor veracious witness.

"Your own admissions," said the colonel, "are sufficient to cause you to lose your life. Both charges against you will be fully established. The testimony as to your guilt is clear and positive." He then read the charges and specifications:

"First charge.—Treason.

"First specification.—That Rev. John H. Aughey, a citizen of the state of Mississippi, and of the Confederate States of America, stated to a member of Hill's cavalry, that if McClellan were defeated the North could raise a much larger army in a short time; that the North would eventually conquer the South, and that he was a Unionist—this for the purpose of giving aid and comfort to the enemy.

"Second specification.—That when said Aughey was requested to take the oath of allegiance to the Confederate States of America, he refused, giving as a reason that England and France and himself had not as yet recognized the Southern Confederacy; stating also that he had voluntarily taken the oath

of allegiance to the United States government, which
he regarded as binding—this in North Mississippi.

"Third specification.—That said Rev. John H.
Aughey was acting as a Federal agent in the purchase of cotton, and that he had received a large sum
of gold from the United States government to pay
for the cotton purchased.

"Second charge.—Enacting the spy.

"That said Aughey, while a citizen of the Confederate States, repeatedly came into our lines for the
purpose of obtaining information for the benefit of the
enemy, and that he passed through the lines of the
enemy at will, holding an unlimited pass from Gen.
Wm. Nelson, of the Federal army, granting that
privilege—this in the vicinity of Corinth, Mississippi,
in '61–2.

"Witnesses—Wallace, Ferdinand Woodruff, J. B.
Coyner, Daniel Barnes, David Hough, —. Williams,
and J. R. Simonson."

I demanded a copy of these charges, which Col.
Walter promised to furnish. He kindly bade me
good-bye, and left the prison.

About 3 o'clock in the afternoon, I approached
two prisoners who were heavily ironed. They were
handcuffed, had bands and chains upon their ankles,
similar to mine, and were also chained together and
to a bolt in the floor. I inquired for what offence
they were incarcerated. The prisoner whom I addressed was a tall gentleman with a very intellectual
expression of countenance and of prepossessing man-
ners. He was pale and sad.

"We are charged with desertion."

"Did you desert?"

"I enlisted in the Confederate service for twelve months. At the expiration of my term of service I asked permission to return home, stating that I had learned from a trustworthy source that my family were suffering from a lack of the necessaries of life; that they lived in Tennessee, which is occupied by Federal troops. Confederate money there has no purchasing power, not being worth the paper on which it is printed; that I desired to relieve my family from their distress, and as my term of service had expired, I demanded my discharge. This they refused, stating that the Confederate congress had passed a law requiring all soldiers who had enlisted for any term, however short, to be held to service during the war, and that all who left before its close would be considered guilty of desertion, and if arrested would be shot. Regarding the law as a tyrannical enactment, and of no binding force, I attempted to return to my family, but was arrested and committed to this prison."

"What will be your fate?"

"I don't know, but fear the worst. At our trial Gen. Bragg said some salutary examples must be made to deter soldiers from deserting, or the army would waste away as snow before the bright beams of the vernal sun. His bile and bitterness overflowed in acrimonious invectives."

The other prisoner's statement was a perfect counterpart of his comrade's.

The first was named Melville Baillie, of Raleigh, Tennessee, and the other Polk Childress, of Hickory Wythe, Tenn. Their friend, Parley Van Horn, of Colliersville, Tenn., they left sick at the home of his cousin, Felix Grundy Ayres, in Byhalia, Miss., who thus escaped. I left them and walked to the opposite side of the prison, when I observed a file of soldiers drawn up in front of the prison. Two officers entered, and walking up to the prisoners with whom I had just been conversing, unfastened their chains, and ordered them to follow. As the officers passed Capt. Bruce, he asked, " What are you going to do with these men ? " " Going to shoot them," was the reply. They then showed him the warrant for their execution, having written across it in red letters, "condemned to death." When the prisoners reached the door, the file of soldiers separated, received the prisoners into the space in their midst, marched them across the railroad, and shot them.

Thus was perpetrated an act of cruel tyranny that cries loudly to heaven for vengeance. Two families, helpless and destitute, were thus each deprived of its head, upon whom they were dependent for support, and abandoned to the cold charity of a selfish world. The wages earned by a year's service in behalf of the wicked, cruel, and vindictive Confederate states, was an ignominious death and a dishonored grave. The widow and the fatherless cry to heaven for vengeance, and their cries have entered into the ears of the Lord of Sabaoth.

12

The judge advocate of the army, Col. H. W. Walter, returned to the prison and called my name. I speedily confronted him. He brought a copy of the charges preferred against me.

He said : " My wife feels a deep interest in you. She is very anxious in some way to secure your acquittal. I received a letter from her to-day, a portion of which I will read you : ' Mr. Aughey's many friends in Holly Springs, and I am of the number, earnestly request you to do all you can for his release, that will comport with the interests of our government. Remember that he is a minister of the gospel, and deserves all the courtesy, consideration, and kind treatment due to one who has faithfully and zealously fulfilled his high calling in our immediate vicinity—at Waterford and Spring Creek. Our dear friend, Mrs. Louis Thompson, has a mother's affection for him, and will visit him if permitted, that she may minister to his comfort and intercede for his release. He has often been our guest and has ever deported himself as a Christian gentleman, *sans peur et sans reproche,*' etc."

He informed me that my trial had been deferred until Monday. He said, " You will be tried on Monday and hanged on Tuesday at 2 o'clock P.M."

"Colonel, if my death is a foregone conclusion, you may as well reverse the order, and hang me on Monday and try me on Tuesday."

"I have examined the testimony against you. I know the intention of the officers. Your own ad-

missions are sufficient to condemn you. It is my
duty as judge advocate to do all I can for the prisoner, and as a friend I would take pleasure ·in
securing your acquittal, if that result would comport
with the interests and safety of the Confederate
states. But you have done us all the harm you
could. Winfrey and Armstrong, young soldiers
from Choctaw county, have informed me all about
your seditious language and conduct while pastor of
churches down there. They will appear against you.
The full extent of the injury you have done our
cause in North Mississippi can only be conjectured,
but it was to the extent of your ability and opportunity. Woodruff, Barnes, Crossland, Capt. George,
David Hough, Wallace, and J. B. Coyner, have
given sufficient testimony to Gens. Bragg, Beauregard, Jordan, and Price, of your treasonable exploits
to fill a volume. At one time Gen Bragg became so
angry at the recital of your Norman Bridge feat,
that he came near ordering a detail to hang you at
once, without the forms or farce of a trial. And he
would have done so, only Gen. Sterling Price interposed and insisted that as you were a minister of the
gospel the right thing to do was to give you a fair
and impartial trial. As you were chained and
closely guarded in the very midst of this great army,
escape was not possible, and a few days' respite could
not by any possibility injure the Southern Confederacy. Gen. Jordan, who is Beauregard's chief of staff,
declared that he ordered and inspected the ironing,

and that he would vouch for the security of the prisoner, for a few days at least. At another time, when Dr. Crossland recounted your insolence to Gen. Pfeiffer, at Brooksville, Gen. Bragg could scarcely restrain his wrath, and was upon the point of ordering your immediate execution. He thought Gen. Pfeiffer did wrong to allow you to express treasonable sentiments and to denounce the Confederate cause. Your execution will be as conspicuous as possible. It will take place in the presence of two brigades, composed of soldiers, many of whom are personally acquainted with you. There are many Unionists up there in North-eastern Mississippi, and a salutary example will not be lost on them. Some of them are in our army here perforce, and will witness an execution suggestive of their own fate if they should be guilty of treasonable language or conduct. Your crimes will be read to them and commented on by Major General Hardee, if present, or Gen. Mark Lowrey, in case of his absence."

"Colonel, I am a civilian. What right have they to try me by military law. The civil court has jurisdiction, and not a court-martial."

"All citizens of the Confederate States between 18 and 35 have been declared in the army, by congressional enactment, and have been required to report themselves at the head-quarters of the commander of the nearest military district within a given time, or be considered deserters. Have you complied with this law?"

THEY HUNG MY SON TO THE LIMB OF A TREE.   Page 187

"No, I have not. You have furnished me a copy of the charges against me, with the specifications. Desertion is not one of the charges."

"No, there are charges enough without that. I only mention it to show you that that enactment gives military jurisdiction over all citizens of military age. All your interests are with the South. It is your adopted home, though like myself you are of northern birth. Why did you not cast in your lot with the dominant class, for whose society you are fitted by literary culture, and not with that class which is giving us so great trouble, and whose treasonable utterances and acts we must suppress with an iron hand. Our own safety requires that we tolerate no longer the traitors in our midst. We must confiscate their property and exterminate them as we would venomous serpents."

"Jefferson Davis, in his inaugural address, quoting from the Declaration of Independence, declares that when governments become destructive to the ends for which they were established it is the right of the people to alter or abolish them. Was it the end for which our government was established to foster the interests of human slavery? If so, and you deem it right to protect those interests, go and fight in their defence, but do not endeavor to compel me and the great majority of the southern people who own no slaves to fight for your interests, and to become the foes of a government that has never trespassed upon our rights, a government which has no superior upon the face of the earth. You may murder me, but you cannot murder the government. If I had a thousand lives I would gladly lay them all upon the altar of my bleeding country."

"Parson, recanting your opinions would not save you now. You have forfeited your life, and I will not insult you by characterizing your crimes by their true names."

"Who said anything about recanting? I have no desire to recant truthful principles. You may express your opinion of my crimes, if you wish, and give their true names."

"Well, your crimes are, treason, enacting the spy, base ingratitude to your benefactors, and those who have heretofore reposed confidence in you, by siding with their enemies."

"Colonel, I have given a fair equivalent for all that I have received, and I have injured no one wittingly, in person, property, or reputation. My present condition indicates that the ingratitude is all upon the other side. I have labored faithfully for eleven years to promote the intellectual and moral and religious interests of the southern people, and they thus repay me with bonds and imprisonment, and they intend to pay the last installment by putting me to an ignominious death on the scaffold."

"Parson, I will call to-morrow, and should you have any requests to make, such as conveying messages to friends, disposition of property, or benefit of clergy at your execution, I will fulfill them for you."

"I would be glad to have Rev. James A. Lyon, D.D., of Columbus, to be present at my execution, also Rev. James Pelan, of Macon."

"I will telegraph them at once."

"I will prepare messages for my wife and other friends by to-morrow evening."

"I will secure their delivery at the earliest possible moment."

"Thanks, Colonel."

Soon after Col. Walter left, Col. Clare came in and asked me whether I had been president of a female college in Rienzi. I replied in the affirmative.

"'Tis strange," said he, "that one who has been so favored, and one who has accumulated property in the South, should prove a traitor to his adopted country and become its enemy."

I replied that I had given a fair equivalent for every dollar I had obtained from the citizens of the South; that for eleven years I had labored faithfully as an educator and minister of the gospel to promote the educational, moral, and spiritual interests of the southern people in the states of Kentucky, Tennessee, Louisiana, and Mississippi, and that now I was receiving my reward by being chained, starved, and insulted, and that they intended soon to pay the last installment by putting me to death ignominiously on the scaffold. I denied being an enemy to my country or to the South, I regarded those who would promote divisions and overthrow the government as the real enemies

of the South who were imperiling all her best interests. If my advice had been followed the South
and the whole country would now be enjoying its
wonted peace and unparalleled prosperity, and would
not have suffered W. L. Yancey and other demagogues to precipitate a desolating and ruinous
revolution.

He replied, "Ingrate, traitor, wretch, I have no
sympathy for you." He then called upon all the
supernal and infernal powers to blast my soul in
everlasting death and confine it forever in fiery
torments.

The prison walls echoed and re-echoed his blatant
blasphemy. The prisoners stood aghast, and with
faces blanched with fear for my safety, plucked me
away and crowded the space between me and this
vile blasphemer, who, with hand upon the hilt of
his sword and pistol belt alternately, seemed ready
to wreak his vengeance upon me.

At this moment Major Irion entered, and was informed by this minion of Jeff Davis that he had relieved his mind by giving me a "good cussen."
He left the prison with this officer, cursing as he
went.

Perhaps I should have been more circumspect—
more reticent, and thus prevented this outpouring of
the vials of Confederate wrath by this cursing
Shimei.

At this moment Gen. Braxton Bragg and several
officers of high rank entered. A distinguished

French officer was visiting this country on a tour of inspection. He desired to visit this prison, and this was the occasion of their visit. When they came to the place where I was standing, Gen. Bragg said, "This man dies on Tuesday next."

"What is his offence?" inquired the officer.

"He is a prisoner of state, and is guilty of treason."

"Are they all state prisoners in this prison?"

"All except a few prisoners of war, who will be removed to Macon, Ga., in a few days."

"This is a bastile, I suppose, but what has this prisoner done?"

"What has he not done, would be a more pertinent question. He has thrown all the influence of his official position as a minister of the gospel into the scale of opposition against our government."

"He is a minister, then?"

"Yes, a Presbyterian minister, of Northern birth and education."

"Ministers are usually regarded as non-combatants."

"Yes, but by word and deed and sermon and pen and every species of treasonable act and utterance, he has done our cause infinite harm. He is far from being a non-combatant."

"What is his name?" [Producing a note-book].

"He spells his name A-u-g-h-e-y. I am not sure of its pronunciation."

"O, yes, General, I recognize that name as of French origin. We have the name in France—a family of Huguenots. Many of that family were banished because of their opposition to the religious traditions of our empire, and some of them, after the revocation of the edict of Nantes, fled to the British Islands, and to Germany and Holland, to avoid the penalty affixed to disobeying the ecclesiastical regula-' tions of our country. He comes by his refractory opinions and conduct legitimately."

Gen. Bragg is a cadaverous, plain-looking man. He has bushy black eyebrows and piercing eyes. He stoops slightly in walking, and his stubby iron-gray beard and his receding forehead give him a plebeian look. He is cruel as the grave. Nearly every day he shoots some of his own soldiers, often for trivial offences. Cruelty is plainly written in indelible characters upon every lineament of his features, which are stern and almost savage in their expression.

After a thorough inspection of the prison our distinguished visitors retired.

I approached two elderly, gray-haired men, who sat in the north-west corner of the prison. These old gentlemen had become fast friends, and wept at the thought of their bleeding country's woes, brought on by designing, scheming politicians (not statesmen) in the interests of an institution subversive of all the inalienable rights of man. They gave me their history. The older gentleman, John Champe, was the youngest son of a revolutionary sire. His father had been chosen by Washington to effect the capture of Benedict Arnold after his treason, so as to save the life of Major André. This, because of untoward circumstances, he could not accomplish. But the effort was a gallant and heroic one, and merited and received high commendation from Gen. Washington. This is his story :

"I resided in Tuscumbia, Ala. I had four sons. Three of them had joined the Federal army. One night an attack was made on my house. My youngest son and I defended ourselves, but after killing four of our assailants, they burst in the door. We fled by the back door, and endeavored to reach the Federal lines. A company pursued us with bloodhounds. They overtook us. We fought with desperation. We killed five hounds and four of the soldiers. We expended all our ammunition. We were both severely wounded. They hung my son to the limb of a tree, and left the body to be devoured by the birds of prey. They put me in irons and brought me here. Why they spared my life I know not. The surgeon informs me that my wound in the breast will prove fatal in a short time. It gives me great pain. I would like much to see my aged wife, who, alone and surrounded by bitter foes, is mourning our absence."

The other said : "My name is Carter Braxton. I was named for my grandfather, a signer of the Declaration of Independence. My home is in Obion county, Tenn. My four sons are all in the Federal army. This is the cause of my imprisonment. They asked me if I were a Unionist, and I replied that it was a principle of law that no one was bound to criminate himself. I have had my trial. They proved that I had refused to take Confederate money, that I have traded with the Yankees, that my four sons were in the Federal army, that I was not a slaveholder, that I refused to take the oath of allegiance to the Confederate states, that after the reduction of Fort Donaldson I had told one George Sarbaugh that it would take more than one Southerner to whip five Yankees."

While he was yet speaking, the officer entered, and this old gentleman and a prisoner named Jason Chenault were unchained and marched to the fatal plat and shot. Chenault was a Kentucky Unionist, who had come to Mississippi to collect money due him for mules sold the year before. He was arrested, charged with enacting the spy, found guilty, and shot. I might record the sad fate of Nicholas Vedder, Bynum, Sorrell, and Oswald, all shot at the same time, for avowed Unionism, but space is wanting. I may place upon permanent record in the near future the biographies of these and other martyrs to the holy cause of our country's integrity imperiled by traitors.

I preached every evening. One evening my text was I. Kings xviii. 21 : "How long halt ye between two opinions." As none of us had a hymn book, I composed these hymns for the occasion. I parceled them out by couplets, and all joined in the singing:

How long! O, sinner, wilt thou halt,
How long! remain in guilty doubt,

While heaven and earth and air and sea
 The Lord is God, responsive shout.

Whilst thou art halting, sin grows strong,
 And lust and passion rule thy soul,
And all the powers of hell combined
 Still hold thee 'neath their stern control.

O, sinner, choose in this thy day
 To serve the Lord who loves thee well,
Oh ! choose to walk in wisdom's way
 And break thy league with death and hell.

Then will the host of heaven rejoice,
 Then will the powers of darkness rage,
But thou, a soldier of the cross,
 Wilt a successful warfare wage.

And when the glorious victory's won,
 Thou wilt a king, a conqueror be,
Wear on thy brow a diadem,
 And have a right to life's fair tree.

HYMN AFTER SERMON.

Spirit of the living God,
 Water now the precious seed,
Slay the sinner with Thy sword,
 Comfort to Thy saints afford.

Satan, like the birds of prey,
 Strives to catch the seed away,
Cares in countless numbers come,
 Shines with scorching heat the sun.

Thus we see our Savior's foes
 Strive to blast the seed he sows.
In the hearts of young and old,
 Prosper it, a hundred fold.

Holy Spirit, Father, Son,
 Aid us till our work is done;
Then, instead of worthless leaves,
 We shall bring our precious sheaves.

Two young men, John N. Maple, of Verona, Miss., and Samuel Melvin, of Tallaloosa, Miss., the former a Primitive Baptist, the latter a Methodist, held a discussion on the doctrine of foreordination. Some point in my sermon occasioned it. They both appeared to believe in the doctrine, since the term was used in the Bible. Melvin said the decrees of God were founded upon His foreknowledge. In the case of Paul, God foresaw all the contingencies and knew because of His prescience how they would eventuate, and based His decree that Paul should stand before Cæsar upon that foreknowledge. Maple affirmed that God knew that Paul would stand before Cæsar because He had decreed it. That He did not stand aside an indifferent spectator to observe how affairs would result, and then decree that they should take place, as He foresaw they would happen anyhow. That all that God does in time He always intended to do, and all that wicked men do He always intended to suffer or permit them to do. He would allow them to do wickedly in the exercise of the freedom of their will, only so far as He chose to overrule their wickedness for the promotion of His declarative glory, and the remainder of wrath He would restrain. Beyond the boundary of His will He would hem them in by His providence, and say, so far shalt thou go and no farther. Foreordination is founded upon the will of God, and not upon His foreknowledge of what man will do or what He foresees will happen. At the close of their debate it was found that neither had convinced the other of his error, nor any one else.

A man of Herculean frame, whose height was six feet eight inches, occupied the space on the floor next to mine as sleeping quarters. This space he called his dormitory. He gave me his history thus:

"I am a native of East Tennessee. I was born in Tellico Plains, Monroe Co., measurably brought up in Conasauga, Polk Co. I married Miss Tennie Paden, bought a farm near Dandridge, of one Geo. Cogsil, and moved on it in the year 1860. My own name is Hermon Bledsoe. I was chosen a delegate to the mass convention of Unionists, held June 17, 1861, in Greenville, Tennessee, to protest against the tyranny inaugurated over us by the rebel authorities. I was a member of the committee which prepared the following address, which was adopted by the convention with entire unanimity. We first detailed the facts of the election, how in Middle and West Tennessee the people were overawed, bullied, persecuted into an adoption of the ordinance; how the secessionists had prepared for the furtherance of their schemes, though the state had voted No Separation; how no provision was made for examining the returns otherwise than by a disunion governor, whose hold on power depended upon the success of the secession program; how volunteers in the secession army were allowed to vote within and *without* the state, contrary to any law; how discussion was forbidden in those sections where the secession vote was triumphant, while every Union paper there was crushed out; how a military despotism was ruling in spite of the wishes and rights of the people. The address then went on to say, in behalf of the loyal Unionist majority:

"'We prefer to remain attached to the Government of our fathers. The Constitution of the United States has done us no wrong. The congress of the United States has passed no law to oppress us. The president of the United States has made no threat against the law abiding people of Tennessee. Under the Government of the United States we have enjoyed, as a nation, more of civil and religious freedom than any other people under the whole heaven. We believe that there is no cause for secession nor rebellion on the part of the people of Tennessee. None was assigned by the legislature in their miscalled declaration of independence. No adequate cause can be assigned. The select committee of that body asserted a gross and inexcusable falsehood in their address to the people of Tennessee, when they declared that the Government of the United States had made war upon them.

"'The secession cause has thus far been sustained by deception and falsehood, by falsehood as to the action of congress; by false dispatches as to battles that were never fought and victories that were never won; by false accounts as to the purpose of the president; by false representations as to the views of Union men; and by false pretenses as to the facility with which the secession troops would take pos-

session of the capital and capture the highest officers
of the Government. The cause of secession or rebellion has no charms for us, and its progress has been
marked by the most alarming and dangerous attacks
upon the public liberty. In other states, as well as
our own, its whole course threatens to annihilate the
last vestige of freedom. While peace and prosperity
have blest us in the Government of the United States,
the following may be enumerated as some of the
fruits of secession.

"'It was urged forward by members of congress
who had sworn to support the Constitution of the
United States, and were themselves supported by the
Government; it was effected without consultation
with all the states interested in the slavery question,
and without exhausting peaceable remedies. It has
plunged the country into civil war, paralyzed our
commerce, interfered with the whole trade and business of our country, lessened the value of our property, destroyed many of the pursuits of life, and bids
fair to involve the whole nation in irretrievable
bankruptcy and ruin. It has changed the entire re-
lations of states, and adopted constitutions without
submitting them to a vote of the people, and where
such a vote has been authorized, it has been upon the
condition prescribed by Senator Mason, of Virginia,
that those who voted the Union ticket must leave the
state. It has advocated a constitutional monarchy, a
king, and a dictator, and is, through the Richmond
press, at this moment recommending to the conven-

13

tion in Virginia a restriction of the right of suffrage,
and in severing connection with the Yankees, to
abolish every vestige of resemblance to the institut-
t'ons of that detested race.   It has formed military
leagues, passed military bills, and opened the door
for oppressive taxation, without consulting the people, and then, in mockery of a free election, has required them by their votes to sanction its usurpations,
under the penalty of moral proscription or at the
point of the bayonet.   It has offered a premium for
crime in directing the discharge of volunteers from
criminal prosecutions, and recommending the judges
not to hold their courts.   It has stained our statute
book with the repudiation of Northern debts, and has
greatly violated the Constitution, by attempting
through its unlawful extension to destroy the right
of suffrage.   It has called upon the people in the
state of Georgia, and may soon require the people of
Tennessee, to contribute all their surplus cotton, corn,
wheat, bacon, beef, etc., to the support of pretended
governments alike destitute of money and credit.   It
has attempted to destroy the accountability of public servants to the people by secret legislation, and
set the obligation of an oath at defiance.   It has
passed laws declaring it treason to say or do anything
in favor of the Government of the United States, or
against the Confederate states, and such a law is now
before, and we apprehend will soon be passed by, the
legislature of Tennessee.   It has attempted to destroy,
and we fear will soon utterly prostrate, the freedom

of speech and of the press. It has involved the
Southern states in a war whose success is hopeless,
and which must ultimately lead to the ruin of the
people. Its bigoted, overbearing, and intolerant
spirit has already subjected the people of East Tennessee to many petty grievances; our people have
been insulted; our flags have been fired upon and
torn down; our houses have been rudely entered;
our families subjected to insult; our peaceable meetings interrupted; our women and children shot by a
merciless soldiery; our towns pillaged; our citizens
robbed and some of them assassinated and murdered.
No effort has been spared to deter the Union men of
East Tennessee from the expression of their free
thoughts. The penalties of treason have been threatened against them, and murder and assassination have
been openly encouraged by leading secession journals.
As secession has been thus overbearing and intolerant while in the minority in East Tennessee, nothing
better can be expected of the pretended majority than
wild, unconstitutional, and oppressive legislation; an
utter contempt and disregard of law; a determination
to force every Unionist in the state to swear to the
support of a constitution he abhors, and to yield his
money and property to aid a cause he detests, and to
become the object of scorn and derision as well as the
victim of intolerable and relentless oppression.

"In view of these considerations, and of the fact
that the people of East Tennessee have declared
their fidelity to the Union by a majority of about

twenty thousand votes, therefore we do resolve and declare.'

"Here followed a series of patriotic resolutions, and the appointment of a committee to prepare a memorial, asking the consent of the legislature of Tennessee to consent to the separation of East Tennessee, and those counties of Middle Tennessee which desired it, from the rest of the state, that they may be formed into a separate state.

"Brownlow, Maynard, Etheridge, Nelson, Hawkins, Johnson, etc., led the Unionists. It was not long before those Unionists and protestants against wrong were flying for their lives, and were hunted down like wild beasts. The leaders disappeared from observation, and the people could only become quiescent in a state of affairs which, in the presence of the armed minions of the Southern Confederacy, they were powerless to prevent.

"I was placed on the proscribed list, and was compelled to hide in a cavern with other Unionists. One night I visited my family, which consisted of my wife and twin babes, Mark and Paul. A band of guerrillas, lying in ambush in the chaparral near my residence, surrounded the house, and rushing through the door, which for the moment I had forgotten to fasten, took me prisoner. They searched my person and found several copies of the address above given, and some letters in a drawer, which were construed unfavorably by these cruel men. They handcuffed me and took me to the chaparral copse. They held

I CALLED, 'HALLO, UNCLE!' AS HE RESTED FOR A MOMENT.   Page 200

a brief trial, which resulted in my conviction and
condemnation to death. Immediate preparations
were made for my execution. Douglas Flinn declared that hanging was too good for such a wretch
as I. Jim Bainbridge coincided with him in opinion. 'What do you want done with him?' said
Bob. Torrence, who commanded the gang. 'Let us
burn him at the stake, like Col. Brown's Sam last
week, for assaulting a white girl.' 'All right,' said
Torrence. 'All in favor of burning this d—d ren-
egade, this Lincolnite, this tory and traitor, say aye.'
A vociferous aye resounded. 'All opposed, no.' Only
two voices responded in the negative. Sam Lovell
took off the handcuffs and bound me to a sapling
with the rope with which they had intended to hang
me. The trial had begun in the gloaming, and now
darkness had enshrouded all the land. Flinn ran
and gathered an armful of dry sticks and deposited
them in a pile at my feet. Soon many were engaged
in gathering fagots. Flinn declared that this was
the happiest night of his existence. He would soon
have the pleasure of seeing this miserable traitor
going up like Elijah in a chariot of fire. 'So mote
it be,' growled Jacob Embry, in a sepulchral tone.
George Goshen, Peter Peters, and J. B. Coyner were
dispatched to Aunt Sylvia Caldwell's for a firebrand
with which to ignite the pile of fagots. I commended
my soul to God and calmly awaited death. Flinn
approached me with a pile of (as he said) very dry
wood. He approached quite near, and dropping the

fagots he placed a knife handle between my teeth. The large blade of the knife was open. He then ran to and mounted a stump about fifty yards distant, and commenced to deliver a harangue laudatory of the Southern Confederacy, and denouncing all traitors, wishing them in the bottom of the lowest hell.

"With some effort I managed to sever the cord binding my wrists. I then cut the cord bound around my waist, and quietly and quickly made my escape. The crowd around Flinn, who was doubtless a Unionist in disguise, were cheering vociferously, which aided my escape, as the noise drowned the crackling of the fagots as I removed or trampled upon them on the farther side from the stump orator and his auditors. Soon the men with the fire arrived and applied it to the heap around the sapling. Looking back from a hill about two miles distant I saw the flames rising higher and higher, till a large space was illuminated. Suddenly I heard fierce yells of disappointment and rage, emanating from the throats of this infuriated and disappointed crowd of demons incarnate, maddened to frenzy by my escape. I traveled by night, but lay concealed during the day.

"When in hiding near Siluria, Shelby county, Alabama, I heard the sound of a wood-chopper's ax, quite near, and peering from the copse in which I was concealed, I saw a slave at work felling a tree. Soon he began to declaim a piece:

" ' The hillsides in places are white I know,
But the white ess is not occasioned by snow.
It is only the petals of apples and cherries
And peaches and plums and all sorts of berries,
Just falling in sport from their bowers,
As if to represent April showers.'

' 'Now,' said he, apparently well satisfied with his effort, 'Dat's 'bout as good as young Massa Josiah hisself could spoke it.' Soon he broke forth in song:

" ' On Jordan's banks we stand,
    An' Jordan's stream roll by,
No bridge de watahs span,
    De flood am risin high.
Heah it foam an' roar, de dark flood tide,
How shel we cross to de oder side.

' De riber deep an' strong,
    De wabes am bery cole,
We see it rush along
    But who can venture bole.
Heah it foam and roar, etc.

'A little chile step down,
    It go in de riber deep,
Kin little feet touch groun'
    Whar mountain billows sweep.
    Heah it foam and roar, etc.

' Dere comes a flash of light
    Ober de cole dark wabes,
Dere come de angel's flight,—
    See, shinin' hands dat sabe,
From de watah's foam, de dark flood tide
Fer de Lawd hab seen from de oder side.

' Heah music swellin' gran',
    Yes, songs of welcome ring.

White wings de riber span,
    De little chile to bring.
Den let old Jordan roar, de dark flood tide,
We'se borne across to de odder side.'

"I called, 'Halloo, uncle!' as he rested for a moment from his labor, with arms akimbo. 'Who am dat calling?' he cried out, with some degree of trepidation. As he looked in my direction, I beckoned him to approach me. When he came near I said, 'To whom do you belong? Where do you live?' He replied, 'I belongs to Major Cayce, of Talladega. He bought me and my wife of Col. Shorter, of Choccolocco, Calhoun county, last year. I was borned the slave of Parson Lagow, of Emuckfaw. When I wuz six months old, master died, an' ole lady Rudisil bought me at the sale fur $500. I lived wid her at Chepultepec till I wuz ten years old, den she died, and I wuz sold agin to Gov. Peyton Claiborne, of Sylacauga. I'se bin around sum, but I'se never bin out en the state of Alabam. I buys my time from my *now* master, Major Cayce, for twenty-five dollars a month. I lives in that cabin up yonder on the hill.' He pointed with the index finger of his right hand to a cabin almost lost to sight in the distance, nestling among the trees in a grove surmounting a hill of great height. He named it cosy cot, and the name was not a misnomer.

"I revealed my condition to this quadroon slave, and he and his kind wife fed and lodged me for a week, till I was sufficiently recovered from my fatigue to continue my journey.

On the broad highway of action,
Friends of worth are far and few;
But when one has proved his friendship,
Cling to him who clings to you.

Should opportunity ever be afforded for reciprocating the kindness of this slave husband and wife, Isam and Tabitha, I will gladly avail myself of it, and do them all the kindness in my power.

"I continued my journey, and with but little of incident or adventure worth narrating, I at length arrived at the home of my cousin, Jerry Humboldt, in Selma, Ala. My cousin was a staunch Unionist, a stalwart, uncompromising friend of the United States government and the old flag, the star-spangled banner, the emblem of freedom and the inalienable rights of man.

"Every day dangers thickened around us. We were compelled to devise a plan of escape to the Federal lines. Twenty-five of us set out together, under the guidance of Leander Browning. At Tallahatta Springs, Clark county, a band of guerrillas, or partisan rangers, as they called themselves, overtook us as we were camping for the night. We fought them long and well, till we had slain nearly twice our number of our pursuers, then, as the darkness grew denser, the remnant of us, wounded and bleeding, fled.

"I was captured at Sanwilpa, was taken to Tuscahoma, put into a guard house. Soon after I was conveyed to Pushmataha; thence I was removed to this dungeon in Tupelo, Miss. I adroitly concealed my identity, and though under violent suspicion nothing definite was proved against me. To save my life, I have agreed to take the oath of allegiance, and join the rebel army. I may soon be able to desert and reach the Union lines. My *nom de guerre* is Ralph Benton."

"Have you any conscientious scruples about the propriety of taking an oath with the deliberate intention of violating it?"

"Not any. It may save my life. At least deliver me from this prison. Deception is certainly justifiable in a case like this. The rebels have violated every oath that they have ever taken. Shall we keep faith with them? Naught but Punic faith for them. As soon trust a rattlesnake as a rebel. I hope to reach the Union lines and offer my services to General Pope as a volunteer in his army."

On the next day my friend was permitted to take the oath and enter the rebel army. He had several copies of the address concealed about his person, as he thought beyond the reach of rebel search, one of which he gave me. I retain it as a sacred memento. A rumor reached me through Philip Henson, a Federal spy, that my friend was under violent suspicion by the rebels, and was caught in his attempt at escape, and shot by order of Gen. N. B. Forrest.

Anent this rumor, Gen. Jefferson C. Davis told me that a soldier in his command bore the name and answered the description of Hermon Bledsoe; that he was a deserter from the enemy; that he was severely wounded in a skirmish, and that his recollection was that his wound proved fatal.

One of my fellow-prisoners became suddenly insane. He frothed at the mouth, rolled his eyes wildly, and butted his head against the walls of the prison. His paroxysms were very violent in the presence of the officers. I sat near him, and after observing him for awhile I came to the conclusion that he was a malingerer. Presently an officer entered, at that instant the crazy man was seized with another paroxysm. He became very violent. The officer watched him for some time and then said, "We must remove him to the hospital that he may die there, for there seems to be but little hope of his ultimate recovery, he is so sick and crazy and fierce." This man's name was Bovard Willis, a Unionist, of Biloxi, Miss. After the officer's departure he quieted down in a very short time. I approached him and said:

"Willis, I do not profess to be an alienist, but I know that you are no more crazy than I am. I will not betray you. What is your motive in feigning madness?"

He replied, "If I am taken to the hospital I will have a by far better opportunity of escaping. I voted against secession, I led the Unionists in our county, I became very obnoxious to the secessionists, and there is no hope for me but in escape."

In the evening he was removed to the hospital. The next morning he was missing. He had unfortunately left some clothing in the hospital. The company that went in search of him let the hounds smell the garment. Soon they struck his trail and followed it to the creek. Willis, upon reaching the creek, waded in it three miles, and thus baffled his pursuers for several hours. In the afternoon they recovered the trail and followed it rapidly for several miles. By this time Willis had reached a house ten miles south-west of Tupelo. He went to it at a venture. He asked for water. The proprietor seemed to know by intuition the character of this wanderer. He told his wife to prepare some food for this stranger. While he was eating, the howling of the hounds was heard. Willis rose in great trepidation. His host at once interpreted the reason. No plan seemed feasible for the concealment of the fugitive. Mrs. Quay suggested the closet as a hiding place, but her husband thought it unsafe, as it was in a part of the house so exposed that it would be among the first places searched. The blood-hounds finding the track fresh were pursuing with great speed.

Mr. Quay said, pointing to a tree about two hundred yards distant, "If you could reach that tree, you would find a secure asylum till your pursuers had gone on, or returned supposing they were on the wrong trail. The horses are in the field, if I can only get one up in time and carry you over to the tree and get back before they reach us you will be safe."

Just then the hounds broke out afresh into loud howls and sharp yelps.

"They are too near for that" said Willis, "I am lost."

"Pa," said little Violetta Quay (who was only six years old), "you just tote that man over to the tree."

"I'll do it," said her pa. He stooped down, and Willis perched himself upon his shoulders and was borne to the tree, and in an incredibly short space of time was concealed amid the foliage of the loftiest branches of this mighty king of the forest.

Quay had just time to return and enter his house when the hounds bounded into his yard, their fierce yelps betokening that they knew that the object of their pursuit was near. Soon the pursuing cavalry entered the yard, and dismounting, began unceremoniously a thorough but bootless search of the house and premises. They questioned strictly each member of the family, but they were all woefully ignorant. The officer in charge asked little Violetta if she had seen any stranger about lately. She replied, "If I had I wouldn't tell you. I just wish the poor man would come here, I'd hide him if I could from those awful dogs." The hounds were completely baffled. They would not leave the track indicated by the scent of Willis' garment for any other. After two hours of fruitless endeavor to recover the track, they left Mr. Quay's house and returned.

Willis was now among friends. After some nights spent in hiding, Willis was conveyed by nocturnal journeys from one friendly post to another, till he reached the Federal lines at Memphis, Tenn. Willis did not change quarters till the guides were ready to enter upon their perilous task of guiding a band of Unionists, of which Willis was one, to the Federal lines. He said, "There is no place so safe as where the hounds have been." And so the experiment proved the adage true. Willis was not molested in this sylvan retreat, though the whole country north to the Federal lines was repeatedly traversed by cavalry and hounds.

M. T. Anderson, of Millersburg, Holmes Co., O., came to me and said:

"Mr. Aughey, I am very sorry for you. There is hope for me. I am a prisoner of war. If I survive the horrors of imprisonment I will be exchanged, but for you, a prisoner of state, there is no hope except by cluding the vigilance of the guards and making your way through this great army, and traversing a long stretch of hostile country to the Federal lines. Now, sir, I am not superstitious, but I had a dream last night that has deeply impressed me. I thought that I was caught up into heaven, into the midst of the Paradise of God, and as I stood dazed amid the splendors of the city of the Great King, and bewildered by the light and resplendent glory that emanated from the great white throne, and Him that is seated thereon, I heard a voice saying, 'Who will go for us to earth, and deliver my servant from bonds and imprisonment and impending death, that he may longer proclaim my gospel?' Suddenly there ap-

peared before the throne a form of wondrous beauty,
apparently a young man—of radiant countenance;
from every feature beamed love and peace and good-
will, who said, 'Here am I. Send me. I will go
and deliver him and bring him safely to the desired
haven.' 'Who art thou?' said the recording angel,
who sat hard by the throne of God. 'I am Ariel,
the lion of Jehovah, who am made strong to deliver
his chosen ones from all their enemies that rise up
against them to destroy them. I delivered Peter
from Herod's dungeon, and many saints who were
shut up in prison have I released,' and he was bidden
to perform the mission. And then I heard the voice
of a multitude saying, 'Go, and Jehovah, merciful
and gracious, mighty and strong to deliver, give thee
abundant success.' And all the host of heaven responded, 'Amen.' Then a voice said to me, 'Return
and make known the vision to my servant, who in
bonds is breaking to thee and those with thee the
bread of eternal life.' I awoke trembling and aston-
ished.

"Now, I entertain more than a mere presentiment
of your escape. I am so fully impressed with the truth
that my dream was a revelation of God's will con-
cerning you, that I firmly believe that these wicked
men will not be suffered in the providence of God to
take your life. I predict that many, many years of
successful labor in your Master's vineyard are before
you; many souls, by your instrumentality, are to be
brought into the fold of Christ and the kingdom of
heaven."

"I wish you may not be a false prophet, and that your dream may be verified. The eye of faith alone can discern a ray of hope. Sight shows a prison, strong and closely guarded, a mighty army of watchful and malignant foes, chains, fetters, guards on the alert, pickets, patrols, videttes, blood-hounds innumerable, my sun of life apparently on the horizon's verge. The hour of my departure fixed. Many, many miles intervening between my prison and a place of safety—a city of refuge. A physical frame enfeebled by starvation and surrounding horrors which have been endured for many weary months, which are lengthening into years. It does indeed require strong faith to discern a ray of hope or glimmer of light to irradiate the future. Next Tuesday ends all, my foes have decreed. If God in his providence has longer life in store for me I will be spared. But I feel that I have received dying grace, and dying grace is reserved for a dying hour. However, should any plan of escape present itself, I will not be slow to avail myself of it. But my only hope is in escape. The vindictive Confederate authorities are determined to put me to death at the hour mentioned by Col. Walter. They are implacable and unmerciful, and it irketh them to await the appointed hour. I would like much to live for my dear wife's sake, and our dear infant's sake. By this cruel deed of rebel hate, my wife will be widowed and my child made fatherless. But God has promised to be the husband of the widow and the

father of the fatherless. To his covenant-keeping
care I commit them both, and the babe unborn."

Feeling assured that my departure from this ter-
restrial sphere was near, I sat down upon the floor of
my dungeon and penned the following letter to my
wife :

TUPELO, MILITARY BASTILE.

My Dear Mary:

The Confederate authorities announce to me that I
have only a few more days to live. When you receive this letter the hand that penned it will be cold
in death. My soul, divested of the body, will have
passed the solemn test before the bar of God; I have
a good hope through grace that I will then be rejoicing amid the sacramental host of God's elect, singing
the new song of redeeming love in the presence of
Him who is the chief among ten thousand and the
one altogether lovely. Mary, meet me in heaven,
where sorrow and tears and temptation and sin are
unknown, and where the wicked cease from troubling
and the weary are at rest. If General Bragg will
permit my body to be taken in charge by my friends,
I will ask your brother, D. R. Paden, and cousin,
Capt. Jas. H. Tankersley, to convey it to you. Bury
me in the cemetery at Bethany church. That was
my first ministerial charge. Plant a cedar at my
head and one at my feet, and there let me repose in
peace till the archangel's trump shall sound, sum-
moning the dead to the judgment of the great day,
and vouchsafing to saints the long hoped for redemp-

14

tion of the body. As to my property, it has all, by Confederate laws, been confiscated, and after years of incessant toil I leave you penniless and dependent, but I implore you to trust in God. To his kind, protecting care I commit you and our dear little Kate. Jehovah has promised to be the widow's husband and the father of the fatherless. Rest assured the Lord will provide. Only trust Him and love Him with your whole heart and soul and mind and strength. I know that it shall be well with them that love God. Be not faithless, but believing, and though clouds and darkness surround you at present, well-nigh obscuring the spiritual sky whence hope emanates, yet be assured a more auspicious day will dawn, and God will bring you safely to your journey's end, and our reunion in heaven will be sweet.

Our dear little daughter, Kate, bring up in the nurture and admonition of the Lord. Teach her to walk in wisdom's ways, for all her ways are pleasantness and all her paths are peace. Her infant mind may be compared to wax in its susceptibility for receiving impressions, and to marble for its power in retaining those impressions. O! that she may be satisfied early with thy mercy, O, God, that she may rejoice and be glad all her days. Teach her to remember her Creator in the days of her youth, before the evil days come in which she shall say, I have no pleasure in them. Make the Bible, the precious Bible, her constant study, and let its words be as household words to her. Inspire her mind with a

love of *the Book* which is able to make wise unto salvation. See to it that the words of Christ dwell
richly in her soul, that she may be filled with knowledge and wisdom and spiritual understanding. Pray
for the Holy Spirit to bless your labors and counsels.
Without his blessing all your labor would be in
vain. Pray that the third Person of the adorable
Trinity, the Spirit of the living God, may take up his
abode in her heart, to abide with her forever. As
my duties in regard to instructing our child will de-
volve solely upon you, take for your guidance in
this respect Deut. vi. 5–9. Let your example be
such as you would wish her to follow. Children
are much more inclined to follow example than
precept. Exercise care in this respect, for as is the
mother so is her daughter. I regret that my family,
from the force of circumstances, will be compelled to
remain in a section where, by many, my course of
conduct which led to my death will be considered
disgraceful. But this cannot be avoided. The
time, I feel sure, will come when, even in Mississippi,
I will be regarded as a patriot martyr. My conscience is void of offence as regards guilt in the
charge preferred against me. When the wicked bear
rule the people mourn. What cruelties are being
perpetrated by rebels against God and their country.
How long, O, Lord, how long shall the wicked triumph? How long will God forbear to execute that
vengeance which is his, and which he will repay in his
own good time? I have an abiding confidence that

the right cause will prevail, and though I shall not live to see it, for my days are numbered, yet I firmly believe since God is a God of justice and an avenger of the righteous who serve him faithfully, that the rebel power will be destroyed utterly.

> "Truth crushed to earth shall rise again—
> The eternal years of God are hers—
> But error wounded writhes in pain
> And dies amid his worshipers."

I write this letter amid the din and confusion incident to a large number of men crowded into a narrow compass and free from all restraint.

This letter will be conveyed to you by friends. The names of those friends you will know hereafter. My real estate will be restored to you when the Union cause triumphs. That it will do so ultimately is beyond the possibility of a doubt. Give my love to all my friends. Remember that I have prayed for you and our dear Kate unceasingly during my imprisonment, and my last utterances on earth will be prayers for your welfare. Farewell, God bless you and keep you and our dear child from all harm.

Your affectionate husband,
JOHN H. AUGHEY.

I then wrote my obituary, which I placed in the hands of Mr. De Grummond, a Federal prisoner, by whom it was to be sent to the *Philadelphia Presbyterian* for publication. I copy a portion of it:

WILLIS WADED IN THE CREEK FOR THREE MILES. Page 204

OBITUARY.

Died in Tupelo, Itawamba county, Miss., July 15, 1862, Rev. John H. Aughey.

The subject of the above notice suffered death on the gallows at the hands of the Confederate military authorities, on the charges of treason and enacting the spy. John H. Aughey was born in New Hartford, Oneida county, N. Y., May 8, 1828. Removed with his parents to Steubenville, O., July 4, 1837. Is an alumnus of Franklin College, New Athens, Ohio. His theological instructors were, Revs. L. A. Lowrey, Winchester, Ky.; Jahleel Woodbridge, Baton Rouge, La.; John H. Gray, D.D., Geo. W. Coons, D.D., and Rev. J. O. Steadman, D.D., Memphis, Tenn.; Rev. Chas. S. Dod, Rev. H. H. Paine, and Rev. S. Irwin Reid, Holly Springs, Miss. Was licensed to preach the gospel by the Presbytery of Chickasaw, October 4, 1856. Ordained to the full work of the ministry by the Presbytery of Tombeckbee, April 19, 1861. Was married January 22, 1857, by Rev. R. Henderson, to Miss Mary J. Paden, of Iuka, Miss., who, with one child, a daughter, born September 3, 1858, survives him. God blessed his labors by giving him many souls as seals to his ministry. After eleven years labor in the South as an educator and minister of the gospel, having never injured a citizen of the South in person or property, he fell a victim to secession hatred, and died a felon's death, because he would not become a traitor to the government which had never in a single instance trespassed upon his rights of person or property. He rests in peace and in the hope of a blessed immortality beyond the grave. "Take ye heed, watch and pray, for ye know not when the time is." Mark xiii. 33.

"Leaves have their time to fall,
And flowers to wither at the north wind's breath,
And stars to set—but all!
Thou hast all seasons for thine own, O! Death."

ADDRESS TO MY SOUL.

O! my soul, thou art about to appear in the presence of thy Creator, who is infinite, eternal, unchangeable in his being, wisdom, power, holiness, justice, goodness, and truth. He cannot look upon sin. He is a sin-avenging God, and thou art defiled by sin. Thy transgressions are numerous as the stars of heaven. Thou art totally debased by sin and thy iniquities abound. Thou art guilty of sins both of omission and commission. Justice would consign thee to banishment from heaven and to everlasting destruction from the presence of the Lord and the Glory of his power. Guilty, helpless, wretched as thou art, what is thy plea that sentence of eternal death should not be pronounced against thee?

THE SOUL'S REPLY.

I plead the merit of the Lord Jesus Christ whose blood cleanses from *all* sin, even from sins of the deepest dye. I plead the atonement made by Him

who made an atonement for sin, who bore my sins
in his own body on the cross of Calvary and wrought
out a perfect righteousness which I may obtain by
simple faith. No money, no price is demanded.
This I could not pay, for all my righteousness is but
filthy rags, and I must perish were any part of the
purchase price demanded. Nothing in my hand I
bring. My salvation must be *all* of *grace*, or to me
it would be hopeless. I trust that Christ will clothe
me in the perfect, spotless robes of his own righteousness and thus present me faultless before the throne.
With this trust I go to the judgment seat, assured
that the soul that implicitly trusts in Jesus shall
never be put to shame. He is faithful who has
promised.

MILITARY DUNGEON,

TUPELO, MISS., July 11, 1862.

My Dear Parents :

Life is sweet, and it is a pleasant thing to behold
the sun. All that a man hath will he give for his
life. Having promise of the life that now is. The
life is more than meat. They hunt for the precious
life. These quotations from the Word of Life show
the high estimate that is placed upon life. My life
is not precious in the eyes of these virulent secessionists, for their military rulers declare that on the 15th
inst. my life must terminate. Yet a few days and
me the all-beholding sun shall see no more in all his
course. Mourn not for me, my dear parents, as
those who have no hope. For me to live is Christ,

and I can say also with the apostle, and to die is gain. I fear not those who, when they have killed the body, have no more that they can do. But I fear Him whose fear casteth out every fear. When these lines are read by you he who penned them will be an inhabitant of the Celestial City, the New Jerusalem. He will have a palace home by the crystal sea, and be the possessor of a kingdom and a crown as eternal in duration as the throne of Jehovah. He will be reposing in his Savior's bosom in the midst of the Paradise of God.

Next to God my thanks are due to you, my dear parents, for guiding my infant feet in the path of wisdom and virtue. In riper. years I have been warned and instructed. By precept and example I have been led, until my habits became fixed, and then, accompanied by your parental blessing, I sought a distant home to engage in the arduous duties of life. Whatever success I have achieved, whatever influence for good I may have exerted, are all due to your pious training. I owe you a debt of gratitude which I can never repay. Though I cannot, God will grant you a reward lasting as eternity. It will add to that exceeding and eternal weight of glory which will be conferred upon you in that day when the heavens shall be dissolved and the elements shall melt with fervent heat. I die for my loyalty to the Federal Government. I know that you would not have me turn traitor to save my life. Life is precious, but death, even death on the scaffold, is preferable to dis-

honor. Remember me kindly to all my friends.
Tell Sallie, Violetta, David, Lizzie, Mary, and
Emma, my dear sisters and brother, to meet me in
heaven. I know that my Redeemer lives. Dying is
but going home. I have taught many how to live
and how to die happily. Now by example I am
called to teach them how to die as becometh the
Christian. May God in mercy grant that as my day
my strength may be, and that in my last moments I
may not by slavish fear bring dishonor upon my
Master's cause, but may glorify Him in the fires.
Remember me to my old, tried, true, and trusted
friend, Henry Spence. I have no doubt you are constantly praying for me. I will soon be in that glorious home where prayer is lost in praise, faith is
changed to sight, and death is swallowed up in
victory. Farewell till we meet beyond the river.

Your affectionate son,

JOHN H. AUGHEY.

*To David and Elizabeth Aughey, Amsterdam, Jeffer-
son county, Ohio.*

CENTRAL MILITARY PRISON,

TUPELO, ITAWAMBA CO., MISS., July 11, 1862.
Hon. Wm. H. Seward:

DEAR SIR—A large number of citizens of Mississippi, holding Union sentiments, and who recognize no such military usurpation as the so-called
Confederate States of America, are confined in a
filthy prison, sadly infested with vermin, and are

famishing from hunger—a sufficient quantity of food not being furnished us. We are separated from our families, and not suffered to hold any communication with them. We are compelled under a strong guard to perform the most menial services; and are often grossly and flagrantly insulted by the officers and guards of the prison. The nights are very cool, after the torrid heat of the day. We are not furnished with bedding, and are compelled to lie down upon the hard floor of our dungeon, where refreshing sleep is not possible. When exhausted nature can hold out no longer our slumbers are broken, restless, and of short duration. Our property is confiscated and our families left destitute of the necessaries of life, all that they possessed, yea, all their living having been seized by the Confederates and converted to their own use. Heavy iron fetters are placed upon our limbs, and daily some of us are led to the scaffold or to death by shooting. Many are forced into the army, instant death being the penalty in case of refusal, thus constraining us to bear arms against our country, to become the executioners of our friends and brethren, or to fall ourselves by their hands.

These evils are intolerable, and we ask protection through you from the United States Government. Please present our humble and earnest petition to his excellency, Abraham Lincoln, president of the United States, that he may take it under advisement and if possible afford us speedy relief. The Federal Government may not now be able to release us, but we ask the protection which the Federal prisoner receives. Were his life taken, swift retribution would be visited upon the rebels by just retaliation ; one or more rebel prisoners would suffer death for every Federal prisoner whom they destroyed.

Let this rule hold good in case of Unionists who are citizens of the states in rebellion. The loyal Mississippian deserves the same protection accorded the loyal Rhode Islander or Pennsylvanian. We ask also that our confiscated property be restored to us, or, in the event of our death, to our families. If it be destroyed, we ask that reparation be demanded from the rebel authorities, or that the property of known and avowed secessionists be sequestered to that use. Before this letter reaches its destination the majority of us will have ceased to be. The judge advocate, Col. H. W. Walter, of the rebel army, has informed the writer that he must die on the 15th inst. We have therefore little hope that we individually can receive any personal benefit from this petition, even though you should regard it favorably and consent to its suggestions, but our families who have been robbed, so cruelly robbed, of all their substance, may, in the future, receive remuneration for their great losses, and should citizens of avowed secession proclivities who are within the Federal lines be arrested and held as hostages for the safety of Unionists who are and may be hereafter incarcerated in Tupelo and elsewhere, the rebels will not dare put another Unionist to death.

Trusting that you will deem it proper to take the prayers presented in our petition under advisement, and afford us the protection desired, we remain with high considerations of respect and esteem your oppressed and imprisoned fellow-citizens,

JOHN H. AUGHEY,

BENJAMIN CLARKE.

B. D. NABORS,

JOHN ROBINSON,

And thirty-eight others.

Two young men, Donald Street and Samuel Maynard, informed me to-day that they had been impressed into the rebel service. They had been taken prisoner at Corinth by General Pope, and had taken the oath of allegiance to the Federal Government, to which their hearts had always been loyal. Recently they had been arrested by Parson Ellis and six other guerrillas, near Rienzi, and being brought by them into the rebel camp, they refused to rejoin their regiments, and in consequence were immured in this dungeon. From the threats of the officers they expected to be shot at any moment. They had used every means to banish the thoughts of death—had forced themselves to engage in pleasantry and mirth to drive away the sadness and gloom which oppressed them when alone, and when they recalled the delights of their happy homes which they would never see again. I counseled them to prepare to meet their God in peace, wisely to improve the short time granted them to make their peace, calling, and election sure. They replied that they hoped all would be well. They had long since confessed Christ before men, and hoped for salvation through his merit alone. Still, they could not help feeling sad, young as they were, in the near prospect of death. They were both in their 20th year.

While I was gone for water, these men were taken to their doom and I never saw them more.

One morning, as I lay restless and sore, endeavoring to find some position which would be sufficiently easy to permit me to secure, even for a few moments, the benefit of tired nature's sweet restorer — balmy sleep, the thought occurred that it would be well to attempt an escape, though it should result in death from the fire of the guards ; this would be by far preferable to death by strangulation at the rope's end, and in the presence of a large concourse of hooting, jeering, yelling, infuriated rebels. I had just finished the preparation of the following address, to be delivered from the scaffold if not forbidden. I gave a copy to M. T. Anderson, who desired it for publication upon his exchange:

ADDRESS TO BE READ FROM THE GALLOWS.

My Unionist Friends:

Hear the words of a man about to die. Last words are of solemn import. Keep them in remembrance. Follow the counsels given, if they commend themselves to your judgment. The Confederate officers have brought you here to witness my fate,

that you may thus learn the penalty they deem
proper to be inflicted for inflexible adherence to patriotic principles.   They declare that I am guilty of
treason.   Who are the traitors ?   I affirm that those
who would subvert the integrity of the government
founded by our patriotic ancestors, are the real
traitors.   Our politicians, I will not call them statesmen, would first overthrow the best of governments,
and then construct from its ruins a government
whose corner-stone shall be human slavery.   Will
it stand?   Forbid it, Almighty God ! forbid it, heaven.
The millennium dawn is too near for God to permit
to prosper a government organized to maintain a
barbaric relic of the dark ages, and to preserve in-
tact an institution subversive of all the rights of man.
Human slavery is made a fundamental feature of the
Confederate States of America—the corner-stone, as
Alexander Stephens terms it.   Should we who have no
slaves risk life and limb in the interests of slave-
holders, and at their bidding war against a government that has never trespassed upon our rights ? I,
for one, prefer death, and gladly welcome its embrace
rather than to violate the monitions of conscience, the
voice of reason, the decision of judgment, and the
teachings of pious and patriotic ancestors.   You believe in state rights, so do I.   State sovereignty and
national supremacy.   They are not incompatible.
State and nation each sovereign in its own sphere.
One needs not and has not trenched upon the prerogatives of the other.   *E pluribus unum*, one com-

posed of many. Distinct as the billows, yet one as
the sea. Forced into the army as conscripts, you are
not warring against the government by choice. Accept deliverance when it comes. See to it that the
republic receives no detriment at your hands. The
time is not far distant when the last assassin's dagger
shall be stricken from his rebellious hand. How earnestly I have prayed to be permitted to see the downfall
of treason, but God in his wisdom declines to grant
my petition. The government will live and flourish
long after all its foes are dead, buried, and forgotten,
for the memory of the wicked shall rot. It will dispense blessings to your posterity and mine, till the
angel of Jehovah, standing with one foot on the sea
and the other on the solid land, shall, with trumpet
voice, proclaim that time shall be no more. It is the
last, the best, and most benign government ever bestowed upon man by Him who establishes the nations and fixes their boundaries and ordains their
duration. Our government would be unworthy of
respect were it impotent to enforce obedience to its
wise, humane, and beneficent laws, and to perpetuate
its existence, if necessary, by the complete overthrow
of all opposing forces. The government under
which we have as a nation so greatly prospered is
the ordinance of God. The wheels of the chariot
which bears it onward will ever revolve. He who
stands in the way of its progress will be crushed as
sure as fate.

Although in durance vile, and in rebellious ranks

perforce, your conscience, your judgment, the teachings of true wisdom, the word of God that enjoins
obedience to lawful authority, the patriotic utterances
of Washington and his compatriots, should be the
chart to direct you in the path of duty in every emergency.   Firmly resolve that the republic, through
you, shall receive no detriment.   The government
has done you no harm.   Reciprocate with grateful
hearts the benefits received from its benignant laws
and beneficent institutions.   When treason dies an
ignominious death, be present to bury its gory corpse
beyond the possibility of a resurrection.   I see before me many who were with us on the high hills
and in the deep glens devising plans to resist the detested conscription.   Many of your comrades are in
the ranks of the patriotic army aiding in crushing
the hydra serpent head of treason and rebellion. See
to it that they suffer no harm at your hands.   May
their lives be precious in your sight.

"Oh, Liberty, how many crimes are committed in
thy name," exclaimed one well known to fame, but
we are murdered by the craven hordes of treason to
promote the fancied interests of chattel slavery, of
human bondage.

I die, but the sacred cause I humbly represent will
not perish with me on this scaffold.   The roots of the
tree of liberty, moistened by the blood of the noble
phalanx of hero-martyrs who have perished here in
Tupelo and on other fields, made classic and sacred
by the outpouring of the precious blood of true

Southern patriots, will strike deep and spread wide, and will send up through every pore the vital fluid which shall keep forever fresh and green the leaves of that sacred tree planted by our fathers in the primeval forest, under whose wide-spreading branches they and their children, and, we trust, their remotest posterity, will find safety and freedom and perennial happiness.

These, our murderers, would dig up the tree of liberty and plant in its stead the deadly upas tree of human bondage. Its roots would reach down and take hold upon perdition. The inalienable rights of man would perish beneath its blighting shade.

Shall we tamely and basely surrender our God-given heritage of freedom to save our lives imperiled by treason's minions? Shall we basely betray a cause dearer to us than life, for the sake of eking out a miserable, cowardly existence, purchased at the cost of our manhood and of every virtuous and holy principle? Shall we sell our birthright for a mess of pottage, and thus ignobly receive, as a boon graciously accorded by these fiends incarnate who are thirsting for our blood, a few years' longer lease of life, till nature calls us to pay the inevitable debt, and we slink into dishonorable graves?

No. A thousand times, no. My free soul, not trammeled by the fetters that bind and torture my body, gladly, joyfully embraces death, exultingly leaping into its outstretched arms in preference to the acceptance of life on terms so vile, so ignominious,

15

that were I to do so, high heaven with ire would
spurn my wretched soul, when seeking admission into
Paradise, from all association with the spirits of the
pure and good, and consign it to the doom of those
who rebelled in heaven and on earth against the God
who ordained the powers that be, to whom, when
ruling by divine appointment, all are commanded to
be subject.

The glorious cause, in the interests of which I lay
down my life, will ultimately triumph. Truth
crushed to earth will rise again. Entertain no doubts
on this subject. Rebellion will be utterly subverted
as sure as the God of justice reigns, who will ever
prosper the cause approved in heaven.

> For right is right, since God is God,
> And right the day must win;
> To doubt would be disloyalty,
> To falter would be sin.

May God subvert rebellion by the speedy overthrow of all its enemies and the restoration of civil
and constitutional liberty to the people of these dis-
tracted, discordant, belligerent, and rebellious Southern states. Liberty calls upon each one of you to do
your duty, that her blessings may be dispensed to
and enjoyed by all.

> . They love her best who to themselves are true,
> And what they dare to dream of dare to do.

Remember my advice heretofore given on many a
high hill and secluded, lonely glen, at the solemn
midnight hour. I am now ready to be offered up,

and the time of my departure has come. I only exchange earth for heaven—a life of warfare for a vic-
tor's crown. Dying is but going home. Farewell,
my friends, till we meet beyond the river where pain
and sorrow, sin and death are felt and feared no more.
My own and my country's enemies cannot reach me
there to harm me. Those holy gates forever bar pol-
lution, sin, and shame. None can obtain admittance
there but followers of the Lamb. My prayer is that
of the good Dr. Valpy:

> In peace let me resign my breath
> And Thy salvation see;
> My sins deserve eternal death,
> But Jesus died for me.

I have complied with the conditions upon which
salvation is promised. I have exercised faith in the
Lord Jesus Christ. I have exercised loving trust
and trusting love, and have the assurance that Jesus
is my loving, precious Savior, in whose delightful
presence I am about to appear. So I have nothing
to fear.

> Once to every man and nation
> Comes a moment to decide,
> In the strife of truth and falsehood
> For the good or evil side;
> Truth is now upon the scaffold,
> Wrong is now upon the throne,
> Yet this scaffold sweeps the future,
> And behind the dim unknown
> Standeth God within the shadow,
> Keeping watch above his own.

Weep not for me but for yourselves and your children. God in his righteous retribution will visit in vengeance for the great sins of this rebellious people. Our blood will be required at their hands. Those of you who can do so, escape for your lives, for this wicked people shall be crushed in the wine-press of Jehovah's wrath, and will be compelled to drink to the dregs the cup of divine vengeance.

> Though the mills of the gods grind slowly they grind exceed-
>   ing small;
> Though with patience He stands waiting, with exactness He
>   grinds all.

I must close. Your friend and fellow-citizen of the state of Mississippi, and the United States of America,   JOHN H. AUGHEY.

The prisoners who were shot suffered death in the following manner: A hole was dug, I can scarcely dignify it by the name of grave. The victim was ordered to sit with his legs dangling in it. The file of soldiers took position in front of their victims, when three balls were fired into the brain and three into the heart, and the body falling into this rude excavation was immediately covered with earth. At first coffins were used, but of late these had been dispensed with, owing to the expense, and the increasing number of executions. In some cases the soldiers purposely missed their aim. It was an odious duty which they endeavored to shun, and only performed it upon compulsion. If the corpse was to be delivered to friends they invariably tried to aim so

THE SOLDIER'S REPRIEVE.

AS I WAS RAPIDLY TRAVELING ALONG A NARROW PATH
I SUDDENLY MET A NEGRO.

Page 240

as to wound without taking life, and many of the condemned have, by feigning death, escaped in this way. Gen. Bragg's name was a synonym for cruelty. He shot many of his o--n soldiers for trivial offenses, and upon the poor Unionists he had no mercy. One of his officers said to me, "So many men are put to death by Bragg, and executions have become so common that now when they occur they scarcely excite remark." He was a martinet who never failed to punish the most trivial offenses with great severity.

I had not long meditated upon this subject when I arose, resolved upon immediate death or liberty. Of two evils I chose the less. My intentions were communicated to several prisoners, who promised me all the aid in their power. My fetters were examined, and it was the opinion of Amos Deane and Amzi Meek that with proper instruments my bonds could be divested of the iron rods which secured the chain rings. A long-handled iron spoon, my knife, which had a file blade, and a file which one of the prisoners had procured from a Unionist visitor, were secured, and two were detached at a time to work upon my manacles. We went to a corner of the prison, and a sufficient number of prisoners stood in front of us to prevent the guards from observing the proceedings. We changed our location frequently to avoid suspicion, and when officers entered, labor was suspended till their exit. Several prisoners were shot to-day, and six Unionists were incarcerated. A reign of terror had been inaugurated only equaled in its appalling enormity by the memorable French revolution.

Spies and informers in the pay of the rebel government prowl through the country, using every artifice and stratagem to lead Unionists to criminate themselves. After this they are dragged to prison and to death. The cavalry dash through the country making daily raids, burning cotton, carrying off or wantonly destroying the property of loyal citizens, and committing depredations of every kind.

Several prisoners resolved to attempt to escape with me. Our plan was to bring in from the enclosure in the rear of the prison the ax with which we cut and split wood for cooking, and if possible to raise a plank in the floor by cutting away the wood and drawing the spikes, a sufficient number to stand around those who did the work to prevent observation, and to make a hilarious noise so as to drown the sound that would be made. Then in the night we would get under the prison and make our way out on the north side through the guards who were off duty. At this time there were three guards in front of each door, and two on the south side of the building. On the north side of the prison there were no guards on duty, it not being thought necessary if the other sides were vigilantly guarded. There were, however, several hundred guards who, when off duty, slept on this side of the prison.

When relieved they came there to sleep, and those whose turn it was went on duty. They were constantly coming and going, and during the whole night they kept up an incessant noise. My friends labored unremittingly during the day to remove the irons that secured the chain ring. Those who stood around us to prevent the observation of the guards standing in front of the doors told stale jokes and laughed at them immoderately, so as to drown the noise of the filing. The sun was now setting, but the ax had not yet been brought into the prison. Jimmie Tevis had hidden it under his blouse and tried to pass the guards with it, but they detected him by the protruding helve, and made him return it. Now the extra guards had gone on duty. There were three in front of each door. The doors had been removed. The apertures we called doors. A guard was seated on each threshold, and one inside the building promenaded the floor backward and forward throughout its entire length all night. During the day no guards were on the thresholds, nor in the building.

While deliberating upon the best plan to pursue, since we had failed in securing the ax, Gen. Jordan and Col. Clare entered. I was standing in the middle of the floor, midway between the doors, eating some rice which had been surreptitiously conveyed to me. A note accompanied the mess, deftly enclosed. It read: "From your sincere and sympathetic friend, Mrs. Lydia Runyan." Gen. Jordan came directly to the place where I stood, and holding a lantern in front of my face, said, "You are here yet, are you?" I gave an affirmative nod. "Well," said he, to Col.

Clare, "I must examine this fellow's irons to see what is their condition." Suiting the action to the word, he put his hands down, and ascertaining that they had been tampered with, he endeavored ineffectually to pull off the bands. He did not notice that I could slip the chain rings off. "These irons," said he, "are very insecure. Who helped you to put them in this condition?" I made no reply. After waiting till he was assured that I intended none, he turned to Col. Clare and said: "Colonel, have these irons welded, put handcuffs upon him, and chain him to that bolt in the floor. The gallows shall not be cheated of their due."

Col. Clare said, "Must I do it to-night?"

"Yes, to-night. Do it at once."

"But," replied the colonel, "it is nearly nine o'clock, and I can't find a blacksmith to weld the irons on his ankles. The forges are out of blast at this hour."

"Well, wait till morning, but do it bright and early."

"All right," replied Col. Clare, "I'll have it done by sunrise or before."

After these officers had taken their departure, the prisoners crowded around me and affirmed that they believed that there was a spy in the house in the guise of a prisoner. With entire unanimity they held the opinion that Aleck Stephens was the man. He was a red-haired, low-browed, grim-visaged, freckle-faced, hard-featured, villainous specimen of

the *genus homo*, who sat reticent in a corner, peering
from under his bushy eyebrows, and rejecting all fa-
miliarity or kind offices tendered by his fellow-prisoners. All realized that I must escape that night or
it would be too late. When chained to a bolt in the
floor, with securely welded anklets and wearing handcuffs, I would be in an utterly helpless condition.
There were eleven guards on duty: three in front of
each door, one seated upon each threshold, and one
promenading the house, which was lighted during the
whole night. There was also a special police force
on duty, as some Federal prisoners who were in prison
till some formalities took place would be sent in the
morning to Columbus, Miss., and it was feared that
they might attempt to escape ere they were sent farther south. I was seated with some Federal prisoners, sending messages to my friends. I told them
that I would slip off my chain, run by the guards,
and that it was more than probable that I would
draw their fire and be shot; that perhaps my mangled corpse would be brought into the prison in a
few minutes. I asked them to be sure to inform my
friends of the manner of my death. With this request they promised faithfully to comply. I said,
"Farewell, perhaps forever," and arose to make the
hazardous attempt.

At this moment a young man whom we nicknamed
"Mississippi" ran up to me and said, "Parson, I
think I have found a way by which you may escape."
His true name, I think, was Leonard Humphrey.

Said I, " What is it?"

He replied, " I was out in the front enclosure, and I saw a hole by the step under the jail, and I think you could get under."

" Why," I replied, " that would be impossible. The three guards standing in front would see me; the guard seated in the doorway would see me; and in their presence it would be impossible to get under the building without discovery."

" I thought of that, and while you was preaching I was fixing up a plan, and by golly, I think we can get you off." We were permitted to go into the front enclosure, three at a time, at pleasure, during the day, and on moonlight nights till ten o'clock. He continued, " I must have help." He soon secured the requisite number, who, at the risk of immediate death, upon discovery, agreed to run the risk for my sake. May the Lord reward them.

He then detailed his plan. When the guard promenading the house approached we talked about the price of cotton or some indifferent topic. When he went from us we resumed the business in hand. We all promised implicit obedience. Just at 9:45 four of us went out. I went out clanking my chains, to lull suspicion, and they did not order me back, as they had done so often before. The rule required that but three be permitted to be in the enclosure at one time, but they providentially did not enforce the rule this time. My three fellow-prisoners stood between me and the guards, and entered into a fierce discussion with them in regard to the comparative merit of Mississippi and Tennessee troops. The enclosures, in front and rear, were formed by stakes surmounted by poles. Their form was a parallelogram, whose dimensions were about ten by sixteen feet. The guards became much excited, and the discussion was becoming loud and acrimonious. Howell Trogden, a prisoner, sat inside and held the guard in conversation, who was seated on the threshold. I sat by the aperture under the building, removed my chain, put my legs under the building, and leaned my head upon my elbow, my elbow upon the step, upon which rested the guard's feet, who was seated upon the threshold of the prison door. My fellow-prisoners, in a wordy war with the guards, were diverting their attention, with every appearance of success. I reflected that a few moments would decide my fate. If detected in this forlorn hope, this last attempt with any prospect of success, I must end my life ignominiously upon the scaffold. In the early morning my anklets would be securely welded; I would be handcuffed and chained to a bolt in the floor of our gloomy dungeon. Then all hope must end, and soon my corpse would be borne into the presence of her whose tears were flowing, and who refused to be comforted, because of my ominous absence.

'Tis ten o'clock; I hear the order for the relief guard. They come; I see their bayonets glittering in the bright moonlight. The set time, the appointed

moment, pregnant with my fate, had arrived. I
offered an ejaculatory prayer to Him who sits upon
the throne of heaven for protection at this critical
moment. The guards stood within ten feet of me.
Now they look steadily at me. I return their gaze.
The relief guard has confronted them. They turn
to receive it. At that moment I moved backward
under the building and disappeared from view. The
new guard enter upon their duty. The old guard,
without a backward glance, march away. The
prisoners are ordered into the dungeon. The guards
see but three, and know that that is the highest number permitted by regulation order within the enclosure. They did not suspect that four had been suffered to be out, in violation of orders. I was under
the prison, but there were vigilant guards on every
side. We were in the midst of the great rebel army.
The din of a multitude sounded in my ears. It seemed
almost impossible even now to escape detection. Bur-
dette Danner had thrown me his canteen, but it struck
against the prison wall. It glittered in the bright
moonlight; I was famishing from thirst, but I feared
to seize it, though I knew that it was full of that
precious liquid whose price was now estimated far
above rubies. I did not wish to take any unneces-
sary risk. The hand protruding from under the
prison would probably be observed by the guards
and excite their suspicion. I could hear their lowest
tones. After awhile one of them said, "Gilmore, I
always do forget the countersign." The other replied,

"It is 'Braxton' for to-night." Though uttered in an undertone, I caught it. "Well," replied his comrade, I thought it was 'Braxton,' or 'Bragg,' or something like that. I won't forgit it agin."

I crawled to the north side of the prison, and found that there were three apertures which would admit my egress. Upon reaching the first, I found that the guards were so numerous and so close, that it would be extremely hazardous to run the risk at this point. Crawling to the second, I remained till there was comparative quiet. But at the instant I was about to creep out, a soldier, who was lying with his face toward me, sat up and commenced coughing, and continued to cough at intervals for more than an hour. Finding it unadvisable to run the risk of detection at this point, I made my way with considerable difficulty to the third and last aperture, near the rear of the prison, and not far distant from the guards in the rear enclosure. Here exhausted nature could hold out no longer, and I slept. How long I know not. The vermin and the cold awoke me. Presently I heard one soldier say to another. "It is 3 o'clock in the morning and we will have to go on duty." I felt confident that then was my time or never. Morning would soon appear, and my escape would be discovered and my re-arrest follow. Commending myself into the hands of God, and pleading that he would mercifully keep me from detection, and grant me safe conduct through this mighty host of watchful foes, I arose from under the building, and in passing two sleeping soldiers lying within four feet of the prison wall, I struck my foot against the head of one of them. I had not walked for so long a time without a chain, which necessarily compelled me to make such short steps, that I reeled as if under the influence of intoxicants, when freed from it. This made me swerve from my intended course and strike with my foot the head of the somnolent guard. He awoke, and looking at me in the bright moonlight, said, "D——n you, don't do that again." He turned over and resumed his slumbers. He doubtless mistook me for one of his comrades, who, in his awkwardness, had made the unintentional assault.

In prison I had purchased a shirt, paying eleven dollars in gold for it, which resembled that worn by many rebel soldiers. This doubtless contributed to my escape, by warding off suspicion, which would have been aroused at once, if I had appeared in their midst in citizen's dress. I was also wearing McHatton's dark-colored pants. After proceeding a few steps I sat down by a stump, around which a number of guards were collected, some standing, some sitting, and some reclining. To appear at ease I took my knife from my pocket and commenced to whittle the stump and to whistle. This apparent unconcern may have deceived them, and contributed to ward off or allay suspicion. It was an almost unparalleled wonder that some of them did not observe me emerge from underneath the prison, as the moon was shining brightly and they were very near the prison wall in great numbers. Doubtless God had held their eyes or obscured their vision. I soon arose, returned my knife to my pocket, and wound my way cautiously among the various groups, endeavoring to reach the corn field to which I had made my first escape. I endeavored to see every vidette before he perceived me. I had some narrow risks in passing them. As I came near the corn field, a vidette, who had been concealed behind a tree, appeared, evidently with the intention of halting me if I approached nearer. I halted without the order. If he had given the command to halt, I should have given the countersign, Braxton, which I had learned while under the prison, and then have made some excuse for wandering away from my comrades. To avoid suspicion I resorted to a ruse which I cannot narrate. It proved successful. I, after a time, started toward the prison, till, seeing videttes in front, I fell upon the ground and deflected from my course toward the prison. After passing through many perils and hair-breadth escapes, as the least blunder would have proved fatal, I reached the dense woods and bore south-west. Kneeling down under a larch tree, I returned God thanks for thus far crowning my efforts with success, and most earnestly besought Him to continue His kind protecting care, to choose my path before me, and make it safe, that I might escape detection and be permitted to rejoin my family and friends in safety. I had asked Him in prison to lengthen my life by fifteen years, as he did Hezekiah's.

I now pursued my journey rapidly in a south-westerly direction, choosing that which led directly from my home for two reasons. The cavalry, with the blood-hounds, would not probably be sent in that direction. After listening attentively while in prison to the reveille and tattoo, and the din from the surrounding camps, I thought the coast was clearest in that direction, and that I could, by taking that route, with the greater ease evade the rebel pickets. I hastened onward with all possible speed, avoiding roads, till the sun arose. As I was rapidly traveling along a narrow path, I suddenly met a negro. He was scared. So was I. I, in a peremptory tone, addressed him in quick succession, the following questions:

"Where are you going? Where have you been? To whom do you belong? Have you a pass?"

"I belong," said the boy, trembling, "to Col. Kohlheim, I have been to wife's house, and am gwine back to Massa's."

He handed me his pass which read: "The bearer, Tabor, has permission to go to Major Smith's to visit his wife and return. Good till to-morrow evening, the —— inst."

"Well, sir," said he, as I handed him his pass, "you see it am all right wid me."

Concluding that it was not *all right* "wid" myself I hurried on. Tabor called to me ere I had gone twenty yards. I halted. He came up and asked me if "dis bill (presenting one on a Tennessee bank) was

good." "Good as the bank," said I, and hurried
onward, speedily leaving the path and turning into
a dense woods. Traveling on till about 12 P.M.,
judging from the vertical rays of the sun, I came to
an open champaign country, through which I could
not travel with safety, in daylight. I sought a place
in which to hide, and discovering a ditch which bisected a corn-field, I concealed myself in that. Many
passed near me during the day. I was very hungry. Sullivan and Soper, Federal prisoners had
each given me, before leaving prison, a small piece of
bread, which they had in their haversacks when captured. I found both pieces were saturated with tobacco. The prisoner with whom I had exchanged
pants used tobacco, and had carried some in both
pockets. As tobacco is very offensive to me, its
presence upon my bread caused me to lose it. I reflected on the best course to pursue in order to secure
the greatest degree of safety in my flight. I thought at
one time that it would be best to go west until I
reached the Mississippi river, then hail a gun-boat
and thus be saved, but I reflected that I was a *long,
long* distance from that river—that there was the great
Mississippi bottom to pass through, which was full
of lagoons, lakes, bayous, and swamps, and that it
was infested with bears, rattlesnakes, vipers, bull-
snakes, centipedes, tarantulas, and venomous reptiles,
and wild beasts of many kinds. I would also have
to swim across the Yazoo and Tallahatchie rivers,
which I feared I could not do, enfeebled as I would

16

be when I reached those rivers, and encumbered as I was with the heavy iron bands. The day ended and the night came. The stars, those beautiful nocturnal luminaries, came out in silent glory, one by one. Fixing my eye upon the polar star, the underground railroad traveler's guide, I set out bearing a little to the west of north. I soon reached the thick woods and found it very difficult to make rapid progress, in consequence of the dense undergrowth and obscure light. The bushes would strike me in the eyes, and often the top of a fallen tree would compel me to make quite a circuit. Soon, however, the moon appeared in her brightness—the old silver moon. But her light I found to be by far less brilliant than that of the sun, and her rays were much obscured by the dense foliage overhead, hence my progress was necessarily slow, labored, and toilsome. During the day I had slept but little, in consequence of the proximity of those who might be bitter foes, and also because of the unpleasant position I occupied, as the ditch in which I had concealed myself was muddy and proved a very uncomfortable bed. I therefore became weary, my limbs stiff from travel and from the pressure of the heavy iron bands. Sleep overpowered me, and I lay down in the leaves and slept till the cold awoke me. I slept an hour and a half, as I judged from the moon's descent. The nights are invariably cool in Mississippi, however sultry may have been the weather during the day. Arising from my uneasy slumber I pressed on. My thirst, which had for some time been increasing, now became absolutely unendurable. I knew not where to get water, not daring to go near a well for fear of arrest. I must obtain water or perish. At length I heard some sucking pigs and their dam at a short distance from me in the woods. There seemed to be no alternative. I must either perish or obtain some fluid to slake my raging thirst, so I resolved to catch one of the little pigs, cut its throat, and drink the blood. I searched for my knife, but ascertained that I had lost it. I was therefore reluctantly compelled to abandon my designs upon the suckling's life. As I went forward, the sow and her brood started up alarmed, and in their fright plunged into water. I followed fast and found a mud-hole—a perfect loblolly. The water was tepid, foul, and mingled with the spawn of frogs. Removing the green scum, I drank deep of the stagnant pool. My thirst was only partially allayed by this foul draught, and soon returned. As day dawned, I found some sassafras leaves, which I chewed to allay the pangs of hunger, but they formed a paste which I could not swallow. I remembered that this day was the holy Sabbath, but it brought neither rest to my weary frame, nor composure to my agitated and excited mind.

The course decided upon as safest and best was to go far to the south and west, and there wait till the cavalry had returned from their search for me, then by a very circuitous route to endeavor to reach the Memphis and Charlestown railroad, find some Fed-

eral outpost on that road, and thus be saved. About
ten o'clock I came to an open country, and sought a
place to conceal myself. I found a dense copse on a
hillside, and hid within its friendly depths. I had
about departed to the realm of dreams when I heard
the voice of song. A human voice quickly aroused
me. I peered out from my lair, and on an opposite
hill I saw a gigantic Ethiopian making his way la-
boriously. He had a plank in his hands, there was
one underneath him upon which he was walking.
When he reached the end of it, he laid down the
plank he bore in his hands, stepped upon it, and
reaching back he lifted the other plank, and thus he
wended his way. He accompanied his task by singing a song heard often upon every southern plantation :

> My ole missus promise me,
> Dat when she die, she'd set me free,
> But she dun dead this many year ago,
> An' yer I'm a hoin de same ole row.
> Run, nigger, run, de patter-roller ketch you,
> Run, nigger, run, hit's almos' day.
>
> I'm a hoin across, I'm a hoin aroun',
> I'm a cleanin up some mo' new groun',
> Whar I lif so hard, I lif so free,
> Dat my sins rises up in fronter me.
> Oh, run, nigger, run, de patter-roller ketch you,
> Run, nigger, run, hit's almos' day.
>
> But some ob dese days my time will come,
> I'll year dat bugle, I'll year dat drum,
> I'll see dem armies a marchin' along,
> I'll lif my head an' jine der song.

I SAW THEM GAZING DOWN UPON ME WITH EVIDENT   Page 248
AMAZEMENT AND ALARM.

IN THE EAST THE TENTS OF A GREAT ENCAMPMENT WERE SPREAD OUT
IN FULL VIEW.   Page 256

I'll hide no more behind dat tree,
When the angels fl)ck t. r wait on me.
Oh, run, nig er, run, de patter-roller ketch you.
Run, nigger, run, hit's almos' day.

As he laid down his plank and stepped upon it,
it slid from under his feet and he fell prone upon
the ground. He jumped up and sang:

"If Charley slip upon his track
Der's danger de hounds will bring him back,
Oh, run nigger, run, de patter-roller ketch you,
Run, nigger, run, hit's almos' day."

Thus he improvised his song as he wended his
weary way. He was trying to evade the hounds by
thus leaving no scent for them to follow. As he
passed me he sang:

"De pore white trash dey lives an' grows,
Dey noze far less dan the nigger noze."

Then he sang the chorus with a will:

"My name's Sam, I don't care a d—n,
I'd radder be a nigger, dan a pore white man."

He look around in alarm, and muttered, "Old
Charley alwa's dun furgit hizsef when he sings dat
song." He then passed onward in silence, carrying
his planks with him.

A singular noise attracting attention, as I gazed
up the hill I saw a man descend from a tree and look
around warily. As he passed near me, I called out,
in a low tone, *Taisez vous.*

Quickly glancing in my direction, he replied,
"*Oui, oui.*"

I bade him come to me. He did so. He had been in hiding for a month, and becoming hungry he left his lofty perch to procure the food that would be left at the designated spot by his wife or eldest daughter. He told me to await his return and he would share his food with me, and he assured me of all possible aid. As he emerged from the jungle, a man with fierce aspect confronted him. He told him to throw up his hands. I had accompanied him and was about to retreat with all possible speed, but the thought of abandoning my friend restrained me. I determined to stand by him and abide the result. My friend refused to throw up his hands. He said he preferred to die there and then in preference to submitting to be bound. This man, who I learned was known as Col. Ned Barry, ordered us to march in front of him, or if we hesitated he would let us have the contents of his revolvers. We obeyed, hoping to escape by darting into the woods at some suitable point, or by some providential deliverance.

As we neared a large tree, Col. Barry said : " Israel Nelson, I've been prowlin' around arter you for more'n three weeks. Now, sir, you got ter go two miles from here, an' Gen. Yerger will be d—d glad ter see yer." He turned around to make this little speech. As he closed, and was about to advance, a dusky form suddenly sprang from behind the tree, a bludgeon descended swiftly upon the Colonel's skull, and our would-be captor lay unconscious at our feet. We found cords in his pockets and securely

bound our fallen foe. Soon he returned to consciousness, and begged piteously for his life. We took
possession of his weapons. A little boy of ten years
of age appeared on the scene. He came to find his
father. He told him that ma. wanted him to come
to the house at once, there was strangers there to see
him. What should we do to secure our own safety.
Nelson proposed shooting both father and son. We
took them both to the copse, and with the aid of this
Ethiopian, who had appeared at an opportune moment, gagged both father and son, and bound them
to the same tree. I urged Nelson to escape with me,
and to leave these persons bound. He replied that
he must see his wife, and that he would go to the
trysting place, and she would probably be there, or
in case she was not there, he would find a note
secreted near by. The note was there, but contained
no special information. Nothing but words of comfort and affectionate sympathy.

We heard hounds, and feared to return to our
prisoners for a long time. The African, Charley,
had left us, and as night had dropped down upon
the scene we cautiously returned to the copse.

I hope never again to witness such a ghastly sight.
The mangled remains of father and son were still ad-
hering to the tree. Fierce hounds had torn them to
pieces. I could no longer stay to gaze upon this sad
tragedy. Nelson told me that he had resolved to shoot
them both, as his safety and mine would be compro-
mised by sparing their lives. I am glad that the

terrible necessity was obviated. Nelson refused to
abandon his family, and I could no longer delay, so
hastened onward.

The dismal night passed away. I found a place
to hide—a ditch as usual. I slept, and saw in my
dreams tables groaning under the weight of the most
delicious viands, and brooks of crystal waters bab-
bling and sparkling as they rushed onward in their
meandering course, but when I attempted to grasp
them they served me as Tantalus of olden time was
served, by vanishing into thin air or receding from
my grasp. While lying here, I was occasionally
aroused by the trampling of horses grazing in the
fields, which I feared might be bringing on my pursuers. Once the voices of men mingled with the sound
of prancing steeds upon a little bridge some twenty
feet distant, induced me to look out from my hiding
place, and lo! two cavalry men, perhaps hunting for
my life, passed along.

When the sun had reached the zenith, I was again
startled by voices, which approached nearer and still
nearer my place of concealment, till at length the
cause was discovered. Several children, both black
and white, had come from a farm house about a
quarter of a mile distant to gather blackberries along
the margin of the ditch. They soon discovered me
and seemed somewhat startled and alarmed at my
appearance. I soon saw them gazing down upon me
in my moist bed, with evident amazement and alarm.
Pallid, haggard, unshaven, and covered with mud, I

must have presented a frightful picture. As soon as the children passed me, fearing the report they would carry home, I arose from my lair and hastened onward. After traveling three or four miles I came to a dense woods bordering a stream, which had ceased running in consequence of the unprecedented drought that had for a long time prevailed throughout this section of Mississippi. The creek had been a large one, and in the deep cavities some water still remained. Though warm and covered with a thick green scum, and mingled with the spawn of frogs, I drank it from sheer necessity, tepid and unwholesome as it was. It did not allay my thirst, but created a nausea which was very unpleasant. After traveling several hours, I came to a place where was a depression in the ground. I thought I might possibly find water. Soon the sight of water gladdened me, but it was stagnant and covered with a thick, greenish, yellowish scum. As I approached it I was startled by seeing the tracks of some one who I thought might have been a fugitive like myself. By closely observing the footsteps and the surroundings, I discerned this to be the place I had left hours ago. I was traveling in a circle. My bewildered brain had lost its power to locate accurately the cardinal points.

About 4 o'clock P.M. I was startled by the baying of blood-hounds behind me, and apparently upon my track. Before escaping from jail I had been advised by my fellow-prisoners to procure some onions, as these rubbed upon the soles of my boots would measurably destroy the scent. These could only be procured by visiting a garden, and I feared to approach so near a house. I had not left any clothing in prison from which the hounds could obtain the scent so as to recognize my track, and my starting in a south-western direction was an additional precaution against blood-hounds. Having heard them almost every night for years, as they hunted down the fugitive slave, I could not mistake the fearful import of their howling. I could devise no plan for breaking the trail. Daniel Boone, when pursued by Indians, succeeded in baffling the dogs with which they pursued him by laying hold of overhanging branches and swinging himself forward. One slave on Dick's river in Kentucky, near Danville, Boyle Co., ran along the brink of a precipice, and dug a recess back from the narrow path. Crawling into it, he remained concealed till the hounds reached that point, when he thrust them from the path. They fell and were dashed to pieces upon the jagged rocks below. Some slaves, before escaping, provide themselves with a large supply of cayenne pepper. When the hounds are heard in pursuit they set down their heels with considerable force so as to make as deep an impression as possible; they then sprinkle their tracks with the cayenne pepper. The hounds, in rapid pursuit, inhale the pepper. It produces such pain and irritation that they will not pursue any fugitive for months, and even then with caution so great that they are nearly worthless as negro dogs.

None of these plans were practicable, and I believed death imminent, either from being torn to pieces by the hounds or by being shot by the cavalry who were following hard after them. Climbing a tree, I resolved to die rather than be taken back to Tupelo to suffer death on the gallows in the presence of a hooting, howling, mixed multitude of infuriate demons. I knew that upon my refusal to come down from the tree a volley from their carbines would end my life. The tree into which I had climbed was a large black oak; a juniper tree stood on a knoll between the oak and the route by which my pursuers would approach. The oak would afford perfect concealment from observation till my pursuers stood underneath the tree, then, by peering into its umbrageous recesses on all sides, my presence would be discovered. Oh! how I wished for my navy repeater, that I might sell my life as dearly as possible—that ere I was slain I might make some secessionist bite the dust. I thought of the couplet in the old song:

> The hounds are baying on my track,
> Christian, will you send me back?

A feeling of deep sympathy arose in my heart for the poor slave who, in his endeavor to escape from the iron furnace of southern slavery, encountered the blood-hounds and was torn to pieces by them. A fellow feeling makes us wondrous kind. A touch of sympathy makes all the world akin. Now I hear the deep-mouthed baying of the hounds. The pack is large, and they realize that the object of their

search is near. I see them now on the crest of the
hill but a mile distant. Down the hill they plunge.
The cavalry follow hard after them. Men and dogs
seem intent upon their fell purpose. Soon they will
seize their prey, their hapless victim is almost within
their grasp. These fierce dragoons are mentally
gloating over the reward which they will receive for
their bloody work. Success will be achieved ere ten
minutes elapse. All hasten forward to be in at the
death. Must I die as the fool dieth? Like Jezebel,
my blood lapped by dogs, and my body devoured by
these fierce blood-hounds and those wild swine feeding near? My friends will never learn how I perished, and 'tis be ter they should not know the
horrible circumstances attending my death. Oh!
that I could see my dear wife and darling Kate, to
kiss them a final farewell ere the tragic scene closes
forever all my hopes of, and aspirations for, a long
and happy life in their society. Now the hounds
appear on the further brink of a ravine, a few hundred yards distant, a ravine I had crossed a short
time before. Their loud baying, their quick, sharp
yelps rang with frightful clearness on the summer
air. All hope of escape died within my bosom.
There seemed to be a pack of forty fierce hounds as
they leaped down the steep declivity. I waited in
terrible suspense their advent on the hither bank.
The cavalry, with rattling sabers and glittering carbines, appeared on the farther bank, and halting on
the brink found the declivity too steep to attempt

the descent on horseback. A number dismounted and speedily disappeared within the ravine. Two gray foxes, driven from their covert by the noise of pursuit, ran by the tree in which I was concealed, and plunged into a cacti copse. A half-dozen men appeared upon the crest nearest me. The hounds were yet howling in the glen. They were bearing eastward, up the ravine, and soon the dismounted dragoons recrossed, and remounting began to follow in that direction. On, on they went, with precipitate speed. The howling of the hounds and the yelling and horrid noise indicated that they were receding in the distance. Fainter and fainter the breezes bore to my ears the echoes of pursuit, till at length they were lost in the distance, and I was mercifully saved from a violent and horrid death. How had Divine Providence interposed in my behalf! It long remained a mystery. A negro fugitive, escaping from slavery, had crossed my path—had gone up the ravine. The hounds will always leave the track of a white man for that of a negro. On the next afternoon they caught the poor slave, who had concealed himself in a tree, and returned him to bondage. His master lived in Natchez, Adams Co., and this boy, Jingo Dick, had absconded three months before his capture.

I climbed down from the oak, and sat under the juniper tree. I sat under it a long time, returning thanks to God for my deliverance from a horrible death, yet depressed with the apparently hopeless prospect of ever evading my pursuers and reaching a place of ultimate safety.

Soon a mocking bird from a neighboring tree began to sing. He seemed to mock me in my agony. When he ceased, a bird perched in the highest branches of the same tree poured from its little throat a song of hope—the sweetest song I ever heard, and then another and another joined in glad refrain, till the whole grove grew vocal with their notes of joy. My soul, responsive to these glad strains, grew hopeful, and I, leaving more than half my weary burden of care, trudged on, homeward bound. After awhile I became bewildered, but soon peeping from a flowery dell I saw the yellow compass flower. Its polary property I knew. And true as the magnetic needle it pointed the way to the desired haven. Coming to a hazel dell I saw the patriotic pimpernel. Its flowers of red, white, and blue were closed, and I knew that a storm was impending. Soon the sky became overcast. Dark, threatening, murky clouds o'erspread the sky and shut out the sun. Oh! that the rain might fall in torr nts. I could then assuage my burning, raging thirst. On a distant hill I saw it falling, but only a few drops reached me, and my consuming thirst remained unquenched. I had the same sensations as Burton, one of the explorers of the Dark Continent. He says, "For twenty hours we did not taste water, the sun parched our brains and the mirage mocked us at every turn." As I jogged along, with eyes shut against the fiery air, every image that came to my mind was of water; water in the cool well, water bubbling from the rock, water rippling in shady streams, water in clear lakes, inviting me to plunge in and bathe. Now a cloud seemed to shower upon me drops more precious than pearls, then an unseen hand seemed to offer me a cup, which I would have given all I was worth to receive. But what a dreary, dreadful contrast. I opened my eyes to a heat-reeking plain and a sky of that deep blue so lovely to painter and poet, so full of death to us whose only desire was rain and tempest. I tried to pray but could not. I tried to think, but I had only one idea—water, water, water. A cup of cold water. Oh! how precious. No comparison is adequate to express its worth. But I will trust Him who is able to supply all my needs.

> " When first before his mercy seat
> I did to him my way commit,
> He gave me warrant from that hour
> To trust his mercy, love, and power."

"Though He slay me, yet will I trust in Him."

Becoming confused again in regard to the cardinal points, I fortunately came to a cemetery. In all Christian lands the headstones at the graves are to the west. I took my bearings and traveled on in a north-easterly direction. The Savior said, in Matt. xxiv. 27, "As the lightning cometh out of the east, and shineth even unto the west, so shall also the coming of the Son of Man be." The early Christians supposed that this verse taught that Christ, at the second advent, would appear in the east. Hence the burial of the dead so that in rising on the resurrection morn they would face the east. While steadily pursuing my weary way the faint howling of a distant pack of hounds coming from the direction in which I was traveling caused me to halt in consternation. I was ascending a lofty hill, and was nearing the summit, when these ominous sounds were heard. It was evident they were not in search of me, for they were coming south, but they might accomplish my destruction as certainly as if they had been commissioned to effect this object. I hastened to the summit of the hill. A lofty umbrageous oak, a venerable forest king, with lateral branches near the ground, stood on the highest eminence. As the increasingly distinct baying of the hounds indicated their rapid approach, I resolved to climb this tree. With less difficulty than I had anticipated I succeeded in doing so. Higher and higher I ascended, till I reached the lofty coronal of leaves that decked this mighty monarch of the woods. A grand panorama was spread out before me. Two miles distant, in the east, the tents of a great encampment were spread out in full view. The sentries were at their posts; the roads on all sides were picketed; a general review was in progress, and the bustle and excitement of camp life was evident in all its appointments. A company of cavalry with blood-hounds were just coming in from the north. They had twenty-five or thirty men in charge, in citizens' dress, evidently Unionists. They were driving these men before them on the double quick. Presently I saw one fall prone upon the earth. Three or four cavalry men dismounted, and pricking him with their bayonets, compelled him to rise. He staggered on a short distance and fell again. A second time they used their bayonets, when one of the prisoners left his companions, and running to the fallen man, thrust aside the bayonets. The guards on foot presented their carbines. A puff of smoke indicated that they had discharged them. This man, who seemed desirous of aiding his fellow-prisoner, fell upon the prostrate form of the fallen man, whom they now transfixed with their bayonets. After a few moments spent in inspecting their victims, they remounted their horses and rejoined their company. But what startled me most was the sight of a large company of hunters, composed of ladies and gentlemen, who, spread over a considerable space, in high glee and with loud and boisterous halloos were pursuing a bear. They were coming rapidly toward me from a point due north. That they would pass near me was evident. The bear was but a half mile in advance of the hounds, and they were gaining rapidly upon him. I perceived that the bear's strength was waning. He seemed to be running in a direct line toward the tree amid whose friendly foliage I was concealed. A planter, whose residence was upon a hill to the west, had heard the hounds, and I saw him hastily make preparations to join in the chase. Colored men brought out several saddled horses; a number of hounds were unleashed and unkenneled, and several men mounted the horses, and with guns in hand has-

17

tened away to join in the chase. I observed that from the direction they took . they would not be likely to intercept the bear. On, on, they rode, and ere long joined the hunters in pursuit. The bear, with failing strength, reached a point about three hundred yards from my tree, and turning his back against a tree, stood at bay. The dogs, as fast as they approached, were driven back, howling in agony. As the bear was on the opposite side of the tree, I could not see the battle. It became fierce, and the mingled growling of the bear and the howls and yells of pain upon the part of the discomfited dogs made for a time a perfect pandemonium. The bear seemed on the point of gaining a victory, but the hunters rode up, called off the not reluctant hounds, and a volley from their carbines laid bruin dead at their feet. I could hear their conversation distinctly. The planter invited the hunters to come over and spend the night with him. He promised to send some of his slaves to flay the bear and care for the meat. The visitors' dogs were taken care of by the planter. They were leashed in his yard; but his own hounds were allowed to roam at will all night. The negroes came down from the house, skinned and dressed the bear, and it seemed to be attractive labor to them. The hounds came under the tree and barked furiously. One of the colored men said he believed there "was coons up dat tree, or dem dogs wouldn't bark so fierce." One of them said he believed he'd "go and tell master dat dere was coons in dat tree." Off he started, and soon came back to tell de boys to "kum up an' take keer of sum dogs dat de bear had almost killed." About ten o'clock I came down from the tree and pursued my journey in the direction of the polar star. I experienced greater difficulty in descending the tree than in the ascent. My limbs were weary; the fetters upon my ankles had become quite galling; my tongue was swollen in my mouth and cracking open from thirst. I had not gotten far from the tree when a hound, which had been lapping the blood of the bear, sprang toward me with open mouth. A well-directed blow from a club, which I took the precaution to secure, sent him howling away. All the hounds within hearing howled in concert, and a more frightful chorus I have never heard. I hastened onward as rapidly as possible, and there seemed to be no pursuit. I feared to deviate from my pathway to the right or left, as I had learned from my lofty point of observation, from my perch in the pinnacle of the lofty monarch of the forest, that there was a large camp to the eastward, and a much less formidable one to the westward; on the one hand was Scylla, on the other Charybdis. Every hour death stared me in the face. Foes were lurking all around. There was but a step between me and death. The days of my appointed time were waning fast. Hunted like a partridge upon the mountains, by blood-hounds and bloody men, a price upon my head, escape seemed impossible. I knew that prayer, fervent prayer, was continually ascending to God in my behalf. Implicitly I believed in the omnipotence of prayer—that no good thing will be denied the prayer of faith. But I had no promise to plead for longer life. It might be the will of the all-wise God to call me from earth, to suffer me to perish, as many patriotic men had done since the inauguration of rebellion, by rebel cruelty. I was never for an hour out of the hearing of howling hounds or yelping dogs. The hound ordinarily used in the pursuit of fugitive slaves is a cross between a mastiff and the bull-dog. It is very fierce, and will assault and tear to pieces the fugitive as soon as caught. A hound sometimes used is the blood-hound of the Talbot or southern breed. He has long, pendulous, drooping ears; he is tall and square-headed; has heavy, drooping lips and jowl. He has a stern expression. He is broad-chested, deep-tongued, and much slower than the cross between the mastiff and bull-dog. His powers of scenting are extraordinary. Let him smell any article of clothing that has been worn by the fugitive, and he will at once recognize his track and follow it, though it should be more than twenty-four hours old. Often one or two of these blood-hounds are kept to guide the pack. They are not so fierce as the other dogs, and any stout negro, by getting his back against a tree, so that he may not be surrounded, could defend himself with a club, and kill his assailants as fast as they approached. But the ordinary dog used to hunt the fugitive—the cross between the mastiff and the bull-dog—is so large, strong,

THE OLD EXPERT WHO PRESIDES OVER EACH KETTLE.

THE DOOR BLEW OPEN AND I STAGGERED IN.   Page 267

and fierce that the fugitive stands but little chance to defend himself from the combined attack of a dozen of them. Were it not for the blood-hounds with them, he could much more readily break the trail and baffle pursuit. The blood-hound is in color tawny, with black muzzles. The former dog has some scenting powers, but it is as inferior in these to the true blood-hound as it is superior to him in blood-thirstiness and cruel, indiscriminate pugnacity. It has no utility except as a man-hunter. In hunting the fugitive slave men always accompany the hounds, and are seldom far in the rear. When the fugitive finds all his skill to baffle pursuit unavailing, he climbs a tree and awaits the arrival of the horsemen, who call off the hounds, order the slave to come down, and they then tie him up and give him one or two hundred lashes, well laid on, on his bare back. Then he is ironed and conveyed home, where he receives the remaining installments of the penalty due to his vain attempt to secure his inalienable rights—life, liberty, and the pursuit of happiness. Life, one of the inalienable rights which God ordains for man, is not servile life. Servile life is induced by the avarice and cruelty of man.

I lay down in the woods and fell asleep ; visions of abundance both to eat and drink haunted me, and every unusual sound would startle me. A fly peculiar to the South, whose buzz sounded like the voice of a man in his senility, often awoke me with the fear that my enemies were near. As soon as Ursa

Minor appeared I took up my line of march. The night was very dark, and I became somewhat bewildered. At length I reached a cross-roads, and as I was emerging from the woods I saw two videttes a few yards distant. As quickly and as noiselessly as possible, I made a retrograde movement. As I was retiring I heard one vidette say to his comrade, "Who is that?" He replied, "It is the corporal of the guard." "What does he want?" said the first. "O," was the reply, "I suspect he's just slipping around here to see if we are asleep."

After I had reached a safe distance in the bushes, I lay down and slept till the moon arose. To the surprise of my bewildered brain it seemed to rise in the west. Taking my bearings I hastened on, through woods, corn-fields, and swamps. Coming to a large pasture in which a number of cows were grazing, I tried to obtain some milk, but the cows would not let me approach near enough to effect my purpose. My face was not of the right color, and my costume belonged to a sex that never milked them. I traveled till day-break, when I concealed myself in a cane-brake. I had scarcely fallen asleep, when I heard the sound of the reveille in a camp near by, and, listening, distinctly heard the soldiers conversing. Arising, I hastily beat a retreat, and cautiously avoiding the videttes I traveled several hours before I dared take any rest. At length I lay down amid the branches of a fallen tree and slept. Visions of home and friends flitted before me. Voices sweet

and kind greeted me on all sides. The bitter taunts
of cruel officers no longer assailed my ears. The
loved ones at home were present, and the joys of the
past were renewed. But, alas! the falling of a limb
dissipated all my fancied pleasures. The reality returned. I was still a fugitive escaping for life, and
in the midst of a hostile country. I fancied the woful
disappointment of the rebel officers when they learned
that the bird had 'flown and that they could no longer
wreak their vengeance upon me, nor have the pleasure of witnessing my execution. I thanked God
and took courage. I was still hopeful and trusting,
often repeating a verse from one of Watts' beautiful
hymns :

> Through many dangers, toils, and snares
> I have already come;
> 'Tis grace has brought me safe thus far,
> And grace will bring me home.

During this night I traveled steadily, crossing
corn-fields, woods, and pastures. I crossed but one
cotton-field. I suspected every bush a secessionist,
though I felt much more secure at night than in daylight. I avoided roads as much as possible, traveling
on none except to cross them, and this I did walking
backward, so that if the hounds found my track the
cavalry would be deceived when the plain tracks in
the road indicated a false direction. Every possible
deception was practiced by Unionists to avoid
detection.

The rising sun still found me pressing onward.

Hunger and thirst were now consuming me. My tongue was swollen and cracking open from thirst. I thought of opening a vein in my arm and drinking the blood. When I had almost despaired of getting water, a presentiment—I may call it an assurance—as if an inspiration from heaven, took possession of my whole soul that soon I would be supplied with water. The sky was clear. No clouds indicated rain. I quietly walked along, as consciously sure of water as if I were being refreshed by it. I came to a road and crossed it. A gin house was visible a few hundred yards distant, and there was a grove near it. I knew that embowered within its sylvan shade was a plantation house. After crossing the road I came to a gorge surrounded by converging hills, from which issued a copious fountain of crystal water. Near it there was no trace of human foot, nor hoof of cattle. I seemed to be the discoverer. On beholding it I wept for joy. I knelt down and in words of thanksgiving expressed my gratitude to Almighty God for this great deliverance, this sparkling, life-giving liquid brewed amid the forest shades by the hand of Jehovah, merciful and gracious. I then stooped down and quaffed the living water, the first pure water I had tasted since my imprisonment. Oh! that men would praise the Lord for his goodness and feel truly grateful for his common benefits. Were water to become scarce men would realize its worth. Blessings brighter as they take their flight. I remained at this spring four hours, quaffing its cool, refreshing waters. I removed my clothing and performed my first ablution since I fell into rebel hands, yet the irons prevented a thorough ablution. I named this spring Fons Vitæ. I was rejoiced when I discovered this spring, but not surprised, for I felt as fully assured of finding water as if an angel had spoken to me from heaven indicating its location. It came into my mind with the force of a revelation. My regret was sincere when I was compelled to leave this spring and continue my wearisome journey.

Three o'clock P.M. arrived. I felt bewildered. I knew not where I was. I might be near friends, I might be near blood-thirsty foes. I could scarcely walk. My iron bands had become very irksome. I felt that I was becoming childish. I could tell all my bones. I tried to pray, but could only utter, "God, be merciful to me a sinner." The sky became overcast with clouds. I could not distinguish the cardinal points. I therefore concealed myself and slept. It was night when I awoke, and the clouds still covered the face of the sky threateningly, concealing my guides, the stars of heaven, and rendering it impossible for me to proceed. Thus when I wished most to advance, my progress was arrested and my distressing suspense prolonged. During the night I was asleep and awake alternately, but could not at any time discern either moon or stars. I slept behind a fallen tree by a roadside. A horseman passed by at midnight. His dog, a large, ferocious animal, came running along by the side of the tree by which

I was lying. When he reached me I rose suddenly, and brandishing a club menacingly, the alarmed and howling dog incontinently and ingloriously fled, leaving me master of the field. The horseman stopped and listened. I lay silent as the grave. After a time, which my suspense and alarm doubtless magnified, he rode onward, when I changed my hiding place for safer quarters farther in the dark forest. The next morning the sun was obscured until nine o'clock. I guess at the time, as I had not my watch. I was then sick. There was a ringing in my ears, and I was afflicted by vertigo, a dimness of vision, and faintness, which rendered me absolutely unfit for travel. It required an hour to walk a quarter of a mile. Before me was a hill, the top of which I reached after two hours laborious ascent. I despaired of getting much farther. Feeling confident that I must be near the point where intersect the counties of Tippah, Pontotoc, Itawamba, and Tishomingo, and knowing that there were many Unionists in that district, I resolved to call at the first house I came to whose appearance indicated that its inmates were not slave-holders. Slave-holders were almost invariably secessionists. If I remained in the woods I must perish, as a great storm was impending. If I met with a Unionist family I would be saved, if with a rebel family I could but perish, and I felt that I could not survive the night and approaching storm.

Soon I came to a cabin by the side of a road, two

miles north of New Albany, Tippah county. The storm had reached me. The wind was blowing a gale, and the rain began to fall in torrents—just such a storm as visits the gulf states after a protracted drought. I went up to the door of the cabin and rapped. "Come," was the laconic response. I pulled the latch-string. The door blew open and I staggered in. When the lady present looked upon me she threw up her hands in terror, and said:

"Are you from Tupelo?"

"I am."

"What is your name?"

"John Hill."

I suppressed my surname. I was not much surprised at the lady's alarm. My hair, long and unkempt, covered with mud, my clothes nearly torn from my body by the thorns and briars in the ditches which bisected the fields that I was compelled necessarily to cross, my face pallid, the iron bands upon my limbs, made me present a frightful apparition to her startled gaze. And coming as the harbinger of a fierce storm, added doubtless to her terror. She, scrutinizing me closely, was about to proceed with her catechising. I forestalled her by turning to her husband, a man of Herculean proportions, sitting near by, saying:

"Sir, the Yankees are overrunning all our country. Why are you not in the army trying to drive them away?"

The lady replied tartly, "He's not there, and he's

not goin' there, either." She then animadverted upon Jeff Davis, the Southern Confederacy, and the conscript law, in terms that pleased me much. I never before delighted so much in hearing Jeff Davis abused. I felt safe, and pointing to the iron bands, told this couple—Mr. and Mrs. Chism—of my escape from the prison at Tupelo and the death preordained by General Bragg.

Their house had been searched for Malone and me, and they were cognizant of our escape. Both husband and wife promised to render all possible aid. Mrs. Chism immediately began to prepare supper. I told her that I could not await the slow process of cooking, that I was too near starvation for that. She turned down the table-cloth which covered the fragments remaining from dinner, and disclosed some corn bread and Irish potatoes. I thought this was the sweetest morsel I had ever tasted. After eating a little I became quite sick, and was compelled to desist. It was so long since I had partaken of any substantial food that my stomach rebelled against it. Soon Mrs. Chism prepared supper, consisting of broiled chicken and other delicacies. The fowl was small, and I ate nearly the whole of it, much to the chagrin of a little daughter of mine hostess, whom I heard complaining to her me in an adjoining room, saying, "Ma, all I could get of that chicken was a tiny piece of a wing, and wasent that gentleman a hoss to eat," with other remarks not very complimentary to my voracious appetite. I ate too heartily after so long a fast, and it caused nausea and vomiting. My stomach was too weak to bear it. After supper mine host endeavored to remove the heavy iron bands with which my ankles were encircled. Fortunately he was a blacksmith by vocation, and with the use of the implements of his trade he succeeded. I keep these as sacred relics. The good lady furnished me with water and a suit of her husband's clothes. After performing a thorough ablution I donned the suit, and was completely metamorphosed and thoroughly disguised, as my new suit was made for a man of vastly larger physical proportions. I spent the night with my new friends, during which a heavy storm passed over, accompanied by vivid lightning and loud, reverberating thunder. Had I been out in the drenching rain in my wretched and enfeebled condition I must certainly have perished.

A rebel camp was within a mile and a half, and horsemen clad in gray passed constantly. In the morning my host informed me of a Unionist who knew the country in the direction of Rienzi, the point which I now determined to reach. This gentleman was a near neighbor, Mr. Sanford by name. Mr. Chism accompanied me to a thicket near his house, in which I concealed myself. Before leaving I handed Mrs. Chism a double eagle. She refused to take it. Said I, " You have saved my life." " I charge you nothing for that," was her laconic reply. I threw the money down upon the table and left with her husband. As we were departing, she said, " Well, if you get to the Federal lines you won't begrudge it, and if you don't you won't need it."

Mr. Chism went to the shop of Mr. Sanford, who was a hatter by trade. There were two rebel soldiers talking with him, so Mr. C. had to wait till they went away of their own accord. As he staid more than two hours I feared treachery—that he might have gone to the rebel camp and given information. I therefore left my place of concealment and ascended an adjacent hill and climbed a eucalyptus tree. When I saw Mr. Chism coming, accompanied by but one man, I descended. The reason for delay was given. Mr. Sanford said, " I am not familiar with the route to Rienzi, but will accompany you to my brother-in-law's, Mr. John Downing's, who I know is well acquainted with the road. He can take you through the woods so as to avoid the Confederate cavalry. As I undertake this at the risk of life, we must use all possible precaution. You will have to spend the day concealed in my barn. I would gladly entertain you at my house, but I have a large family and many of them are girls, and you know that girls will talk, and might say something that would lead to suspicion and search, for these rebels are lynx-eyed and are on the alert. There are many notices affixed to trees and shops and posts in the most public places describing you and offering a large reward for your capture. I will carry you provisions during the day, and at midnight we will start to Mr. Downing's. We will be compelled to make a large circuit to avoid the rebel camp, and to go around a spur of the mountain. We will have to travel forty-five miles of a circuit, while it is only nine miles as the raven flies."

At one time Mr. Sanford's twin daughters came into the barn in search of eggs. They approached near my place of concealment, but did not discover me. When Mr. S. came with delicacies his wife had prepared, I informed him of it. He said, "I will send all my girls to their uncle's on a visit, so that there may be no danger of their suspicions being aroused. We are in daily, imminent peril. I do hope that the Federal troops will make haste to occupy the country and save us from our bitter and malignant foes, who will soon attempt to force all Unionists into their army; then it will be necessary to leave home and escape to the Union lines." He brought his wife up to see me, and we sat sadly discussing the perils and troubles surrounding the loyal people of the South. At length night came, and I slept. At midnight Mr. S. awoke me. He told me to mount the horse he held by the bridle. Said he, "That is a blooded animal of high mettle and good bottom, one of the swiftest horses in Tippah Co. He runs like a streak of lightning." I provided a good whip, resolving in case of danger to put my horse to his utmost speed. We traveled rapidly till nine o'clock in the morning, having to make a detour on account of discovering an unexpected camp. We must have traveled over fifty miles. When we reached Mr. Downing's we partook of an excellent

breakfast. The guerrillas had a few nights before
murdered a Unionist—a Mr. Newsom. His sentiments had become known to the rebels. They
watched his house till they knew of his presence at
home. He had been in concealment, but run the risk
of going home to see a sick daughter. They offered
him the oath of allegiance to the Confederate states.
He refused to take it. In their anger they resolved
upon his immediate death. Some proposed hanging,
some shooting, but the majority prevailed, and these
fiends in human form, these devils incarnate, then
deliberately heated water, and in the presence of his
weeping, pleading wife and helpless children they
scalded to death their chained and defenceless victim.
They then suspended the corpse from a tree, with a
label attached threatening a similar death to any who
should remove the corpse or bury it. Thus perished
a patriot of whom the state was not worthy. These,
my friends, cut down the corpse by night and buried
it in the forest. May God reward them. Oh, the
inhumanity of man to his fellow-man. The mother-
in-law of Mr. Newsom was a daughter of Gen. Nathaniel Green of revolutionary fame. She was very
aged. I asked her, for we stopped at her house, if
she remembered much about the war of the revolution. She kept repeating, "Oh, it was dreadful times.
The British before, the Indians behind, and the tories
in the middle."

Ere I left Mr. Downing's there were more than
fifty Unionists called to see me. They held a coun-

cil, and Mr. Downing was deputed to convey me to the Federal lines. We immediately set out upon our perilous journey.

Mr. John Downing, my guide, thought it best to travel by day, as the recent rains had raised the waters of the Hatchie and Tallahatchie rivers, both of which we must cross. Fording would be quite dangerous at night. We must follow trails, and thus avoid, if possible, the rebel cavalry and camps. There was one point of special danger at a place where stood a mill, at the base of converging lofty hills. We were traveling in a semi-mountainous country. We at length reached the summit of a very high hill. Far below us, winding around the base of this hill, which might not inappropriately be termed a mountain, ran the clear waters of a consid-erable creek. This was the dangerous point. Here was a large grist mill. We hitched our horses in a copse and reconnoitered. Believing the coast to be clear, we warily descended the steep declivities, till at length we reached the mill. The miller appeared at the door and poured forth a torrent of interroga-tories, to all of which my guide answered warily and discreetly, and I thought measurably allayed his sus-picions. Presently we espied a covered wagon drawn by Sumpter mules approaching. The saddle marks were visible. It halted at the mill, and eleven Confederate soldiers emerged from underneath the low, dingy covering. We were about to ride on, when they halted us, and the following dialogue ensued

18

between my guide and the soldiers, who had been out on sick furlough ever since the battle of Shiloh, and were now returning to camp at Ripley, Miss.:

"Hello! strangers, whar are ye from?"

"From New Albany, Tippah county."

"Whar ye gwine?"

"On the hunt of stray oxen. Hev ye seen nothin' of a black ox and a pided (pied) ox nowhar in yer travels?"

"No, we hain't."

"Is ther any danger of meeting any Yanks on that road over yender?"

"No, ther ain't. But ther's a road turns offen it 'bout three mile from here, to ther right, that is a mighty dangerous road. The Yankee cavalry's on it most every day. Say, who's that feller with ye? He jes' looks like death on a pale hoss."

"He's my brother-in-law from Alabam. He's hed the aiger for more'n a year, an' ther ain't no quinine in the country an' he can't git it stopt. Some of 'em thinks he's purty well gone with quick consumption."

"Golly, he looks like it. But what's that air notis up thar on the mill?"

The miller replies, "It's a notis of a reward fer a prisoner that broke jail at Tupelo. Jes' read it. I can't."

"Nun of us kin read. Jim Colquitt stopped back a piece thar to see his sister, Missis Curlee. He'll be along dreckly. We is to wait for him hyar. He kin read, an' rite, too."

The miller replied, "The officer that axed me to stick this notis up said a prisoner that hed escaped before wuz follered with blood-hounds an' tuck back an' put in irons, but he'd broke jail agin the day before he wuz to be hung. That old Bragg wuz all-fired mad about it, and offers a big reward to whosomever brings him back dead or alive. His name is Mohave or suthin like that. He is a parson an' lives in Rienzi, an' it's thought he's makin' fer that point."

We were about to start, when one of the soldiers said, "Stranger, what mout your name be?"

"My name is Jim Chalmette, and my brother-in-law's name is Oliver Folsom Brownlee, from Florence, Alabam," said my guide.

The soldier then said, "Can't one of you fellers read that air notis?"

We rode up in front of it and Mr. Downing read it thus: "Ten thousand dollars reward will be paid for the return, dead or alive, of a prisoner who escaped from the military prison at Tupelo, Miss. His name is John Mohave. He is over six feet high, of dark complexion, heavy beard, black eyes, high cheek bones, and was dressed in broadcloth, somewhat the worse for prison wear. Any soldier who captures him will, in addition to the cash reward, receive suitable promotion.

"BRAXTON BRAGG,
"*Major General Commanding.*"

I thought Downing had read it correctly, till I rode up and read it. I felt some tremor when I recognized an exact description of myself. Even the missing molar had been noticed.

One of the soldiers said, "Well, stranger, that settles it. I thought afore yer read that notis as how yer brother-in-law mought a ben the feller what broke jail, but he don't fill the bill, by odds. But he's got on awful fine boots an' hat. They don't suit them cloze, an' his cloze don't nigh fit him. They wuz made fer a long sight bigger man."

"Them's a suit of my cloze he put on this mornin' so my wife could wash an' mend hizzen."

"Well, I s'pose yer all right, but ther's a camp about three mile from hyar. You an' yer brother-in-law hed better let them oxen go fer awhile an' come with us to camp. Chalmers or Baxter will be thar, or mebbe old Forrest hisself. He'll be mighty glad to see ye, I reckon. Then ye kin explain some things about ye that we don't zackly understand."

At this time we were surrounded by them, and Downing thought it best to express his acquiescence. One of the soldiers presently went to the wagon, and producing a jug, asked us to drink with him. We rode to the further side of the wagon. The soldier then said, "Here's to Jeff Davis and the Southern Confederacy, wishin' 'em success and that we may kill a hundred Yankees apiece an' all git home safe."

At this moment Downing said, "We must go on," and putting spurs to our horses we soon put considerable space between us and these soldiers. They called after us to halt. Downing said, "We haven't

SLAVES WORKING IN THE COTTON FIELD.

THE MEN RAN UP THE KNOLL AND FIRED AT US. Page 277

time, howsomever we're all right." We rode on rapidly, thankful that we had escaped imminent peril. We soon came to a turn in the road. Just as we made the turn, we saw two men, with guns in their hands, on a knoll covered with a heavy growth of walnut trees. We were not sure whether they were hunters or guerrillas. They called to us to halt. We did so and asked them what they wanted. They replied that they would come to the road and tell us, and said, " Wait till we come to you." Downing said, in a low tone, " We are in danger, as we are in range, and they can bring us down with their guns. We will wait till they get to the bottom of the hill, among the chaparral which will intercept the shot if they fire." He then called to them to come on. They started toward us, and when they had reached the dense chaparral, we put spurs to our horses and galloped rapidly away. When we started, the men ran back up the knoll and taking aim fired at us. The shot from one of the guns whistled harmlessly through the branches of a mulberry tree under which we were passing. The shot from the other gun was more effective. One shot struck my horse in the flank. He reared and plunged wildly. I managed, however, to keep my seat. A shot struck Downing's saddle, and glancing inflicted a wound in the thigh. The men then hastened through the chaparral, and upon reaching the road, both fired the two undis- charged barrels of their guns. We were now so far away, and had turned a slight bend in the road, that the shot did us no injury. We, however, heard their patter and whistle as they passed through the branches of the trees in close proximity to us. Neither Downing nor I felt the least fear. The excitement of the moment and the comical and excited appearance of our would-be captors, both of whom had lost their hats in the bushes, excited our mirth. Downing said he believed the men were Porter Rucker and Albert Braddock, guerrillas, or partisan rangers, as Jeff Davis styled those who were engaged in hunting down Unionists, and capturing and returning to camp deserters.

"Perhaps," said I to Downing, "it will delight us hereafter to recall even the present things to mind." "Yes, if we outlive this terrible war and survive its horrors. But there is not much pleasure in them now."

In a short time we came to the road designated as dangerous by our would-be captors at the mill. As we reached it we saw in the distance ahead of us, on the road we were now traveling, a few straggling cavalrymen. They saw us and halted, apparently to await our overtaking them. We turned off on the road which the Yankee cavalry were said to frequent ere we reached them. A boy whom we overtook informed us that Baxter's rebel cavalry had just passed. They would have swift steeds to follow with any prospect of overtaking us. A former classmate in Richmond College, Ohio, Matthew Thompson by name, was an officer under Baxter, and would have recognized me had we been a few minutes earlier at that point, and been captured by this doughty rebel. Baxter's scouts infested this section for a long time, murdering Unionists and hunting with blood-hounds the poor conscripts who, having been forced into the Confederate service, endeavored to escape to the Federal lines. Baxter concocted a plot to capture Gen. U. S. Grant, but failed to accomplish his nefarious purpose.

Having traveled several hours after escaping Baxter's cavalry, we rode into the woods, dismounted, and sat down to rest and take an inventory of our injuries. Downing's boot had some blood in it and his thigh was beginning to be quite painful. The left leg of his pantaloons was completely saturated. I examined his wound, and used Downing's knife as a probe, but I could not find the shot. I cut off a piece of cloth from one of my under garments and bandaged the wound to stop the hemorrhage. My horse had bled considerably from the wound in his flank, but did not show any perceptible sign of weakness or flagging gait. We remounted and rode on to Antioch or Hinkle. I think we passed through both these hamlets. Here Downing left me to return home. He must travel by a different route in returning. He would lodge that night at the house of a stalwart Unionist, Elihu Noble, who had recently moved from Ingomar, Issaquena county, to Molino Del Rey. I gave him a double eagle, and we parted with fervent adieus and good wishes for each other's welfare. I again assumed the role of a pedestrian, and ere long reached Rienzi.

When I gazed on the star spangled banner, emblem of my country's glory and power, beneath whose ample folds there was safety and protection for the poor, pursued, panting, perishing Unionist, and saw around me the loyal hosts of brave men, eager to subvert rebellion and afford protection to the wronged and persecuted southern patriot, I shed tears of joy. I felt that I was safe, my perils o'er, and from the depths of a grateful heart I returned thanks to Almighty God, who had given me my life in answer to importunate prayer, preserving me amid peculiar dangers, seen and unseen, till now I had reached the desired haven and was safe amid hosts of friends. When I reached the picket line, a horse was furnished me, and I was taken to the head-quarters of Col. Mizener. My brother, David H. Aughey, and brother-in-law, Prof. Robert K. Knight, residents of Rienzi, heard of my arrival and came at once to see and convey me to their homes. Col. M. had sent an orderly to report my presence. Col. Mizener requested me to report all that would be of service to Gen. Rosecrans, who was ten miles south at Booneville, which I did, he copying my report as I gave it. I reported the particulars of my escape, the probable number of Confederate troops in and around Tupelo, the topography of the country, the probable intentions of the rebels, the putative number of troops sent to Richmond to re-inforce Gen. Lee; the harsh, cruel, and vindictive treatment of the southern Unionists incarcerated in the bastile in Tupelo, etc. The Colonel requested me to go with him to visit Gen. Rosecrans at his head-quarters in Booneville the next morning, but at the hour specified reaction had taken place, and I was very sick. My report was carried up to Gen. Rosecrans by Col. Mizener, who immediately forwarded it to Gen. Grant at Memphis, who noted it and placed it on file. It has been published in official Records of the War of the Rebellion, Union and Confederate, Vol. 17, page 107.

Gen. W. S. Rosecrans, upon hearing that I was sick, sent Surgeon Berridge Lucas, of an Illinois brigade, raised in Peoria, Ill., and Dr. Hawley, of the 36th Ill. Infantry, to attend me during my illness. Under their skillful and efficient treatment I measurably regained health, though for some time I was apparently upon the border land, and it was feared that I would be a mental and physical wreck. My sufferings at the hands of the rebels produced a lesion from which I will never fully recover. Two of my soldier comrades have recently succumbed to a similar malady, and I cannot hope to resist it much longer. The citadel of life must eventually yield to its force, and death supervene. Skillful medical treatment and extremely temperate habits alone have thus far held it in abeyance. Hardships incurred afterward in the service, as chaplain, aggravated the malady.

But why should I repine since my country's integrity and permanence has been secured, never more to be imperiled by traitors to their government and their God? The salutary lesson they have learned will prevent a repetition of their folly.

When I recovered sufficiently to leave my room I was honored with a serenade by a brigade brass band, through the politeness of Col. Bryner and Lieut. Col. Thrush, of the 47th Ill. regiment. At the close they called for a speech, to which call I thus responded:

GENTLEMEN—I desire to express my sincere thanks for the honor conferred. In the language of the last tune played by your band, I truly feel at home again, and it fills my soul with joy to meet my friends once more. What a vast difference between Tupelo and Rienzi. There I was regarded as a base ingrate, as a despicable traitor, an enemy to the country, chained as a felon, doomed to die, and before the execution of the sentence subjected to every species of insult and contumely. Here I meet with the kindest expressions of sympathy from officers of all ranks, from the subaltern to the general, and there is not a private soldier who has heard my tale of woe that does not manifest a kindly sympathy. I hope you will speedily pass south of Tupelo, but in your victorious march to the gulf I wish you to fare better than I did in my journey from Tupelo to Rienzi. Traveling day after day without food or water would cause you to present the emaciated appearance that I do. On your route, call upon the secession sympathizers and compel them to furnish you with all the viands

that you need. My good horse, Bucephalus, I left
at Tupelo. He is an animal of pure blood and high
mettle. The rebel general Hardee, in the true spirit
of secession, appropriated—that is, stole him. He
often insolently rode him by our prison, surrounded
by his staff. He did not return him to me when I
left. However, I did not call to demand him upon
leaving. Being in haste I did not choose to spare
the time, as I am a great economist of time, and leaving in the night I did not wish to disturb the slumbers of the Tupelonians. He is a bright bay. If
you find him you may have him gratis. I would
much prefer that he serve the Federal army. I
bought him of Gen. Lionel Colquitt, at West Point,
Miss., for three hundred and fifty dollars.

If you take Gen. Jordan prisoner, send me word,
and I will furnish you with the irons with which he
bound me, by which you may secure him till he
meets the just penalty of his crimes, even death,
which he richly deserves for the murder of many
Unionists.

When I became convalescent I rode to Jacinto, the
Federal outpost nearest to my family. I called upon
Gen. Jefferson C. Davis, who at once ordered eight
regiments of cavalry, accompanied by a section of
artillery, to bring them into Jacinto. I soon had
the pleasure of beholding my wife and child, whose
faces I recently had given up all hope of ever seeing
upon earth. The meeting was mutually a joyful one.
Gen. Davis ushered them into his office, where I was

awaiting them, and then considerately retired. My little daughter, during my ominous absence, would often try to comfort her ma by telling her, when she was weeping, "Ma, I think they will let pa loose, 'cause we pray so much for him. Don't cry, I think God will send him to us soon. He has said He will hear us when we pray."

Richard Malone lived in Jacinto. Gen. Davis and I called to see him. He rejoiced greatly upon seeing me. He had informed Gen. Davis of my capture and re-arrest. Gen. Davis had ordered the arrest of four prominent citizens of Jacinto, to be held as hostages for my safety. The officer was just about to start to execute the order when I arrived at his head-quarters. The citizens were named John G. Barton, Col. Runnels, Barton Key, and Calvin Taylor.

When Malone reached the point where we agreed to meet he awaited my arrival. He gave the pre-concerted signals, but I came not. We agreed to meet at a point where a garment was suspended from a post of the corn-field fence. But as there may have been more than one garment suspended from the posts, as many rebel soldiers, after washing, hung their clothes out to dry, we mistook the place, and reached the corn-field at different points, and so were compelled to set out alone on the hazardous journey. At one time Malone resolved upon the risk of walking upon a road a few hundred yards to reach a forest. A company of cavalry came suddenly upon him and ordered him to go before them, declaring that they would gladly return him to prison. They made him go on the double-quick. He said, presently, "I am very thirsty; will you give me some water?" They replied that they were going to that house on the distant hill to get water. When they reached the house and drew the water, Malone noticed that there was no dipper at the well with which to lift the water from the bucket. He said, "I will go into the house and ask for a dipper." Two cavalry men followed him, and stationed themselves at the door. Malone went into the house, shut the door, and the back door being open, he ran through the house, opened the garden gate, ran through the garden, leaped over the palings at the farther end into a corn-field. Two women who were in the house ran to the door clapping their hands and exclaiming, "O! your Yankee is gone, your prisoner has escaped." The cavalry men ran round the house, and seeing Malone running through the corn-field called to him to halt. Malone, not heeding the order, ran onward. They fired. Malone ran zigzag to avoid the bullets which whistled uncomfortably close to his ears. They failed to bring him down. They followed, but Malone outran them to a swamp, and after many other narrow risks reached his home in Jacinto.

I returned to Rienzi. I reached Rienzi from prison on the day that the 2d Michigan regiment made a present of a fine black cavalry horse to Gen. Philip Sheridan. As the presentation was made in

Rienzi, the general named the horse after the town, calling him Rienzi. This was the horse he rode in his famous ride from Winchester, Va., to Cedar creek, when he turned the tide of battle, changing an inglorious rout into a glorious victory over Jubal Early We soon left Rienzi for the North. When we reached the home of my parents the rejoicing was as if one who was dead had been restored to life. They had heard through war correspondents with the army of my imprisonment, escape, re-arrest, and re-incarceration. They had not heard of my second escape. Thirteen days after our arrival at my father's house a son was born to us, August 20th, 1862, whom we named John Knox. Our third child, Gertrude Evangeline, was born February 12, 1867. Our first child, Anna Katharine, now Mrs. Ferguson, of Congress, O., was born September 3, 1858.

As soon as I felt able to do so, I accepted the position of chaplain, first in the army of the Potomac, afterwards in the western army. The officers of the 6th Ill. calvary, of which I was chaplain, asked me at one time to give them an address on the subject of my arrest, imprisonment, and escapes. I complied with their invitation. At the close of the address, a soldier who had deserted from the rebel army and was now a member of a company in our regiment, came to Col. Lynch, who at this time commanded the 6th Ill. calvary (Col. Benjamin Grierson was the 1st colonel), and informed him that he was one

of the guards on duty at the prison in Tupelo on the
night of my escape. He said that I was missed in
the morning, very early. One of the guards noticed
my chain, which I had coiled up and left by the side
of a little stump, inadvertently placing it on the side
next the guards. He called the officer of the guard
and showed him the chain. Soon many officers
came into the prison. All the guards who had been
on duty during the night were brought into the
prison in irons. They thought that some of them must
have been in collusion with the prisoner, or he could
not have escaped. The prisoners were strictly questioned as to whether they knew anything in regard to
the escape, or if any of them had rendered any assistance. They denied all knowledge of or complication
in the matter. One of the officers said,"God Almighty
alone must have known and helped him. He could
not have gotten away without assistance, and you all
deny having rendered any." Col. Lynch said, "If
you had known of his intention to escape, would you
have helped him?" "No," said the soldier, "I was
a rebel in sentiment then, and would have done my
duty and taken stringent measures to prevent his
escape, had I known of his intention to do so. Two
companies of cavalry were sent in pursuit, with strict
orders to shoot him on sight and not bring him back
alive." But providentially they never got the sight.
One went north toward the Federal lines. The
other north-east. One went in sight of the Federal
pickets near Rienzi. The other visited my father-in-

law's, at Paden's mills, south-east of Iuka. They again, as upon their first visit, searched the house, mills, negro quarters, and every crevice capable of secreting a hare.

A Unionist, Washington Gortney, whose name I have mentioned, was murdered by a band of guerrillas under the lead of his nearest neighbor, one Bill Robinson. Gortney and Reece had enlisted in the Union army. Gortney desired to visit his family, one mile from Paden's mills. Reece accompanied him. Robinson heard of it, and gathering a few partisan rangers, murdered Gortney in the midst of his family. Reece was left for dead, but recovered. In retaliation, a company of Federal soldiers were sent out to burn Paden's, Vawter's, and Robinson's mills and ten houses. This they accomplished, and returned. This salutary proceeding had the effect of checking guerrilla murders and predatory raids by them for a time.

How terrible for a family to see and hear the howling hounds in search of one of their number, and to hear the horrid and blasphemous oaths of the fierce dragoons, swearing what terrible vengeance they will wreak upon their victim when caught and in their power.

"Oh! the inhumanity of man to his fellow-man
Makes countless millions mourn."—
"Oh! Freedom! How we love thy name,
We who thy choicest blessings claim.
No servile hordes now sweat and toil
Upon our consecrated soil;

No bondman's cries fall on our ears,
No master's lash wrings scalding tears
From women's eyes; none wildly flee
From threatened scourge of a Legree.
Exempt from slavery's fearful thrall,
Sweet Freedom's gifts now bless us all.
And those who once did meekly bow
Beneath the yoke are voters now."

MEMPHIS, TENNESSEE, February 12, 1888.
Rev. John H. Aughey, Chariton, Ia.:

DEAR SIR—I take the *National Tribune,* that most excellent soldiers' paper. In it I noticed your request for the address of Leslie Barksdale and others who were your fellow-prisoners in the South. I am now known as Melvin Estill, having changed my name for reasons which will be hereinafter given. I was a fellow-prisoner with you in that miserable den at Tupelo, Miss. Delevan Morgan, John Truesdale, Byron Porter, Ulysses Chenault, and I were conscripted, and because of our refusal to take the oath and enlist we were immured in prison. We were tried by court-martial, and condemned to death, with the proviso that if we took the oath and entered the army the sentence would be suspended. We were given twelve hours for deliberation. You will remember we consulted you, and you advised us to take the oath, enter the army, and desert the first favorable opportunity and escape to the Federal lines. We accordingly took the oath. I think our motive was suspected. We were taken to Saltillo and

19

placed under guard in an old rickety building, with a number of other prisoners.

That same night we evaded the guards and escaped. Guided by the north star, we hastened northward with all possible speed. Soon after daylight we heard the baying of the blood-hounds; nearer and nearer they came. When they came in sight three of our number climbed a tree. Delevan Morgan and I essayed to climb a large tree that stood near. Morgan caught hold of a withered branch. It broke in his grasp and he fell to the ground. He arose and ran. I jumped down and followed him. The hounds and cavalry appeared upon the scene. Our three companions were shot, and as they fell the hounds tore them limb from limb. Morgan had sprained his ankle, and his progress was quite slow. I made a detour and concealed myself behind the huge trunk of a fallen tree. Soon the hounds overtook my friend and tore him to pieces. These hounds were under the care of a miscreant named Jasper Cain, who was assisted by one Laverty Grier, John Graham, and others.

I supposed that death was inevitable. Cain and his men held a council of war. Cain enquired, "How many prisoners did old Bragg say there wuz?" "Four," replied Grier. "Well we've got 'em all," replied Cain. Some one said he believed General Bragg said, "there wuz five," but it was decided that "it wuz only four." Cain said, "Our orders wuz, to take' em dead or alive. Now how will we prove to old Bragg that we killed 'em all, an' git the reward?" "Take their scalps," suggested Grier. "Good, that is a bright idea," said Cain. "Now, Laverty, you scalp 'em with that 'ere knife that's in your belt." The order was obeyed, the scalps stuck in Grier's belt, and the cavalcade returned to camp.

I now hastened onward. After traveling about four miles I came to a cabin in a clearing. I knew that pursuit would not long be delayed. I went to the cabin and knocked. A lady came and opened the door. She bade me enter. I asked her if she was Union or Secesh. She assumed an air of great ignorance and stupidity, and replied, "I ain't neither, I'm a Baptist." That was enough for me. I felt sure she was all right. I at once revealed my condition, and told of my imminent peril. She and her daughter and her sick husband at once set about devising a plan of escape. There was a cave in the hillside about a half a mile distant. This lady, who was of Amazonian proportions, and her daughter, carried me to this cave. I found a cot within it and a little table. This lady, Mrs. Cameron, gave me a pair of her daughter's shoes in exchange for mine. Her daughter, Miss Alverna Cameron, put on my shoes and traveled five miles northward to a swamp. She then took off my shoes and put on a pair of her mother's, which she had carried in her apron, and returned.

Jasper Cain, after considerable delay reported to General Braxton Bragg, and told him of the fate of the prisoners, whom he had left unburied, to be devoured by wild hogs and buzzards. He then displayed exultingly the scalps which he bore as a trophy and as a proof of having carried out the orders of his commanding general. "But there are only four scalps," said the general, "where is the fifth?" "You said there wuz four prisoners what escaped," said Cain. Gen. Bragg ordered Cain to start in pursuit of the fifth at once and to bring in his scalp or consequences might follow not pleasant for Cain to contemplate. This infuriate demon obeyed with alacrity, and ere long the domicile of the Camerons was surrounded by howling hounds and blaspheming rebels. Soon, however, they seemed to have discovered the track, and off they went pell-mell on the route which Miss Alverna had taken to mislead them.

Miss Alverna and her mother visited me in the cave, bringing with them hoe cake, butter, and milk. The rebel soldiers had robbed them of all other provisions. I feasted upon the regale these kind ladies furnished me. They were delicious viands indeed to one who brought the sauce of hunger to the repast. Starvation in the rebel camp and prison had so improved my appetite that it required all they brought to appease it. Miss Alverna told me of the pursuit by Cain with his blood-hounds, and how she had misled them. They then prepared to take their departure. Mrs. Cameron and her daughter sang "Jesus, lover of my soul," and a hymn, one stanza of which I shall ever remember.

"MA, I THINK THEY WILL LET PA LOOSE, 'CAUSE WE
PRAY SO MUCH FOR HIM."   Page 284

I Asked For Something To Eat.   Page 294

"Savior, I look to thee,
Be thou not far from me
Mid storms that lower;
On me thy care bestow,
Thy loving kindness show,
Thine arms around me throw
This trying hour."

Miss Alverna then read the 31st Psalm. Two verses, the 35-6, seemed very pertinent. "My times are in thy hand; deliver me from the hands of mine enemies and from them that persecute me. Make thy face to shine upon thy servant and save me for thy mercy's sake." Also the 13th verse, etc., "Fear was on every side, while they took counsel together against me, they devised to take away my life. But I trusted in thee, O Lord, I said thou art my God. Have mercy upon me, O Lord, for I am in trouble. Thou art my rock and my fortress, therefore for thy name's sake lead me and guide me." Mrs. Cameron then led in prayer, asking the Lord to deliver me from surrounding foes, the bears, venomous serpents, and still more venomous Confederates. They then bade me good-bye and returned home. When night came I feared to stay longer in my cave. I started off on my perilous journey toward the Federal lines. I lay concealed by day and traveled by night, guided by the polar star.

One night I felt that I must run a great risk to procure some food, as I was in a starving condition. I found a cabin inhabited by slaves. I went to the door and rapped. Soon a venerable aunty appeared at the door. I asked her for something to eat. She appeared alarmed, and calling a little colored boy she bade him guide me to a place where I should be fed. When I reached the terminus of my journey under this boy's guidance, I found a man about my own age, who was, like me, a fugitive bound for the Union army. Soon a number of kind colored people appeared, and in this swamp we were fed with all the luxuries procurable by these kind friends who bore the image of God carved in ebony. My fugitive friend said his name was Johnny Peterson, and that he lived on the Taccalceche in North Mississippi. After many thrilling adventures we reached the Union lines and were joyfully welcomed. A minister of your church informs me that, by examining the year book or minutes of your general assembly, he learns that you are pastor of the Presbyterian church in the city of Chariton, Iowa. My address will be Memphis, Tenn., for a few months. Write me at your earliest convenience.

After reaching the Federal lines both Peterson and I enlisted and fought through the war. Through fear that I might be taken prisoner and recognized, I changed my name, and found it almost impossible to resume my old name after the war.

I am glad to know that you made your escape. Tell me all about it at your earliest convenience.

Your friend,
MELVIN ESTILL.

"THE BONES OF THE DEAD."

BY MARY DALE CULVER EVANS.

We'll cover them over, the bones of the dead;
Bring laurels and myrtle to strew o'er his bed—
The bones that were bleaching now honored shall be,
By patriot hearts in the land of the free.

Twice a decade of years had passed o'er his form,
Full twenty long summers and winters of storm,
Ere the lone spot was found where martyr he died,
Cut down by assassins in manhood's full pride.

He died for his country—the holiest cause—
For Union, for Freedom, for Liberty's laws,
When treason ran rampant and sought to destroy
The gift of our fathers unmixed with alloy.

The land next to heaven we prize as our own,
Where religion and science twin sisters have grown.
'Neath the stars and the stripes, we love as a friend
The time-honored banner he sought to defend.

Bring out from the forest the mouldering bones,
From the gloom of the rock house, those sentinel stones,
Mute witnesses they of the torturing pain
When the victim to treason by ruffians was slain.

Oh, cover them over and leave them to rest,
With memorial honors over his breast;
And rear a just tablet the story to tell
To the youth of our country, the fate of Journell.

—*Wilkes-Barre Record.*

LETTER FROM PROF. FRANKLIN BREVOORT, FOUND IN HIS
BROTHER GIDEON'S TENT AFTER HIS BURIAL.

MEMPHIS, TENN., Dec. 16, 1864.

Dear Brother:

I have just learned your address. I, too,
made my escape to the Federal lines. When
the tocsin of war sounded I was teaching in Pensacola,
Florida. Teachers and ministers employed in their
vocation were by Confederate law exempt from service
in the army. When the summer vacation of 1861
came I felt that body, soul, and spirit with united
voice demanded rest—a period of absolute freedom
from all secular cares and avocations. The duties of
the class-room had been peculiarly severe and exacting
during the academic year just closed. But the trying
ordeal was passed, and vacation had come. Homer
and Horace, Virgil and Xenophon, Legendre and
Bourdon, Watts and Whately, and all the tomes of
ancient and modern lore were consigned for the time
to the gloomy alcoves of the library, there to rest in
silent companionship till vacation ended and schol-
astic duties were resumed.

The young men have donned their hunting apparel and hied away to the forest, where the red deer wander, and to the rivers, where the finny tribes abound, and I, whither shall I go? The bow that is kept continually in a high state of tension, and the mind that is never relaxed, lose elasticity and become permanently impaired. The environment has a tendency to recall the duties performed in it, which one wishes wholly to throw off for a time, and thus the benefits of recreation are diminished. It is better, therefore, that needful rest be taken at some place remote from the scenes of labor. New scenes, new faces, new employments divert the mind, and call into action other faculties, and give those that have been overburdened the desired rest. With this end in view I prepared to leave our classic shades and hie away to the home of one of my students, whose warm invitation I felt happy in accepting. On a beautiful morning, just as the auroral brightness was assuming a vermilion hue, sure harbinger of coming day, the colored coachman drove to my door and I was soon outward bound for the home of Jasper Pettigru, whose hospitable residence I was never to reach. The oriole, the mocking-bird, the paroquet flitted from tree to tree, and a great variety of feathered songsters made the forests vocal with their harmony, and by the brilliancy of their plumage encircled our pathway with a halo of glory. One could readily imagine himself in the enchanted land. The balmy air, the fragrant flowers, the silvery, sparkling waters, the odor-laden breeze, all contributed to the highest happiness, the most ecstatic delight of the votaries of pleasure—a crowd of whom were with me in the diligence. But ever and anon there came borne upon the unwilling breeze an agonizing sigh, proceeding from the inmost recesses of a bleeding, broken heart—a heart crushed by some sorrow too great to be sustained long and the victim live. I thought perhaps it is a fugitive slave on the top of the diligence who is being returned to his master. When we arrived at Daphne, Ala., where I intended lodging for the night with an old friend, Joe Poindexter, an officer got out of the diligence, ordered a carriage from the livery stable, and obtaining assistance, took a white man from the top of the stage and placed him on the rear seat of the carriage. He said this was a state prisoner whom he was conveying into the presence of Col. Bonham, at Tensas, to be dealt with as he was accustomed to deal with all tories. As my friend lived near Tensas, I mentioned this fact to this man, whose name was Major Samuel Rodney. Major Rodney said he would be glad to have me go with him for company. I at once accepted the proffered favor, having a desire to assist, if possible, this suffering Unionist. When within two miles of Tensas we came to the residence of a gentleman, a friend of Major Rodney, Col. Wardlaw by name (if my memory is correct). A dance was in progress at his house, and he insisted upon Major Rodney's attending the dance. The

major said this d—d tory must be delivered to-
night to Col. Bonham. "Can't your friend take
him in?" replied the colonel. "Yes, or I can drive
in and return," said the major. "You'd miss oceans
of fun if you were to do that. Just send him in and
let your friend put the team in the livery stable at
Tensas. I'll send for it in the morning." I cordially assented to this arrangement.

After driving a few hundred yards I asked my
prisoner to give me his story. He replied that his
name was Isaac Simpson, that he was a Unionist,
and supposed that this would be the last night of his
life, as Col. Bonham spared the lives of no Unionists,
and that he would not recant his opinions to save his
life. I replied, " I, too, am a Unionist." " Glory
to God," said the prisoner, " then there is yet hope
for me." " Yes, we will survive or perish together."
Col. Rodney had given me the key of the prisoner's
manacles. I had no difficulty in liberating him.
There was no road by which to turn off, so we were
compelled to go into Tensas, then bear north, and
trust in God for divine guidance. We drove rapidly,
and were far, very far from Tensas by daylight. Near
Shongalo, Smith Co., Miss., we sold our horses and
carriage to a planter for $500, Confederate money.
At Tougaloo, Hinds Co., we bought suits of clothes
in order to conceal our identity. At Brandon, Miss.,
we bought tickets for Grand Junction, Tenn., and
without any further special adventures reached Cairo,
Ill., where we both enlisted in the Federal service.

At Brandon I bought a newspaper which gave a description of us, and offered a large reward for our capture.

Prof. Simpson has never yet been able to correspond with his family, nor has he heard what may have befallen them since his arrest; nor have I been able to visit my student friend for whose hospitable mansion I started in what appears, because of the thronging events and various vicissitudes of the past years, to be the "auld lang syne." We hope that soon the bottom will fall out of that rotten old hulk —the Southern Confederacy.

Please write to me at your very earliest convenience and tell me all about yourself.

Your affectionate brother,
FRANKLIN BREVOORT.

The song of war shall echo through the mountains
   Till not one hateful link remains
   Of slavery's lingering chains,
   Till not one tyrant treads our plains,
Nor traitor lips pollute our fountains.

FROM A SOLDIER'S LETTER.

THE SOLDIER'S LOT.

The feigned retreat, the nightly ambuscade,
The daily harass and the fight delayed,
The long privation of the hoped supply,
The tentless rest beneath the humid sky,
The stubborn wall that mocks the leaguer's art,
And palls the patience of his baffled heart,
Of these they had not deemed. The battle day
They could encounter as a veteran may ;
But more preferred the fray, the strife,
And present death, to hourly suffering life. "

THE SOUTHERN BARBECUE.

Twenty-four hours before the feast is to be served
the preparations are under way. Seventy-two South-
down sheep have been slaughtered and suspended
in undivided carcasses. Twenty-five shoats bear the
mutton company. While the butchers are doing their
work, a gang of darkeys, whose shovels fly as if it
was a labor of love, have excavated three trenches,
sixty feet long, three and a half feet wide, and four
feet deep. They are side by side, clean cut through
sod and clay, and if a surveyor had gone over them
he could not have found fault with the symmetry.
Then the wood is hauled. It is only the best seasoned
hickory which goes into the pits, and cord after cord

is piled in, until there is an amount which would stock a wood yard in a northern city. Stick after stick is laid on until the wood rises above the surface. Coal oil is brought and poured on the wood. Then fire is applied in a dozen places and the contents of the trenches blaze from end to end. From midnight till daylight the smoke and flames and the trenches are not approachable. It is Gehenna in miniature. At five o'clock the contents have settled down to a bed of coals a foot thick, from which arises a fervent heat. In the waiting hours the spits, long, smooth-shaven poles of hickory, have been made ready, and in pairs have been run through the carcasses length-wise. They form stretchers, and as they rest on sup-porters the sheep or shoat is stretched out flat. Grasping these hickory poles the darkies, one at each end, carry the carcasses and lay them over the trenches, the spits holding them in position. Over the intense heat, the surface flesh begins to sputter and fly, and then ensues a lively scene. To prevent scorching the carcasses have to be turned over every ten minutes, and the attendants fairly rushed along the sides of the trenches grasping and flopping over the roasting pork and mutton. At one end of the pits is a great cauldron, where the seasoning, salt and pepper and other condiments, is mixed in water and boiled. This compound is dipped out in buckets, and men go from carcass to carcass with great swabbing cloths tied on sticks. In this way they apply the seasoning. As the embers drop lower the heat becomes less intense,

and the barbecuing goes on more soberly. Occasionally
a little water is thrown on the coals, and steam relieves
the cooking of too much dryness, but the basting goes
on unceasingly. In ordinary times Uncle Jake Hostetter may be an humble citizen in Lexington. Now,
as master of the barbecuing, he rules supreme in the
cooking lot, for the trenches are enclosed by a tight
board fence, and it requires some persuasion to get
past the guards. There are only a few favored persons within. The thousands who sniff the odors, and
look longingly toward the incense arising from the
fires, are wandering through the park wondering when
dinner will be ready. The master of the barbecue
moves among the trenches and his word is law. He
served his apprenticeship away back when presidents
came to these Kentucky festivities. Barbecues have
not been so frequent of late years. But Uncle Jake
feels safe in his experience, and he shows no uneasi-
ness over the fact that 5,000 people are holding him
responsible for their dinners, and some of them have
gone breakfastless to stimulate appetite. Now and
then two of the cooking corps bring up from the
trenches to the table under the big tree a carcass to
inspect. He cuts into it, slices off bits of the flesh,
tastes, and looks knowing. Even the president of the
day, Hon. W. C. P. Breckenridge, recognizes the
authority. The speaking has commenced from a
stand in the park, and somebody wants to know when
the orators are going to stop for dinner. " Just when
Uncle Jake Hostetter says the mutton is done to a

turn," replies Mr. Breckenridge, and another statesman is let loose to say a great many pretty compli-
ments about Kentucky, and a very few words about
national politics.

The Blue Grass country has contributed to this
occasion three great caldrons. Whatever useful purpose they may have subserved about hog killing time,
they are now doing duty in the manufacture of 900
gallons of burgoo. Burgoo has a basis, as the
chemist says. The basis on this occasion consists of
150 chickens and 225 pounds of beef in joints, and
other forms best suited for soup. To this has been
added a bushel or two of tomatoes. The heap of
shaven roasting ears tells of another accessory before
the fact. Cabbage and potatoes and probably other
things in small quantities, but too numerous to mention, have gone into the pots. The fires were lighted
under the vats before the roasting commenced on the
trenches, and the burgoo has been steadily boiling
ever since. This boiling necessitates steady stirring,
and next to Uncle Jake's ministerial powers the old
expert who presides over each kettle comes in for due
respect and glorification. "You might not think it,"
says the old grey-headed Kentuckian whose eye is
on the largest of the pots where 500 gallons of burgoo are bubbling, "but a piece of mutton suet as
large as my hand thrown into the pot would spoil
the whole mess. That shows you that there are
some things you can't put in burgoo. Sometimes out
in the woods we put in squirrels and turkeys, but we

didn't have any this time. I think they've got a lectle too much pepper in that pot down there, so if you don't find what you get is just right come to me and I'll fix you up with some of this." As the meat boils from the bones the latter are raised from the bottom of the kettle by the paddle and thrown out. Gradually vegetables lose all distinctive form and appearance, and the compound is reduced to a homogeneous liquid, about the consistency of molasses. "Burgoo ought to boil about 14 hours," says the old expert, "we've only had about 8 for this, but I think they'll be able to eat it."

Gradually the heap of barbecued meat accumulates before Uncle Jake. He goes over and looks at the burgoo, and consults with the old expert. Then he glances over the fence at the long tables, and finds that two wagon loads of bread have been hewn into rations and strewn along the pine boards. The tin cups, 3,000 of them, are hurriedly scattered with the bread. From all parts of the grounds there is a sudden but decorous movement toward the tables, and the orator on tap runs off a peroration and stops. Uncle Jake's corps of assistants bring out the carcasses still on the stretchers, and every rod of table length finds a smoking sheep and a shoat. Gus Jaubert and a dozen butchers, with their long, sharp knives, shave and cut and deal out with all the speed that long practice has given them. The burgoo, steaming hot in new wooden buckets, is brought in, and as the attendants pass along the lines the hungry people dip

out cupfuls and sip it as it cools. There are no knives
nor forks. Nobody asks for or expects them.
Neither are there spoons for the burgoo. The great
slices of bread serve as plates for the meat. There
are 5,000 people eating together, and all busy at once.
Not a basket has been brought. All types and classes
of Blue Grass people are facing those tables, and
handling their bread and meat and burgoo with mani-
festations of appetite which tell of the relish of the
fare. Finally, nothing but skeletons remain of the
sheep and shoats, and the tables are swept. Uncle
Jake moves among the throng, and men like Senator
Beck and Gov. Blackburn and Gen. Wm. Preston
shake his hand, and tell him he has eclipsed his
former efforts. It is the proud happy hour of Uncle
Jacob's life. He is the hero of the hour. Don
Piatt and several other reporters were present taking
notes of this wonderful institution, the southern barbecue, and graphic reports find their way to the
northern papers. The southerner, notably the Kentuckian, regards the man's life a failure who has not
attended a barbecue.

Winchester, Clark Co., Ky.

"STRIKE FOR THE RIGHT."

Be bold, be firm, be strong, be true,
And dare to stand alone;
Strike for the right whate'er you do,
Though helpers there be none.

Strike for the right, and with clean hands,
Exalt the truth on high;
Thou'lt find warm sympathizing hearts
Among the passers by.

Those who have thought and felt and prayed,
Yet could not singly dare
The battle's brunt, but by thy side
Will every danger share.

Then learn this truth, the base of all,
That all are equal, so they fill
Their proper sphere and do God's will,
There is no other great or small.

There is a tear for all that die,
A mourner o'er the humblest grave,
But nations swell the funeral cry,
And triumph weeps above the brave.

Cowards are cruel, but the brave
Love mercy, and delight to save.

THE DEATH OF SLAVERY.

WILLIAM CULLEN BRYANT.

O thou great wrong that through the slow-paced years,
Didst hold thy millions fettered, and didst wield
The scourge that drove the laborer to the field,
And turn a stony gaze on human tears,
 Thy cruel reign is o'er ;
 Thy bondmen crouch no more
In terror at the menace of thine eye ;
For He who marks the bounds of guilty power,
Long suffering hath heard the captive's cry
And touched his shackles at the appointed hour,
And lo ! they fall, and he whose limbs they galled
Stands in his native manhood disenthralled.

A shout of joy from the redeemed is sent :
Ten thousand hamlets swell the hymn of thanks ;
Our rivers roll exulting and their banks
Send up hosannas to the firmament !
 Fields where the bondman's toil
 No more shall trench the soil,
Seem now to bask in a serener day ;
The meadow-birds sing sweeter, and the airs
Of heaven with more caressing softness play,
Welcoming man to liberty like theirs.
A glory clothes the land from sea to sea,
For the great land and all its coasts are free.

Within that land wert thou enthroned of late,
And they by whom the nation's laws were made,
And they who filled its judgment seats obeyed
Thy mandate, rigid as the will of fate.
 Fierce men at thy right hand
 With gesture of command,
Gave forth the word that none might dare gainsay ;
And grave and reverend ones who loved thee not
Shrank from thy presence, and in blank dismay
Choked down unuttered the rebellious thought,

THE COLORED ELDER.

While meaner cowards mingling with thy train,
Proved from the book of God thy right to reign.

Great as thou wert and feared from shore to shore,
The wrath of heaven o'ertook thee in thy pride :
Thou sitt'st a ghostly shadow : by thy side
Thy once strong arms hang nerveless evermore.
    And they who quailed but now
    Before thy lowering brow
Devote thy memory to scorn and shame,
And scoff at the pale powerless thing thou art,
And they who ruled in thy imperial name,
Subdued, and standing sullenly apart,
Scowled at the hands that overthrew thy reign
And shattered at a blow the prisoner's chain.

Well was thy doom deserved ; thou didst not spare
Life's tenderest ties, but cruelly didst part
Husband and wife, and from the mother's heart
Didst wrest her children, deaf to shriek and prayer ;
    Thy inner lair became
    The haunt of guilty shame ;
Thy lash dropped blood ; the murderer at thy side,
Showed his red hands, nor feared the vengeance due.
Thou didst sow earth with crimes, and far and wide,
A harvest of uncounted miseries grew
Until the measure of thy sins at last
Was full, and then the avenging bolt was cast !

Go now accursed of God, and take thy place
With hateful memories of the elder time,
With many a wasting plague, and nameless crime,
And bloody war that thinned the human race ;
    With the Black Death, whose way
    Through wailing cities lay,
Worship of Moloch, tyrannies that built
The Pyramids, and cruel deeds that taught
To avenge a fancied guilt by deeper guilt—
Death at the stake to them that held them not.

Lo! The foul phantoms, silent in the gloom
Of the flown ages, part to yield thee room.

I see the better years that hasten by
Carry thee back into the shadowy past,
Where, in the dusty spaces, void and vast,
The graves of those whom thou hast murdered lie.
  The slave-pen, through whose door
  Thy victims pass no more,
Is there, and there shall the grim block remain
At which the slave was sold; while at thy feet
Scourges and engines of restraint and pain
Moulder and rust by thine eternal seat.
There, mid the symbols that proclaim thy crimes,
 Dwell thou a warning to the coming times.
May, 1866.

WILL CARLETON'S FAMOUS MEMORIAL DAY POEM— "COVER THEM OVER."

Cover them over with beautiful flowers;
Deck them with garlands, these brothers of ours;
Lying so silent by night and by day,
Sleeping the years of their manhood away;
Years they had marked for the joys of the brave;
Years that must waste in the sloth of the grave.
All the bright laurels they fought to make bloom
Fell to the earth when they went to the tomb.
Give them the meed they have won in the past;
Give them the honors their merits forecast;

Give them the chaplets they won in the strife,
Give them the laurels they lost with their life.
Cover them over, yes, cover them over—
Parent, and husband, and brother, and lover:
Crown in your heart these dead heroes of ours,
And cover them over with beautiful flowers.

Cover the faces that motionless lie,
Shut from the blue of the glorious sky:
Faces once light with the smiles of the gay—
Faces now marred with the frown of decay.
Eyes that beamed friendship and love to your own;
Lips that sweet thoughts of affection made known;
Brows you have soothed in the day of distress;
Cheeks you have flushed by the tender caress;
Faces that brightened at war's stirring cry;
Faces that streamed when they bade you good-bye;
Faces that glowed in the battle's red flame,
Paling for naught, till the death angel came.
Cover them over—yes, cover them over—
Parent, and husband, and brother, and lover:
Kiss in your heart these dead heroes of ours,
And cover them over with beautiful flowers.

Cover the hands that are resting half-tried,
Crossed on the bosom or low by the side:
Hands to you, mother, in infancy thrown;
Hands that you, father, close hid in your own;
Hands where you, sister, when tried and dismayed,
Hung for protection, and counsel, and aid;
Hands that you, brother, for faithfulness knew;
Hands that you, wife, wrung in bitter adieu.
Bravely the cross of their country they bore;
Words of devotion they wrote with their gore;
Grandly they grasped for a garland of light,
Catching the mantle of death-darkened night.
Cover them over—yes, cover them over—
Parent, and husband, and brother, and lover:

Clasp in your hearts these dead heroes of ours,
And cover them over with beautiful flowers.

Cover the feet that, all weary and torn,
Hither by comrades were tenderly borne;
Feet that have trodden through love-lighted ways,
Near to your own, in the old happy days;
Feet that have pressed, in life's open morn,
Roses of pleasure and death's poison thorn.
Swiftly they rush to the help of the right,
Firmly they stood in the shock of the fight.
Ne'er shall the enemy's hurrying tramp
Summon them forth from their death-guarded camp;
Ne'er till Eternity's bugle shall sound,
Will they come out from their couch in the ground.
Cover them over—yes, cover them over—
Parent, and husband, and brother, and lover:
Rough were the paths of these heroes of ours—
Now cover them over with beautiful flowers.

Cover the hearts that have beaten so high,
Beaten with hopes that were born but to die;
Hearts that have burned in the heat of the fray;
Hearts that have yearned for the homes far away;
Hearts that beat high in the charge's loud tramp;
Hearts that low fell in the prison's foul damp.
Once they were swelling with courage and will,
Now they are lying all pulseless and still;
Once they were glowing with friendship and love,
Now the great souls have gone soaring above.
Bravely their blood to the nation they gave,
Then in her bosom they found them a grave.
Cover them over—yes, cover them over—
Parent, and husband, and brother, and lover:
Press to your hearts these dead heroes of ours,
And cover them over with beautiful flowers.

One there is, sleeping, in yonder low tomb,
Worthy the brightest of flowers that bloom.

Weakness o.' womanhood's life was her part;
Tenderly strong was her generous heart.
Bravely she stood by the sufferer's side,
Checking the pain and the life-bearing tide:
Fighting the swift-sweeping phantom of death,
Easing the dying man's fluttering breath.
Then when the strife that had nerved her was o'er,
Calmly she went to where wars are no more.
Voices have blessed her now silent and dumb;
Voices will bless her in long years to come.
Cover them over—yes, cover them over—
Blessings, like angels, around her shall hover:
Treasure the name of that sister of ours,
And cover them over with beautiful flowers.

Cover the thousands that sleep far away—
Sleep where their friends cannot find them to-day;
They who in mountain, and hillside, and dell,
Rest where they wearied, and lie where they fell.
Softly the grass-blade creeps round their repose;
Sweetly above them the wild flow'ret blows;
Zephyrs of freedom fly gently o'er head,
Whispering names for the patriot dead.
So in our minds we will name them once more,
So in our hearts we will cover them o'er;
Roses and lilies and violets blue
Bloom in our souls for the brave and the true.
Cover them over—yes, cover them over—
Parent, and husband, and brother, and lover,
Think of those far-away heroes of ours,
And cover them over with beautiful flowers.

When the long years have crept slowly away,
E'en to the dawn of earth's funeral day;
When at the Archangel's trumpet and tread
Rise up the faces and forms of the dead;
When the great world its last judgment awaits;
When the blue sky shall swing open its gates,

And our long columns march silently through,
Past the Great Captain for final review—
Then for the blood that has flowed for the right,
Crowns shall be given, untarnished and bright;
Then the glad ear of each war-martyred son,
Proudly shall hear the good judgment, " Well done."
Blessings for garlands shall cover them over—
Parent, and husband, and brother, and lover:
God will reward these dead heroes of ours,
And cover them over with beautiful flowers.

HOW SLEEP THE BRAVE!

How sleep the brave who sink to rest
By all their country's wishes blessed !
When spring, with dewy fingers cold,
Returns to deck their hallowed mould,
She there shall dress a sweeter sod
Than fancy's feet have ever trod.

By fairy hands their knell is rung,
By forms unseen their dirge is sung;
There honor comes, a pilgrim gray,
To bless the turf that wraps their clay;
And freedom shall awhile repair,
To dwell a weeping hermit there !

DECORATION DAY.

The muffled drum's sad roll has beat
The soldier's last tattoo;
No more on life's parade shall meet
The brave but fallen few.
On fame's eternal camping ground
Their silent tents are spread,
And glory guards with solemn round
The bivouac of the dead.

No rumor of the foe's advance
Now sweeps upon the wind;

No troubled thoughts at midnight haunt,
   Of loved ones left behind;
No vision of the morrow's strife
   The warrior's dream alarms;
Nor braying horn, nor screaming fife
   At dawn shall call to arms.

Their shivered swords are red with rust,
   Their plumed heads are bowed;
Their haughty banner trailed in dust
   Is now their martial shroud,
And plenteous funeral tears have washed
   The red stains from each brow,
And the proud forms by battle gashed
   Are freed from anguish now.

Now 'neath their parent turf they rest,
   Far from the gory field.
Borne to a Spartan mother's breast
   On many a bloody shield;
The sunshine of their native sky
   Smiles sadly on them here,
And hundred eyes and hearts watch by
   The soldier's sepulcher.

Rest on, embalmed and sainted dead,
   Dear as the blood ye gave!
No impious footsteps here shall tread
   The herbage of your grave;
Nor shall your glory be forgot
   While fame her record keeps,
Or honor points the hallowed spot
   Where valor proudly sleeps.

Yon faithful herald's blazoned stone
   With mournful pride shall tell,
When many a vanished age hath flown,
   The story how ye fell!

Nor wreck, nor change, nor winter's flight,
　　Nor time's remorseless doom
Shall mar one ray of glory's light
　　That guilds your deathless tomb.

THE BLUE AND THE GRAY.

By the flow of the inland river,
　　Whence the fleets of iron have fled,
Where the blades of grave-grass quiver,
　　Asleep are the ranks of the dead.
Under the sod and the dew,
　　Waiting the judgment day—
Under the one the Blue,
　　Under the other the Gray.

These in the robings of glory,
　　Those in the gloom of defeat,
All, with the battle blood gory,
　　In the dusk of eternity meet.
Under the sod and the dew
　　Waiting the judgment day—
Under the laurel the Blue,
　　Under the willow the Gray.

From the silence of sorrowful hours
　　The desolate mourners go,
Lovingly laden with flowers
　　Alike for the friend and the foe.
Under the sod and the dew
　　Waiting the judgment day—
Under the roses the Blue,
　　Under the lilies the Gray.

So with an equal splendor
　　The morning sun-rays fall,
With a touch impartially tender
　　On the blossoms blooming for all.

Under the sod and the dew
    Waiting the judgment day—
Broidered with gold the Blue,
    Mellowed with gold the Gray.

So when the summer calleth
    On forest and field of grain,
With an equal murmur falleth
    The cooling drip of the rain.
Under the sod and the dew
    Waiting the judgment day—
Wet with the rain the Blue,
    Wet with the rain the Gray.

Sadly, but not with upbraiding,
    The generous deed was done;
In the storm of the years that are fading
    No braver battle was won.
Under the sod and the dew
    Waiting the judgment day—
Under the blossoms the Blue,
    Under the garlands the Gray.

No more shall the war cry sever,
    Or the winding rivers be red—
They banish our anger forever
    When they laurel the graves of our dead.
Under the sod and the dew
    Waiting the judgment day—
Love and tears for the Blue,
    Tears and love for the Gray.

AN ANSWER TO THE "BLUE AND GRAY."

WRITTEN BY A LOYAL LADY.

The loyal Blue and the traitor Gray,
    Alike in the grave are sleeping.
Lying side by side in the sunlight's ray
    And under the storm cloud's weeping.

'Tis well to forgive the past,
　God giving us grace we may,
But never while life shall last
　Can we honor or love the Gray.

Our boys in Blue were loyal and true,
　For their God and their country dying;
With a grateful pride that ever is new
　We garland their graves where they're lying.
　　They were murdered by rebel bands,
　　　They fell in the fearful fray,
　　Guarding our flag from traitor's hands;
　　　We do not *love* the Gray.

We would not *hate* them, our hearts would fain
　Cast a vail o'er their shameful story—
It will not bring back our loyal slain,
　To recall their treason gory;
　　But barriers deep and wide,
　　　Divide the false from the true;
　　Shall treason and honor stand side by side.
　　　Is the Gray the peer of the Blue?

Answers each loyal heart to-day,
　They are peers and equals never;
No wreath on a traitor's grave we lay—
　Let shame be his weed forever.
　　Give love where love is due.
　　To the loyal all honor pay;
　　Love and honor belong to the Blue,
　　　But what do we owe the Gray?

We owe them three hundred thousand graves,
　Where the loved and lost are lying,
We owe them where'er our banner waves,
　Homes filled with tears and sighing.
　　Do they think that we forget our dead,
　　　Our boys who wore the Blue—
　　That because they sleep in the same cold bed
　　　We know not the false from the true?

Believe it not; where our *heroes* lie
  The very ground is holy;
His name who dared for the right to die
  Is sacred, however lowly;
    But honor the traitor Gray—
      Make it the peer of the Blue—
    One flower at the feet of treason lay?
      Never! while God is true.

THE NATION'S DEAD.

Four hundred thousand men—
  The brave, the good, the true—
In tangled wood, in mountain glen,
On battle plain, in prison pen,
  Lie dead for me and you!
Four hundred thousand of the brave
Have made our ransomed soil their grave
    For me and you!
Good friend, for me and you!

In many a fevered swamp,
  By many a black bayou,
In many a cold and frozen camp,
The weary sentinel ceased his tramp,
  And died for me and you!
From western plain to ocean tide
Are stretched the graves of those who died
    For me and you!
Good friend, for me and you!

On many a bloody plain
  Their ready swords they drew,
And poured their life-blood like the rain,
A home, a heritage to gain—
  To gain for me and you!
Our brothers mustered by our side,
They marched, they fought, and bravely died
    For me and you!
Good friend, for me and you!

Up many a fortress wall
  They charged—those boys in blue;
'Mid surging smoke and volley'd ball,
The bravest were the first to fall—
  To fall for me and you !
The noble men—the nation's pride—
Four hundred thousand men have died
      For me and you !
Good friend, for me and you !

In treason's prison-hold
  Their martyr spirits grew
To stature like the saints of old,
And 'mid dark agonies untold
  They starved for me and you !
The good, the patient, and the tried—
Four hundred thousand men have died
      For me and you !
Good friend, for me and you !

A debt we ne'er can pay
  To them is justly due,
And to the nation's latest day
Our children's children still shall say,
  "They died for me and you !"
Four hundred thousand of the brave
Made this, our ransomed soil, their grave,
      For me and you !
Good friend, for me and you !

SLEEP, COMRADES, SLEEP !

I.

Sleep, comrades, sleep ! The clinging rust
  Lies thick upon the blade,
And valor is obscured by lust
  Of money and of trade;
The fife is mute; no more the drum
  The drowsy camp alarms;

The piping times of peace have come,
And Pleasure spreads her charms.

II.

Sleep, comrades, sleep! The cannon's roar
  No longer fills the air;
The rifle volley routs no more
  The rebel from his lair.
Where once the beacon brightly shone,
  The sentry walked his round,
The crumbling headstone marks alone
  The consecrated ground.

III.

Sleep, comrades, sleep! The battle flag
  Is rotting on the staff,
And soon, perchance, the tattered rag
  Will waken but a laugh;
The peaceful plowshare cleaves the sod
  Once wet with War's red stain,
And fields that mighty armies trod
  Are starred with flowers again.

IV.

Sleep, comrades, sleep! Though soon forgot
  By some, while life endures,
Forget our loving hearts will not
  To keep their tryst with yours;
The general muster of the dead,
  Whate'er on earth betide,
Shall find us still by Glory led
  And marching by your side.

THE VETERAN'S REQUEST.

BY BAYARD TAYLOR.

I.

An old and crippled veteran to the war department came,
He sought the Chief who led him, on many a field of fame,
The Chief who shouted "Forward!" where'er his banner goes,
And bore its stars in triumph behind the flying foes.

II.

"Have you forgotten, General," the battered soldier cried,
"The day of eighteen hundred twelve, when I was at your
    side?
"Have you forgotten Johnson, that fought at Lundy's Lane?
'Tis true I'm old and pensioned, but I want to fight again."

III.

"Have I forgotten?" said the Chief; "my brave old soldier,
    No!
And here's the hand I gave you then, and let it tell you so;
But you have done your share, my friend; you're crippled, old,
    and gray,
And we have need of younger arms and fresher blood to-day."

IV.

"But, General," cried the veteran, a flush upon his brow,
"The very men who fought with us, they say, are traitors now;
They've torn the flag of Lundy's Lane, our old red, white, and
    blue,
And while a drop of blood is left, I'll show that drop is true.

V.

"I'm not so weak but I can strike, and I've a good old gun,
To get the range of traitors' hearts, and pick them, one by one;
Your minie-rifles and such arms it ain't worth while to try,
I couldn't get the hang of them, but I'll keep my powder dry."

VI.

"God bless you, comrade!" said the Chief—"God bless your
    loyal heart!
But younger men are in the field, and claim to have their part.

They'll plant our sacred banner in each rebellious town,
And woe, henceforth, to any hand that dares to pull it down."

VII.

"But, General!"—still persisting, the weeping veteran cried;
"I'm young enough to follow, so long as you're my guide;
And some, you know, must bite the dust, and that at least
 can I;
So, give the young ones place to fight, but me a place to die!

VIII.

"If they should fire on Pickens, let the colonel in command
Put me upon the rampart, with the flag-staff in my hand;
No odds how hot the cannon smoke, or how hot the shells may
 fly,
I'll hold the Stars and Stripes aloft, and hold them till I die.

IX.

"I'm ready, General, so you let a post to me be given,
Where Washington can see me, as he looks from highest
 Heaven,
And say to Putnam at his side, or, may be, General Wayne,
'There stands old Billy Johnson, that fought at Lundy's Lane.'

X.

"And when the fight is hottest, before the traitors fly,
When shell and ball are screeching, and bursting in the sky,
If any shot should hit me, and lay me on my face,
My soul would go to Washington's, and not to Arnold's place."

THE SOLDIER'S REPRIEVE.

"My Fred! I can't understand it,"
 And his voice it quivered with pain,
While the tears kept slowly dropping
 On his trembling hands like rain.
"For Fred was so brave and loyal,
 So true; but my eyes are dim,
And I cannot read the letter,
 The last I shall get from him.

Please read it, sir, while I listen—
  In fancy I see him—dead ;
My boy, shot down like a traitor,
  My noble, my brave boy, Fred !''

'' Dear father,'' so ran the letter,
  '' To morrow when twilight creeps
Along the hill to the churchyard,
  O'er the grave where mother sleeps,
When the dusky shadows gather,
  They'll lay your boy in his grave,
For nearly betraying the country
  He would give his life to save.
And, father, I tell you truly,
  With almost my latest breath,
That your boy is not a traitor,
  Though he dies a traitor's death.

'' You remember Bennie Wilson ?
  He's suffered a deal of pain,
He was only *that* day ordered
  Back into the ranks again.
I carried all of his luggage,
  With mine on the march that day ;
I gave him my arm to lean on,
  Else he had dropped by the way.
'Twas Bennie's turn to be sentry ;
  But I took his place, and I—
Father, I dropped asleep, and now
  I must die as traitor's die. ''

'' The Colonel is kind and thoughtful,
  He has done the best he can,
And they will not bind or blind me—
  I shall meet death like a man.
Kiss little Blossom ; but, father,
  Need you tell her how I fall ?''—
A sob from the shadowed corner—
  Yes, Blossom had heard it all.

As she kissed the precious letter,
　She said, with faltering breath :
" Our Fred was never a traitor,
　Though he dies a traitor's death."

And a little sun-brown maiden,
　In a shabby, time-worn dress,
Took her seat a half hour later
　In the crowded night-express.
The conductor heard her story
　As he held her dimpled hand,
And sighed for the sad hearts breaking
　All over the troubled land,
He tenderly wiped the tear drops
　From the blue eyes brimming o'er,
And guarded her footsteps safely
　Till she reached the White House door.

The President sat at his writing;
　But the eyes were kind and mild
That turned with a look of wonder
　On the little shy faced child.
And he read Fred's farewell letter,
　With a look of sad regret,
" 'Tis a brave, young life," he murmured,
　" And his country needs him yet,
From an honored place in battle
　He shall bid the world good-by,
If that brave young life is needed,
　He shall die as heroes die."
　　—[*Rose Hartwick Thorpe, in the Detroit Free Press.*

"FEAR NOT YE."

In the sun, and moon, and stars,
   Signs and wonders there shall be;
Earth shall quake with inward wars,
   Nations with perplexity.

Soon shall ocean's hoary deep,
   Tossed with stronger tempests, rise;
Wilder storms the mountains sweep,
   Louder thunders rock the skies.

Dread alarms shall shake the proud,
   Pale amazement, restless fear;
And, amid the thunder-cloud,
   Shall the Judge of men appear.

But though from his awful face,
   Heaven shall fade, and earth shall fly.
Fear not ye, his chosen race,
   Your redemption draweth nigh.

"WELL DONE."

" When the long years have rolled slowly away,
E'en to the dawn of earth's funeral day,
When at the Archangel's trumpet and tread,
Rise up the faces and forms of the dead ;
When the great world its last judgment awaits,
When the blue sky shall swing open the gates,
And our long columns march silently through,
Past the great Captain for final review,
Then from the blood that has flowed for the right
Crowns shall spring upward, untarnished and bright.
Then the glad ears of each war-martyred son
Proudly shall hear the glad tidings —" Well done."

GALESBURG, KNOX CO., ILL., June 21, 1888.
Rev. John H. Aughey, Mountain Top, Luzerne Co., Pa.:
DEAR SIR—Yours of recent date was received in
due course of mail. I am glad to hear from you.
I was at a soldiers' reunion two years ago, and while
there met our old friend and fellow-prisoner, Alexander Spear, of Ellisville, Fulton Co., Ill. I was
very glad to meet him, as we had not met before
since we were paroled. I have forgotten whether I
told you what General Jordan said to me when he
came into prison the morning of your escape. He
came up to me as I stood on the floor. He said,
" How did that preacher get away? What do you
know about his escape?" I did as the rest of the
prisoners did. I denied knowing anything about
your escape, either as to the time of it, or the man-

ner by which it was effected. He said, "God Almighty helped him get away, for no living white man could." After studying a minute he said, "Did you render him any aid in liberating him from the chain?" I replied, "I am not God Almighty." He then rejoined the officers. They sent out two companies of cavalry with blood-hounds, with strict orders to leave you wherever they found you.

Please present my kind regards to your wife and family. I think of you and your wife often. You, as you were standing in the center of Tupelo prison, declaring that you will run past the guards and take the risk of making your escape, or die in the attempt, which you said you would prefer to the certainty of death on the scaffold in a few days; and her, overwhelmed with sorrow at your prolonged absence. I am now very busy at work for the city.

How terrible is war. As my mind reverts to the past, I almost feel like saying with Cowper—

> "Arms through the vanity and brainless rage
> Of those that bear them, in whatever cause,
> Seem most at variance with all moral good,
> And incompatible with all serious thought."

An offensive war is always wrong. A war in defense of country and liberty alone is justifiable. Please answer at your earliest convenience.

Your sincere friend and fellow-prisoner,

JOHN J. DeGRUMMOND.

Late Private Co. C, 47th Regt., Ill. Vol. Inf

WHILE THE YOUNG PATRIOT WAS DRINKING SHE DREW A PISTOL
AND IMMEDIATELY SHOT HIM.

P. S.—Howell Trogdon, our fellow-prisoner at
'Tupelo, wrote me that when you were pastor of the
Fairmount church in Saint Louis, Mo., he lived near
you, and saw you almost every day. Trogdon held
the guard, seated on the threshold of our prison, in
conversation while you made your final escape.

Can you give me Trogdon's address? I have some
good news to write him. Yours truly,

JOHN J. DeGRUMMOND.

THE MUSTERING.

BY MRS. SARAH S. SOCWELL.

Ho! Freemen of the loyal North, come to the rescue now—
See! basely trampled in the dust, our glorious flag lies low!
That flag which led our fathers on to victory and fame—
Will ye stand tamely by and see that banner brought to shame?

No! like the rushing tempest's roar I hear the answer come,
From princely hall, from homestead fair, from lowly cottage
    home;
And, borne on every breeze, I hear, from mountain, plain, and
    glen,
The stirring drum and bugle call, and tramp of armed men.

The cry hath reached the lake-gemmed wilds and rugged shores
    of Maine—
The woodman drops his gleaming ax—the fisher leaves his
    seine;
And from New Hampshire's hills and vales pours down a gal-
    lant band,
Who, firm as their own granite rocks, beneath our flag will
    stand.

Old Massachusetts gladly sends the sons whose noble sires
At Lexington and Bunker Hill first kindled Freedom's fires;
And from Connecticut's fair vales—Rhode Island's sea-girt
    shore,
Comes forth a hardy band to strike for Liberty once more.

Vermont's green mountain peaks have caught spirit-stirring
    tones;
And prompt and dauntless, as of yore, pour down her sturdy
    sons;
New York remembers Arnold now, when traitors claim the
    sway,
And her brave sons by thousands come to mingle in the fray.

Staid Pennsylvania rises, majestic in her might,
And like a solid bulwark turns from Freedom's soil the fight;
New Jersey, with her gallant Blues, is promptly in the field—
The soil made sacred with her blood, she'll be the last to yield.

And Delaware keeps, still unquenched, her sacred altar fires,
Her children still remember the lessons of their sires.
The Maryland line has not yet lost its ancient patriot pride,
Though treason, with unblushing front, holds back the swelling
    tide.

And from the young, but mighty West, comes back a quick
    reply—
"Beneath our flag we'll conquer, or beneath it we will die;"
Along her noble rivers, o'er all her verdant plains,
I hear the drum's deep clangor, the march of armed trains.

The Freedom-loving Germans, remembering Fatherland,
For Liberty and Union have taken valiant stand;
And Erin's quivering harpstrings thrill with a wild refrain,
As forth her sturdy children come to swell the thronging train.

God bless the noble patriots, who are gathering in their might,
The Lord of Hosts shall guard them in Freedom's holy fight;
Ne'er may the gleaming sword be sheathed till treason finds
    its grave,
And over our whole country our good old flag shall wave.
    La Prairie Center, Marshall Co., Illinois.

BATTLE OF CORINTH.

Generals Price and Van Dorn, having been defeated at Iuka, Miss., by Gen. Rosecrans, resolved to avenge themselves of their adversary by his utter annihilation at Corinth. But they reckoned without their host. On Oct. 1st, 2d, and 3d, 1862, the sanguinary battle of Corinth was fought. The Confederates, although outnumbering the Nationals more than two to one, suffered an overwhelming defeat, losing in killed, officers and men, one thousand four hundred and twenty three. Their wounded amounted to nearly six thousand. They lost in prisoners, in the battle and subsequent pursuit, two thousand two hundred and forty-eight. Fourteen stand of colors, two pieces of artillery, three thousand three hundred stand of arms, four thousand five hundred rounds of ammunition, together with a large quantity of accoutrements, fell into the hands of the victors. Thus Rust, Price, Villipigue, Van Dorn, and Lovell were beaten with heavy loss by a force one half their number. These rebels, however, fought like brave men, long and well. Loyal history must accord to the rebel the acknowledgment of the bravery which he displayed, while it abhors his treason. The defeated rebel army returned to Tupelo, broken and dispirited, to recuperate and re-organize for another attempt to defeat the patriot army. General Hackleman fell in this battle, lamented by the whole army. General Oglesby was severely (and at the time thought to be fatally) wounded. And many brave and loyal men surrendered life in defence of their country's imperiled integrity on this bloody field.

BATTLE OF TUPELO.

The battle of Tupelo was one of the most important battles of the civil war fought in the Southwest. Gen. W. T. Sherman was attempting to reach the strategic stronghold of Atlanta. Between Chattanooga and Atlanta he must drive before him or destroy the efficient and disciplined army of that able commander, Gen. Jo. Johnston, who, carrying out the Fabian policy, endeavored to delay his adversary till he could throw upon his line of communication a cavalry force sufficient to sever it, and thus cut him off from his base of supplies. This would make a retreat compulsory. Between Nashville and the point where Sherman was slowly driving the Confederate army, by flanking its positions successively, there was but a single track railroad upon which supplies might be brought. Wheeler, with a considerable force of cavalry, was endeavoring to destroy this road, confident of success as soon as he could be reinforced by Forrest, Chalmers, Rhoddy, Kirby, Smith, and Baxter, who were in Tupelo. To avoid this disastrous result, Sherman directed Gen. Washburn to send Gen. S. D. Sturgis with a large force to attack Forrest. The Rebels, learning that this force was approaching, moved out to meet it. A battle ensued, June 10th, 1864, at Tishomingo Creek, near Guntown.

Sturgis proved incompetent. He suffered Forrest and Kirby Smith to succeed by a well executed flank movement in reaching the rear of his army, where his wagons were parked, and in destroying or capturing all his supplies, including the caissons containing his ammunition. A retreat was ordered, which soon became a pitiable and disastrous rout. *Sauve qui peut* became the watchword, as, panic-stricken and helpless because of the loss of their commissariat and ammunition, they fled before the cruel and victorious rebel hordes, who shot down without mercy or compunction all whom they overtook. The pursuit of this dispersed army, these scattered fugitives, was continued as long as any remained alive. Guerrillas with blood-hounds joined in the hunt. As a squad of these panting fugitives passed through Ripley, the women from their windows and doors shot them as they passed along. A young soldier begged a young lady who was seated on a veranda to give him a glass of water, as he was perishing from thirst. She walked into the house, brought a glass of water, and while this young patriot was drinking she drew a pistol and immediately shot him. Thus perished Ralph Erskine, of near Golconda, Pope Co., Ill. Two thousand two hundred perished thus cruelly at the hands of their merciless fellow countrymen. This savage and protracted pursuit occupied time which Sherman was improving in making progress towards Atlanta, which he was destined to reach if his communication with his base of supplies could be kept open. The persistency with which the rebels followed up their success exhausted them, and time was required for recuperation. At this junction Gen. A. J. Smith arrived at Memphis from Red River, with the troops of the Army of the Tennessee, which Gen. Sherman had sent to reinforce Banks, whom they rendered very efficient service. Smith was directed by Sherman immediately to move upon the Confederates at Tupelo. This he did, Gen. Grant says, with the promptness and effect which has characterized his whole military career. On the 14th of July, 1864, he met the enemy at Tupelo, and gained a glorious victory, whipping the enemy badly and routing him completely, after three days' hard fighting, yet losing few compared with the loss of the enemy. He thus contributed materially to the grand success achieved by Sherman, who was, by the utter overthrow of the rebel cavalry commanders at Tupelo, enabled to keep open communication with his depot of supplies at Nashville, and thus the defeat of Sturgis and the decisive victory of Smith rendered possible the capture of Atlanta, and all the victories that followed in its train.

When Gen. A. J. Smith had accomplished the object of his expedition, he returned to Memphis, remembering to chastise the rebels and guerrillas by the way who had so atrociously maltreated Sturgis' defeated troops in their disastrous retreat. The inglorious defeat of Sturgis and the decisive victory of Smith both inured to the salvation of Sherman, the declarative glory of God, and the utter subversion of rebellion. In the battle of Tupelo, including Guntown or Tishomingo Creek, the Federals lost in killed, wounded, and captured, more than eleven thousand men, but the results achieved more than compensated this loss.

The battle of Tupelo stands in the same relation to the capture of Atlanta, and the triumphant march of Sherman to the sea, that the battle of Oriskany does to the capture of Burgoyne. *Vide* Official Report of Lieut.-General Ulysses S. Grant, 1864—1865.

Paoli, Orange Co., Ind.

"I'LL WHIP THE STORY OUT OF HIM."

I GAVE HIM A PRESENT OF FIFTY DOLLARS IN GOLD.

THE OCTOROON, THOMAS GRIMKE.

" With peaceful mind thy path of duty run;
God nothing does, nor suffers to be done,
But what thou wouldst thyself, if thou couldst see
Through all events of things as well as he."

Thomas Grimké was one of those who were guarding my house when attacked, as recorded on page 62 of this volume. In the summer of 1853 I traveled by stage from Holly Springs, Miss., to Grenada, in the same state. In order to better observe the scenery through which we were passing, I asked and obtained permission to ride with the driver. A planter who resided near Grenada sat on one side of the driver, and I was invited to be seated between them. Behind us, on the stage, lay a manacled slave. Agony was depicted upon his countenance. It seemed to be the pangs of bitter disappointment rather than of pain, though his position was apparently a very uneasy one. Both hands and feet were fettered. I found the planter, Dr. Bailie Peyton, a very loquacious gentleman. After we had established an acquaintance I said casually, casting a backward glance, " Is this your boy ? " (Male slaves are called boys until they are forty or forty-five years old, after which they are called uncle.)

" Yes," said the doctor, " and he's a troublesome one."

" What has he done? "

" This makes ten times that he has run away, and it has cost me five hundred dollars to catch him. I have sworn to give him one thousand lashes, well laid on, in four installments, when I get him home."

"Why, that will kill him, won't it?"

"I don't care if it does."

"Why, he's worth fifteen hundred dollars."

"Fifteen hundred! I wouldn't take any man's three thousand for him. He's a splendid overseer, and he has no bad habits except running away."

"Doctor, what induces him to run away."

"Well, parson, ain't you a parson?"

"Yes, sir."

"Well, pardon me for making use of some pretty strong expletives in your presence. Thinking of the trouble and expense Le Roy has put me to is very provoking. Parson, I think he has some high notions about freedom. My aunt, Annetta Peyton, took quite a fancy to Le Roy, and, being a religious old maid, she took it into her head (her heart she always said) to violate our state laws, and teach him to read and write. It's a whim of hers that he looks like the Peytons, and isn't any common nigger. This is what it ends in. Since her death he has been continually running away."

"Where did you find him this time?"

"Near Bowling Green, Ky. He was heading straight for Canada. I hired Derrick Louray, with his famous nigger dogs, and Barley Bird, with his imported Cuban blood-hounds. I hired them when his track was fresh, and they were out a month, and hunted all over Grenada, Yalobusha, and Panola counties. They scoured the country a whole month, and came back wofully crestfallen. They both swore that it was the first time they had failed to bring back the nigger dead or alive. After this, this slave will work with a ball and chain attached to his ankle, and under a vigilant overseer; that is, if he stands the thousand lashes."

"Doctor, it would be merciful to remit a part of the penalty."

"Why, parson, would you want me to swear to a lie? I've sworn to give him a thousand, well laid on, and he'll get them, if he dies at the post."

"Some oaths are more honored in the breach than in the observance."

"Parson, you may rest assured this one will not be honored in the breach, and I may order the overseer to carry one for every ten, so that there will not be any mistake about the thousand."

"He seems to be as white as either you or I?"

"Yes, he's an octoroon. I think that accounts for his remarkable success in evading the hounds, and getting so far north. I think he passed himself off for a white man, and with his glib tongue imposed upon the white people, and got lodging, and so traveled north. He was working in Bowling Green as a white porter in a grocery. His employer saw a description of him as a runaway slave in the *Memphis Eagle and Enquirer*, and his suspicion being aroused, in order to secure the reward, he wrote me.

"As soon as I received his letter I went up post-haste, and sure enough found that it was Le Roy. His story was that he was a stevedore, lived in Mobile, Alabama, and was on his way to visit friends in Cincinnati, Ohio, and having lost his pocket-book at the hands of a pick-pocket he was compelled to work awhile to make up the loss. I'm thinking that it will be some considerable time before he visits his friends in Cincinnati. I have no doubt that every fugitive slave has friends in Cincinnati. I'll whip the story out of him when I get him home, and find out if any villain knowingly helped him on his way toward the polar star. And if any one did, woe to him. His abolition carcass will soon be filled with more lead than it can easily tote. I bought a wife for him that he took a fancy to, of Senator Washington, my neighbor. She, like himself, is an octoroon. However, I sold her last year to General Jo. Jefferson, of Grenada. I hated to sell her from her husband, but the General wanted a woman. He's a lustful old fellow, and I got a cool $3,000 for her. My stars! how mad Leroy was. He acted as though he wanted to kill somebody for awhile, and then I feared he'd commit suicide by slow starvation. He has never been the same man since. If I did get a pretty good price for the girl, I came near losing Le Roy by it, and so did not make much in the long run. The boy became discontented, and my other niggers seemed to sympathize with him, and I overheard them saying that I would never have any luck. Things did go wrong. I think

HOW THE DARKIES SHOUTED.

they tried to make their prophecies come true. The cotton crop turned out poorly, and corn was almost a failure. Some of my best working mules were killed by buffalo gnats in the Taccaleeche swamp.

"I tied Le Roy up and gave him two hundred lashes on the bare back, thinking I would whip the sulks out of him. Then he ran away, and it has cost fearfully to hire hounds and to go all the way up to Bowling Green, Ky., after him, and to pay the large reward I offered for his recovery. A general gloom has settled down upon my family, and upon the whole plantation. I have had the devil to pay all around. I sometimes wish that I had not sold Dilsie, but she was my property and I had the right to dispose of her to whomever I chose. Had I known what was to follow from the meanness and superstition of my hands, as a matter of policy I should have declined the $3,000 and kept Dilsie. Dilsie had a baby, blue-eyed and light-haired. She called her Minnie. She is three years old. I sold her last week to Major Madison, of Grenada, for $500. Girl babies that are white and pretty bring a fearful price in this neck of woods. She will bring the Major $3,000 if he wishes to sell her when she is fourteen years old."

"Fourteen, Doctor, that is quite a high price for one so young."

"Parson, I have known them to be used at twelve."

"But is it quite right to traffic in female virtue?"

"A slave has no rights that a white man is bound to respect. This is the view of the South, and it is the doctrine of the Bible, too. I heard Parson Angus Johnson, of Water Valley, preach a sermon on the duties of slaves. He told us that it was their duty to obey in all things their masters, and that if in chastising a slave his master killed him, according to the Bible he ought not to be punished, because he is his money. Oh! he gave us some mighty good doctrine.

"I am not a Christian, far from it, but I have some respect for a religion that teaches such wholesome doctrine, and I will help support any minister that preaches like Parson Johnson. I did once order my overseer to give a girl a hundred lashes. She was *enciente* and the fright and pain brought on premature labor, and she died the next day. I felt very bad. If I had been a murderer I could not have felt worse for awhile. But as providence would have it, though I seldom attend church, I went the next Sabbath. I wanted to hear what hope there was in the gospel for such a great sinner as I felt myself to be. There was a burden on my soul that I felt I must get rid of or die. When I heard the parson say that God had ordained slavery, and that slaves must obey their masters, in all things, I felt better, and when he said the Bible tells us if a man smite his servant or his maid with a rod and he die under his hand, he shall not be punished, for he is his money, I received that as a special message from

heaven addressed to myself. My conscience was quieted and I returned home a happier man. Parson
Johnson had heard of Dinah's death and the cause of
it, and he preached a special sermon to fit the case. I
do not remember the text, but I think it was the usual
text against the abolitionists, 'Cursed be Canaan, a
servant of servants shall he be for ever and ever, amen;
and whosoever findeth him shall enslave him.' Dinah
was worth $1,500. She was a good field hand. The
loss of the money I can stand. The thought that I
was a murderer was killing me, but the gospel, as
dispensed by Parson Johnson, healed that trouble, as
the parson said, there is a balm in Gilead to heal the
wounded and troubled conscience. He further said
that Christ and his apostles approved the slavery that
existed in their day, when the power of life and death
was vested in the master, and that they required slaves
to be obedient, not only to the good and gentle, but
also to the froward. When beaten they were to take
it patiently, they were not even to answer again or
to talk back. All power, according to the Bible, was
vested in the master; submission in all things was
the duty of the slave. The parson said the abolitionists of the North said, for we don't allow any in the
South, by way of argument against slavery, that
some of our slaves were white and that many of them
were our own children. In Christ's day, he replied,
all the slaves were of the same color as their masters
and many of them were their master's children, and
Christ and his apostles did not disapprove it for that

reason. Ah! my friend, the parson is a powerful preacher. He preaches the gospel that suits me. I subscribed $100 to his salary the next day. Before he left my house—for he dined with me that day—I gave him a present of fifty dollars in gold, and assured . him he should never be destitute of a true friend while I lived. He preaches a gospel that makes a man feel good and happy from the bottom of his heart; he feels like thanking God for such a gospel. If our slaves had this gospel preached to them, and they would receive it, they would be far less discontented."

At this moment the wheels of a heavily laden wagon collided with the wheels of our coach. We soon after reached a relay house, when the driver discovered that one of the wheels of the coach was injured by the collision and needed repair. This occasioned a delay of two hours. The passengers sauntered hither and yonder at will. Le Roy was carried into the yard in the rear of the relay house and laid upon a plat of ground near the palings.

After the lapse of an hour I approached him. From my look of compassion and from my conversation with his master, he was led to hope that I might be a friend to him in this hour of sorest need. As I drew near he said:

"Master, for the love of God bring me some water."

I supplied his urgent need from a pump hard by. His next question:

MOVED OVER THE COUNTRY WITH FIRE AND ROPE.

"Master, where was you born?"

"In New Hartford, near Utica, N. Y."

"Is that in the North?"

"Yes."

"Master, I'm in great distress."

"Do you suffer much pain?"

"Some in body, but more in mind."

"What troubles your mind?"

"Unless I can get away before master gets me home he will murder me, for there's murder in his eye and in his heart."

Agony was depicted upon his countenance, and his voice quivered with emotion. I left him, and walked to and fro in a grove of Norway spruce a short distance from the hotel. I reflected thus: This man has a wife and child, though bereft of them for the present. I have no family. He is doomed to a cruel death, for he cannot survive a thousand lashes laid on by one who is prompted by wrath and hatred and malice. Is it my duty to risk my life to save his? These passages occurred to my mind: "Remember those that are in bonds as bound with them," and "He that saveth his life shall lose it." My duty in the premises seemed plain. I returned and said:

"Le Roy, what can I do to save you?"

"Master, you can get me a file. My wrists are larger than my hands. I can slip the handcuffs off at any time, and having a file I can soon rid my ankles of the chain, and I can without much difficulty travel with the bands on my ankles."

"If I help you at the risk of my life will you betray me?"

"Never, so help me God.

"If you are overtaken and caught by the hounds can they compel you by whipping to tell who helped you?"

"I will die at the post before I would tell on you or any one who helps me."

"Well, I will run the awful risk. I will get you a file and will assist you all I can."

"When we reach Grenada it will be night. Master will lodge at the Grenada House till morning. You can get the file at a hardware store in the city, and pass it to me in some way   I will be on the lookout."

I left Le Roy to his meditations. When we entered the coach I noticed Le Roy's face beaming with a new-born hope. We reached Grenada at seven o'clock. After supper I visited a hardware store and made a few purchases, and managed to secrete a file on my person. I feared to purchase one. At another store I purchased a ball of twine. Dr. Peyton and I registered together, and at his request were assigned to the same room. Le Roy was carried by two stalwart colored servants to an unfurnished room in the second story, the Doctor and I accompanying them. The Doctor locked the door and put the key in his pocket. I obtained reluctant leave of the Doctor to procure some corn bread and meat for Le Roy. I went to the kitchen and bought

the food from one of the servants. I asked the
Doctor to accompany me to the room. He handed
me the key, saying that he must visit the barber. I
procured a lamp, and going to Le Roy's dark, dismal, little room, gave him the food, together with
the file and twine.

I told him I dared not purchase a rope, and knew
not how he could descend from the window of his
room to the ground, as the twine was not strong
enough to bear his weight. He replied:

"My wife is at General Jefferson's. Call there.
She will answer the bell. Tell her to bring a rope
and come under the window of this room with it at
midnight, that I will let down the twine, she can tie
the rope to it, and I can get down in that way."

I called at General Jefferson's at nine o'clock. An
octoroon came to the door. Said I:

"What is your name?"

She replied, "Dilsie."

"Do you know Dr. Peyton's Le Roy?"

"He is my husband."

I gave her her husband's message. She promised
compliance. I had told Le Roy that if he could
reach Ripley, Miss., to inquire for Mr. Faulkner,
who would render him all possible aid, and would
send me any information he might have for me. I
returned to the hotel at half past ten. I asked Dr.
Peyton to visit Le Roy to see that he was still there.
We did so, and found him as we had left him. The
Doctor assured him that he would get the city

whipper to give him the first installment of the thousand lashes bright and early in the morning, before starting for home. Le Roy said:

"Master, please be merciful."

"You do not deserve mercy," rejoined the Doctor.

We then returned to our room and retired. We did not wake till half past seven in the morning. As we were dressing we heard a great tumult in the hotel. Presently the landlord knocked loudly at our door. Upon being admitted he said:

"Doctor, your nigger absconded in the night, a rope, apparently a bed-rope, hangs dangling from the window of his room, the only clew as yet as to the manner of his escape. Who furnished the rope or aided him in getting rid of his irons is as yet a mystery. I have given the alarm in the city and the authorities are on the alert and your slave will doubtless soon be brought in."

The doctor lost all control of his temper and swore terribly. He started a messenger off for Barley Bird, and his imported Cuban blood-hounds, ordering him to make all possible haste. He declared with a terrible oath that when caught he would tie Le Roy up by the thumbs and administer the thousand lashes at once. He closely scrutinized the room and the yard below. He secured the rope by which the descent had been made. He found the door of the room locked as when he had left it. An air of impenetrable mystery surrounded the whole affair. The servants at the hotel professed profound ignorance of the

matter. The night had been very dark. It was the
dark of the moon and lowering clouds had obscured
the starlight. One of the guests reported that having occasion to go out near midnight he encountered
a colored woman not far from the ground underneath
the window whence Le Roy had escaped. He asked
her who she was and what she was doing out there at
so late an hour. She replied that she was a cham-
bermaid and that she was waiting upon the sick lady
in room No. 30, and that she was out in her service.
The servants were all required to put in an appearance in the dining-room, but the investigation elicited
no information. Barley Bird arrived with his hounds
but could not get them to scent Le Roy's track. Many
colored persons had visited the yard, and when the
hounds found a track it would terminate on the steps
or lead into the kitchen or dining-room. All Grenada
was on the *qui vive*. After a few visits to the bar the
doctor became furious and reckless. He offered $500
for the arrest of the fugitive. Soon eight companies,
each with a pack of blood-hounds, were scouring the
country near and far in search of the fugitive, each
bent on securing the reward. They visited General
Jefferson's mansion, but the general positively declared that Dilsie had not left his premises during
the night, of this he was absolutely certain. A thorough search was instituted. At fifteen minutes of
twelve Dilsie had quietly and unperceived slipped out
of the house, leaving the general asleep, and in half
an hour she had accomplished the dangerous task.

She secreted Le Roy in the chicken-coop, in a box underneath a lot of straw on which two hens were incubating, one at each end of the box. It was a difficult feat to get under the straw without disturbing the fowls, but it was nevertheless accomplished by the dexterous aid of this devoted woman. The baying of the hounds and the shouting and yelling of the infuriated pursuers made the general's premises a perfect pandemonium for the space of two hours. They were loth to leave the place, and remained till every recess and crevice capable of sheltering a human being had been examined. Descrying the chicken-coop they sent a colored boy into it, and bade him toss up the straw in the box, but the disturbed hens pecked and squawked furiously. The boy thrust his arm down into the straw, when one of the hens pecked him in the eye, causing him to beat a hasty retreat. The crowd ordered him to return to the search. He did so, thrusting his arm down at various points, but apparently made no discovery. He came out declaring:

"Dat box am empty ob eberyting but straw an' fitin' hens."

His hand had come in contact with the face and limbs of Le Roy. He certainly knew that the fugitive was in that box, but young as he was he kept his own counsel. He was a quadroon twelve years old, and a special favorite of Dilsie's. That same evening he approached Dilsie and quietly said:

"Dilsie, you's been good to me, an' I b'leve dat

it's right to do good to dem what duz good to you, so
I saved yer husband's life fer you."

Dilsie looked up in alarm and said, "Why, Sar-
nem, what do you mean?"

"Oh," said he, "I node Roy was in dat box in de
chicken-coop, 'cause why, I feeled um, but duz yer
tink ize gwine ter tell an' let dem dogs kill um?
No, sur, I'd dide fust. I give Roy's ear a good pull·
to let him no I node he wuz dar, an' needn't be
afeard ob me a tellin'. Now, Aunt Dilsie, give me a
cooky."

"Yes, you shall have a dozen."

"O, glory! duz you mean it?"

"Yes, I do, and I'll trust you to help me to save
Roy."

"Yes, I will, you may 'pend on me."

It is only necessary to say further that Le Roy was
concealed for a month on the general's premises, till
the search for him was abandoned. He then made
his way to Ripley, was received by friends who informed him of my whereabouts. He visited me. I
advanced him money, and passing himself for a white
man (he was white) he purchased some land near
Tuscumbia, Alabama. With great difficulty and risk
I succeeded in abducting his wife and child. On his
land he lived happily with them, securing the respect
of his neighbors and the esteem of his brethren in
the church, of which himself and wife became members. When I removed to Choctaw county he sold
out his farm, and purchasing a few acres of land in

this county, he located near me. He now lives near Los Angeles, California. He has become wealthy, and he has given his children a good education. He has six children, three boys and three girls. One of his sons (named for me) is a lawyer, one a physician. One daughter, Minnie, is married. Her husband is a state senator. Le Roy was a half brother of Dr. Bailie Peyton. His mother, though white, was a slave and the mistress of the doctor's father. Such is slavery in itself. Is it any wonder that Thomas Grimké expressed a willingness to serve me to the extent of his ability and at the risk of his life. Le Roy assumed this name by my direction to conceal his identity. He intends, if his life is spared, to visit me next spring. The above episode is true, except a change of names in some instances.

Dallas, Marshall County, West Virginia.

THE ANIMAL PERSISTENTLY REFUSED TO STEP OVER HIS PROSTRATE BODY.

THE SOUTHERN UNIONIST.

" Faithful found
Among the faithless, faithful he
Among innumerable false, unmoved,
Unshaken, unseduced, unterrified
His loyalty he kept, his love, his zeal,
Nor numbers nor example with him wrought
To swerve from truth, or change his constant mind
Though single."

PRISONER'S HOPE.

TRAMP! TRAMP! TRAMP!

In the prison cell I sit,
  Thinking, mother dear, of you,
And our bright and happy home so far away;
  And the tears, they fill my eyes,
Spite of all that I can do,
  Tho' I try to cheer my comrades, and be gay.

Tramp! tramp! tramp! the boys are marching,
  Cheer up, comrades, they will come,
And beneath the starry flag
  We shall breathe the air again,
Of the free land in our own beloved home.

In the battle front we stood,
  When their fiercest charge they made,
And they swept us off a hundred men or more,
  But before we reach'd their lines,
They were beaten back dismayed,
  And we heard the cry of vict'ry o'er and o'er.
    Tramp! tramp! tramp! etc.

So within the prison cell,
  We are waiting for the day,
That shall come to open wide the iron door;
  And the hollow eye grows bright,
And the poor heart almost gay,
  As we think of seeing home and friends once more.
    Tramp! tramp! tramp! etc.

JOHN BROWN, OF OSAWATOMIE, KANSAS.

John Brown's body lies mouldering in the grave,
While weep the sons of bondage whom he ventured all to
save.
And though he lost his life in struggling for the slave.
His soul is marching on.

CHORUS—Glory, Hallelujah !

John Brown was a hero, undaunted, true, and brave.
Kansas knew his valor when he fought her rights to save,
And though the grass grows green above his northern grave,
His soul is marching on.

CHORUS—Glory, Hallelujah !

He captured Harper's Ferry, with his nineteen men so few,
And frightened old Virginia till she trembled through and
through.
They hung him for a traitor—themselves a traitor crew,
But his soul is marching on.

CHORUS—Glory, Hallelujah !

The conflict that he heralded, he looks from heaven to view,
On the army of the Union, with her flag red, white, and blue
And heaven shall ring with anthems o'er the deeds we mean
to do,
As we go marching on.

CHORUS—Glory, Hallelujah !

O soldiers of Columbia, then strike, while strike you may
The death-blow of oppression in this better time and way.
And the dawn of old John Brown will brighten into day,
As we go marching on.

CHORUS—Glory, Hallelujah !

New Athens, Harrison Co., Ohio.

MARCHING THROUGH GEORGIA.

Bring the good old bugle, boys! we'll sing another song—
Sing it with a spirit that will start the world along—
Sing it as we used to sing it, fifty thousand strong,
   While we were marching through Georgia.

     Hurrah! hurrah! we bring the Jubilee!
     Hurrah! hurrah! the flag that makes you free!
     So we sang the chorus from Atlanta to the sea,
       While we were marching through Georgia.

How the darkeys shouted when they heard the joyful sound!
How the turkeys gobbled which our commissary found!
How the sweet potatoes even started from the ground,
   While we were marching through Georgia.

       Hurrah! hurrah! etc.

Yes, and there were Union men who wept with joyful tears
When they saw the honor'd flag they had not seen for years;
And they could not be restrained from breaking forth in
   cheers,
   While we were marching through Georgia.

       Hurrah! hurrah! etc.

"Sherman's dashing Yankee boys will never reach the coast!"
So the saucy rebels said, and 'twas a handsome boast,
Had they not forgot, alas! to reckon with the host,
   While we were marching through Georgia.

       Hurrah! hurrah! etc.

So we made a thoroughfare for freedom and her train,
Sixty miles in latitude—three hundred to the main;
Treason fled before us, for resistance was in vain,
   While we were marching through Georgia.

       Hurrah! hurrah! etc.

HE RAN AT THE FIRST FIRE.

THE COLORED PHILOSOPHER.

Upon the hurricane deck of one of our gunboats an elderly darkey, with a very philosophical and retrospective cast of countenance, squatted on his bundle, toasting his shins against the chimney, and apparently plunged into a state of profound meditation. Finding, upon inquiry, that he belonged to the Ninth Illinois, one of the most gallantly behaved and heavily losing regiments at the Fort Donaldson battle, I began to interrogate him upon the subject.

"You were in the fight, Uncle?"

"Had a little taste of it, sa."

"Stood your ground, did you?"

"No, sa; I runs."

"Run at the first fire, did you?"

"Yes, sa, and would hab run sooner if I had node it was comin'."

"That wasn't very creditable to your courage."

"Massa, dat isn't in my line; cookin's my profession."

"Well, but have you no regard for your reputation?"

"Reputation is nuffin to me by de side of life."

"Do you consider your life worth more than other people's?"

"It's worth more to me, sa."

"Then you must value it very highly?"

"Yes, sa, I does—more dan all dis world, more dan a million of dollars, sa; for what would dat be worth to a man wid de breath out of him? Self-preservation am de fust law wid me."

"But why should you act upon a different rule from other men?"

"Because different men set different values upon their lives. Mine, sa, is not in de market."

"But if you lost it you would have the satisfaction of knowing that you died for your country."

"What satisfaction would dat be to me when de power of feeling was gone?"

"Then patriotism and honor are nothing to you?"

"Nuffin whatever, sa; I regard dem as among de vanities."

"If our soldiers were like you, traitors might have broken up the government without resistance."

"Yes, sa; dere would hab been no help for it; but I reckon if dey was all like me de country would be safe."

"Do you think any of your company would have missed you if you had been killed?"

"May be not, sa; a dead white man ain't much to dese sojers, much less a dead nigger. But I'd miss myself, and dat was de pint wid me."

It is safe to say that the corpse of Uncle Pete will never darken the field of carnage.

Petersburg, Pike Co., Indiana.

"BETTER THAN THE BAYONET."

" There is a weapon surer set
And better than the bayonet,
A weapon that comes down as still
As snow-flakes fall upon the sod,
Yet executes a freeman's will
As lightning does the will of God;
Nor from its force nor bolts nor locks
Can shield them—'tis the ballot-box."

MY COUNTRY.

I love my country's vine-clad hills,
Her thousand bright and gushing rills,
    Her sunshine and her storms;
Her rough and rugged rocks that rear,
Their hoary heads high in the air,
    In wild, fantastic forms.

I love her rivers deep and wide,
Their mighty streams that seaward glide,
    To seek the ocean's breast;
Her smiling fields, her flowery dales—
Her shady dells, her pleasant vales,
    Abodes of peaceful rest.

I love her forests, dark and lone,
For there the wild bird's merry tone,
    I hear from morn to night;
And lovelier flowers are there I ween,
Then e'er in eastern lands were seen,
    In varied colors bright.

Her forests and her valleys fair,
Her flowers that scent the morning air,
    All have their charms for me;—
But more I love my country's name,
Those words that echo deathless fame,
    The Land of Liberty !

THE SHIP OF STATE.

THOU too, sail on, O ship of State !
Sail on, oh Union, strong and great !
Humanity with all its fears,
With all the hopes of future years,
Is hanging breathless on thy fate.
We know what Master laid thy keel,
What workman wrought thy ribs of steel,
    Who made each mast, and sail, and rope,
What anvils rang, what hammers beat,
In what a forge, and what a heat,
    Were shaped the anchors of thy hope.

Fear not each sudden sound and shock;
'Tis of the wave, and not the rock;
'Tis but the flapping of the sail,
And not a rent made by the gale.

Spite of rock and tempest roar
In spite of false lights on the shore,
Sail on, nor fear to breast the sea;
Our hearts, our hopes, are all with thee,
Our hearts, our hopes, our prayers, our tears.
Our faith triumphant o'er our fears,
Are all with thee—are all with thee.—*Longfellow.*

TESTIMONIALS.

No novel ever conceived and written by human genius possesses one-half the fascination, elements of humor, pathos and moving power of "the plain, unvarnished tale" of the Rev. Mr. Aughey.

JAMES A. WORDEN, D. D.,
Superintendent Missionary Department of the Presbyterian Board of Publication, Philadelphia, Pa.

It is as fascinating as any romance, and yet it bears the impress of truthfulness in every sentence.   D. J. M'MILLAN, D. D.,
Secretary of the Board of Home Missions, New York.

The story is a stirring narrative of suffering and thrilling adventure, and will be found intensely interesting.   JOHN GILLESPIE, D. D.,
Secretary of the Board of Foreign Missions, New York.

I thank thee sincerely for the book, and hope it will be read in all parts of the Union. With all good wishes for thy welfare, I am thy aged friend,   JOHN G. WHITTIER.

It bears the marks of truthfulness in its details, and the vividness of a record of personal experiences which none can question.

S. F. SMITH, D. D.,
Author of "My Country, 'Tis of Thee."

The lessons that it teaches, written in tears and blood, will ever live as mile-posts in the nation's history.   JAMES H. SCARR,
Weather Bureau, St. Louis, Mo.

It is a vivid and indeed a lurid tale, and is the testimony of one who was right in the cyclone.   M. W. STRYKER, D. D., LL. D.,
President of Hamilton College, Clinton, N. Y.

Its style is terse, vigorous, chaste and pure, and the book is replete with information which all who read it will highly prize.

MRS. DARWIN R. JAMES,
President of the Woman's Home Missionary Society of the Presbyterian Church in the United States of America.

www.ingramcontent.com/pod-product-compliance
Lightning Source LLC
Chambersburg PA
CBHW020238110726
47898CB00004B/1311